PRAISE FOR *THE RULE OF ONE*

"Ava and Mira's world is an all-too-believable mix of advanced technology and environmental collapse. In their debut, Saunders and Saunders, themselves twins, lend an authentic voice to the girls' first-person narration . . . Readers are in for a fast-paced ride, poised for a sequel, as the twins embrace their father's call, in the words of Walt Whitman, to 'resist much, obey little.'"

—*Kirkus Reviews*

"Utilizing an SF-fantasy setting and a survival-oriented plot, the Saunders sisters are careful to promote growth and differentiation between the twins . . . There are parallels to current news stories, such as immigration, environmental resources, and an autocratic political system."

—*Booklist*

"The apocryphal nature, strong female heroes, and similar concepts to the movie *What Happened to Monday* and to Margaret Haddix's book series Shadow Children, are reflected in this plot-driven book. Readers of the genre will appreciate the page-turning action, the close calls, and the authors' development of distinct personality differences between the twins."

—*VOYA*

"The descriptions of everything are incredibly vivid and make you feel as if you are running for your life . . . This story was completely compelling."

—The Nerd Daily

"Twin storytellers Ashley and Leslie Saunders are modern-day soothsayers who beautifully spin a suspenseful tale of the not-so-distant future. Pay attention—this could be what 1984 was to 1949."

—Richard Linklater, Academy Award–nominated screenwriter and director

EXILES

Also by Ashley Saunders & Leslie Saunders

The Rule of One Trilogy

The Rule of One

The Rule of Many

The Rule of All

EXILES

ASHLEY SAUNDERS
LESLIE SAUNDERS

47NORTH

Text copyright © 2022 by Ashley Saunders and Leslie Saunders
All rights reserved.

Published by 47North, Seattle

www.apub.com

Amazon, the Amazon logo, and 47North are trademarks of Amazon.com, Inc., or its affiliates.

ISBN-13: 9781542033961
ISBN-10: 1542033969

Cover design by David Curtis

Printed in the United States of America

This one's for each other

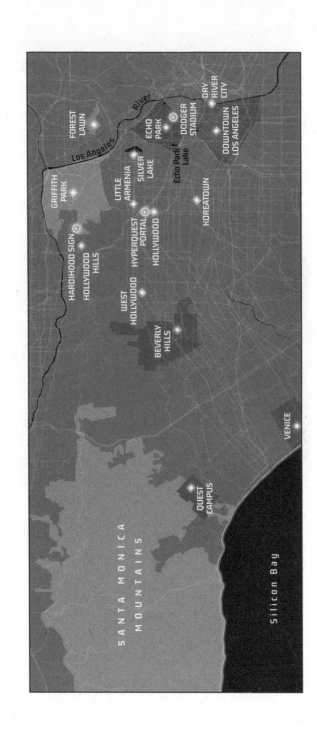

PROLOGUE

It was a gorgeous night for trespassing. A thick coastal fog had just rolled in, veiling the chilly valley and the soaring peaks above. Rhett imagined the thin, whitish curve of the crescent moon hanging somewhere overhead as the tip of Mother Nature's fingernail, trying to scratch away the low-lying cloud obscuring her view.

Haven't you learned by now? Rhett silently taunted her. *These are Yates's private mountains. No one gets to see what goes on in there.*

At least, not until tonight.

Rhett stood at the center of the press of prying minds that had gathered outside the South Entrance of Quest Campus. The diffuse glow of red and blue strobe lights gave him the sensation of being trapped on a machine-fogged dance floor in some Sunset Boulevard club, but the rabid shouts of a dozen police officers snapped him from the trance. All around, reporters, gawkers, and a dozen or so tourists in "Hardihood" shirts held their arms aloft like tripods, trying to capture a glimpse over the solid iron gate with their cameras.

An elbow slammed into Rhett's kidney as the mob pushed him nearer to the gate. He felt an eye-watering tug of his hair, then pain across his back as a pair of feet awkwardly attempted to scale his shoulders for a better look. Rhett tossed aside an enthusiastic teen who had the look of a budding Quester about him, then fended off a paparazzo who'd grabbed him by his throat, striving to take his place.

The snoops were turning barbarous. Everyone smelled blood. And the pack of ravenous inquisitors would have their scandal fresh and unadulterated. Before Yates's PR team could cut away all the juicy bits, scrub up all the stains.

"Get back!" the nearest cop warned, taking out his baton.

"Sir—" a woman in full makeup and hair shouted, holding out a selfie stick to film the exchange. "Can you confirm that a distress call was placed from inside Adsum Academy?"

"Home or jail, take your pick!" a second officer bellowed.

Would they really arrest those with media IDs? Rhett had his own forged press badge pinned to his sweater, but it was no matter. He had his own way in. He moved unnoticed to the edge of the hullabaloo and slipped into the mist.

A security fence loomed out of the haze to his right. Steel pickets, six inches wide. Rhett squinted upward, noting the deceptively handsome bougainvillea trees lining the barrier. Vines wrapped arches over the high fence tops, their savage thorns masked by plush magenta petals that deterred any would-be climbers—in style, of course.

Rhett hugged close to the fence, his fingers brushing the cold thickset pickets as he tiptoed farther into the dark. "Forty, forty-one, forty-two . . ." he whispered aloud. Finally, after picket fifty-five, his fingers grazed only air, and he halted, smiling impishly.

Rhett had created this secret, person-sized entryway himself. Two nights prior, at the tail end of a weeks-long bender. Turned out, sleep deprivation and the anniversary of his pops's funeral were the perfect combination to help Rhett upgrade from stalker to burglar.

He'd been watching Yates for months, desperate to dig up dirt, find a crack in his seemingly shatterproof reputation. But a man who could not only profit from disaster—the Yates Empire grew 50 percent richer in the aftermath of the 2040 Quake—but rebuild a demolished Los Angeles into his own image? That kind of man would not be so easily laid bare.

The wail of an ambulance drifted down from Adsum Peak. Music to Rhett's ears—a siren's call of intrigue. He glanced behind him, yanked a neck gaiter over his lower face, and squeezed through the double-gap pickets and onto the Quest Campus grounds.

Before he could even brush the fallen bougainvillea petals from his shoulders, he heard a bright, silvery trill as something—no, *two* some-things—zoomed past overhead.

Rhett ducked, cursing, thinking security was onto him. But the drones were headed *up* Adsum Peak, not down. Just more snoops, then. "Amateurs," he sighed, stretching his quads and groin before setting off at a brisk run toward the narrow switchback road that led up the dusty mountainside.

In truth, Rhett was a sleuthing amateur himself. Self-taught, self-funded. A one-man team whose sole job and purpose was to damage Damon Yates. Not to kill him—no, that would be too easy. For Damon, not for Rhett.

Rhett wanted the tech billionaire humiliated, disgraced, baking in an overheated prison cell. Friendless and penniless, forced to spend the rest of his purposeless life remembering Rhett Wood and his pops.

It was a mile and a half to the top. Rhett ignored the cruel, relent-less incline, the burn in his lungs and thighs, focusing on the road, watching for the headlights of autonomous vehicles. Quest AVs were stealth on wheels; you never heard one coming until it was too late.

He bolstered his nerve. He hoped *he* wasn't too late.

For what exactly, he wasn't sure. But a midnight distress call from the exclusive mountaintop boarding school, whose inaugural class was made up of a bunch of no-name street urchins? That had the sweet stench of scandal, ripe for the picking. Rhett could almost taste it. The revenge. The blackmail. He closed his eyes, picturing the axe he'd been grinding, all these long months, finally swinging loose, singing through the air as he took down a god.

3

Who had made the SOS call? Was it one of the Unfortunate kids Yates had plucked from the city's quake-ravaged neighborhoods for his academy? Or maybe it was a Quester—no, a *defector*, ready to rip the protective veil off Yates's mountain of secrets.

Grinning like a loon, Rhett split through the fog, the long dry fronds of the palm trees clapping boisterously in the wind, encouraging him onward. But the higher he ran, twisting his way up the peak, the more he lost his bearings. Was the sandy arc of Silicon Bay, the world's hottest tech scene, to his right or left? Was the luminous haze hundreds of feet below him the clustered factories of Quest Motors, or was he staring down toward HyperQuest, Yates's pioneering hyperloop company?

"We get you where you need at near supersonic speed." Rhett muttered the aggravating tune, locking his eyes back onto the road ahead, certain at least where this strip of concrete led. After he made a last hairpin turn, Adsum Academy took shape on the blanketed horizon. He slowed to a prowl, barely flinching when he heard the muted buzz of another drone speeding toward the sprawling property.

Ever heard of a no-fly zone? he silently jeered at the surveillance drone. The thing hit an invisible shield of signal disruptors before it spun to the ground with a pathetic crash, joining the litter of other incapacitated aircraft that had been downed by the geofence. Rhett kept up his pace as he moved along the wide tree-lined drive, until he spotted a vacant police cruiser and ambulance parked just inside the open wrought-iron gate.

Where was the chaos of lights, the raised voices? Had he made it all this way for a false alarm?

The axe in Rhett's mind began to dull, his promise of retribution slipping fast from his hands. He halted, on the verge of turning back, when a shrill, sputtering laugh reached him on the wind.

He bounded toward the sound. Within seconds he was scaling a ten-foot-tall stone fence, peering surreptitiously into a great, fanciful garden made all the more breathtaking by the pale figure at its center.

A strapping boy, no more than twelve, stood at the top of a three-tiered marble fountain dressed in nothing but a pair of lustrous boxer shorts with Adsum's coat of arms on each thigh. One hand brandished a gun, the other tore at his dark, tangled mane. He howled tearful, incoherent words at a small huddle of students cowering in their silk pajamas on the damp grass below.

Rhett fumbled for his phone. Tapped to open its camera. Hit record.

A line of officers and paramedics stood by, empty-handed, deferring to a towering figure in billowy ocean-blue robes. Rhett zoomed in on the woman's face and recognized her immediately as Yates's second wife. The dean of the new academy. Rhett cocked his head, listening for fragments on the breeze.

"Darling, put the gun down," the dean coaxed the boy. "Let's figure this out together."

"Stay back!" the boy roared. He kicked water at her with his bare feet before launching into another tirade directed at his classmates. "They're listening to all of my thoughts . . . transmitting them . . . enemies of my father!"

"Maxen, please!" the dean pleaded.

Rhett couldn't believe his luck. This wasn't just any Adsum student. Maxen was Gen 2, the dean's kid, *Yates's* youngest son. Rhett aimed his camera at Maxen as he pointed the gun at anyone that moved.

"The Doc . . . where is she?" Maxen shouted. "We have to get her out. I have to get rid of her!"

The students shrieked, clinging together like a school of fish trying to scare off a predator. Maxen flew off the fountain, tackling the dean to the ground. "I won't let them take my mind!" As his mother struggled to wrestle the weapon from his hands, a shot rang out, reverberating through the mist-covered mountains.

The students scattered toward the dormitory—all except a pair of twin girls, scrawny as stray kittens. They wore their hair in loose, chestnut-colored curls around their bony shoulders. The hems of their oversize silk pajamas were cuffed to their pint-size frames. They were identical in every way, except for the blood that leaked down one twin's chest.

She clutched at her collarbone before collapsing into her sister's arms.

Rhett must have made a noise. He might have even screamed "*No!*" Maxen's turbulent eyes locked on Rhett's. He jolted, attempting to scramble down from the wall, but his movements were too quick. Too careless. *One slip was all it took,* his pops once warned him. The tip of his boot slid off the slick stone. Rhett's sweaty fingers grasped for purchase. Clutched nothing but empty air.

His stomach dropped first. Then his body. As he fell backward toward the pavement, he caught a glimpse of the scythe-shaped moon. *Haven't you learned by now?* it taunted back at him. *No one gets to see.*

Rhett felt a vicious *crack*. And then nothing.

SIX YEARS LATER

ONE

Crys was six when she'd heard the earth scream. The 2040 Quake had unleashed a monstrous rock roar that made all of Los Angeles tremble and half of it break. At the time, Crys had thought the ground rippling beneath her feet like waves was a kind of magic trick. Or a game her birth parents had conjured to make her forget about her hunger. But then the roof of her family's motor home caved in and silenced her laughter.

Now, when the pearly papered walls of Aevitas House's common room shook, a sudden tremor vibrating up through the heated floor and into Crys's chest, she wasn't afraid. She was protected in a house that Damon Yates had built.

Besides, she reassured herself, *that wasn't a quake.* Just the arrival of Adsum Academy's fresh selection of first-years.

Crys cocked an ear, tracking the sharp whirring over the high domed skylight, then out the open double doors to the veranda. There, past a sandstone patio dotted with lithe bodies stretched in Sun Salutation yoga poses, a golden field of wild California grassland danced under the powerful wind of Damon Yates's private auto-copter.

Even from inside the dormitory, Crys could see the new foster sibs' faces through the cabin's panoramic windows. So could her classmates, who were huddled around the crisp electric flames of a suspended glass fireplace near the window, clad in variations of the academy's ocean-blue uniform. Culotte trousers, luxe pinafores, pleated skirts, tailored blazers, patch-pocket cardigans, and ruffled white blouses, each uniform styled as uniquely as the person who wore it. Crys and the other seventh-years had been working on their latest critical-thinking assignment, but the incoming sibs had now captured their full attention.

"They look so ungainly—"

"So wretched—"

"So . . . *germ ridden.*"

Crys frowned. "No more than we were."

"Well, you look stunning now," Nico purred. Impeccably dressed and smelling of bergamot and panache, he holstered his powder brushes and texturizing sprays and stepped back, admiring his work. "Iconic, as always."

"I'll take your word for it," Crys said, rising to her feet and avoiding the mirror he held up to her face. She paid Nico a small fortune to maintain her glamorous image precisely so that she didn't have to look at herself. "I won't need you again until the morning, thank you."

At the veranda doors, Crys slipped out of her plush silk house slippers and into a pair of platform oxfords. After one of his many spiritual retreats abroad, Damon had implemented a personal shoes-off policy inside all Quest Campus buildings, a practice every Quester was eager to emulate, Crys included. When she reached the far end of the patio, her eyes swept past the lap-lane pool toward the west end of Adsum Peak.

She had expected a windswept Zoe Reeves strolling up from the podcar station, flush with colorful excuses for her delay. The academy's prefect had snuck off campus for a furtive weekend with her latest fling in the city, but she had promised to return to coguide the yearly Adsum welcome tour. She was never flighty—she knew Crys needed her friend's relentlessly sunny disposition to face the uncouth first-years. Their hollow cheeks, unkempt manes, tattered hand-me-down clothes, and stench of the Unfortunate encampments they'd been plucked from were all evidence of a cruel and humble past Crys was loath to revisit alone.

Expect me when you see me, kisses.

That was all Zoe had texted since Friday. Two days fielding questions from the dean and foster sibs, and this was Crys's reward? She unholstered her phone and punched out a response, then tightened her silk ribbon tie and moved for the auto-copter.

A row of grinning twelve-year-olds clutched duffel bags stitched with the Adsum coat of arms. They stood at the edge of the meadow, gaping up at the gleaming academy. Crys hung back, watching their eyes take in the curved glass exteriors designed to mimic the elegance of the surrounding Santa Monica Mountains, and the vivid bougainvillea vines that draped each building's roof garden. A boy with half-healed bruises on his arms nodded toward the saltwater pools in front of each of the three dormitories, where students clad in tiny swimsuits sipped Arnold Palmers. The first-years broke out in a chorus of whispers.

"I feel like the kid in *Charlie and the Chocolate Factory*."

"Yeah, only, we get to *live* here."

"Think Mr. Yates is really cracked like that Wonka?"

"He's called the Savior, dipshit. That means he's one of the good ones."

A reedy girl spoke up from the front. "You can't send us back, right?"

A silken voice laughed from the steps of the auto-copter. "No, darling." Poppy Szeto resembled the native flower she was named after. Long-stemmed and exquisite in her sundown-orange pantsuit, she descended and stood at the center of the wide-eyed first-years. "You're all a part of the Adsum family now. I'll serve as both your dean and foster parent, for as long as you each will have me."

Crys was surprised to find Poppy here and not Damon. After the golden couple's less than amicable divorce, Poppy had refused to abandon her commitments as educator and guardian at the academy.

Though day-to-day operations belonged to Poppy Szeto, escorting the first-years to Adsum Peak was a tradition of Damon's, a celebration he never missed. Damon had once told Crys that his students, "his aspiring young innovators," meant more to him than all his companies combined. He was equal parts genius business magnate and devoted philanthropist, known citywide as the Savior. And Crys loved him for it.

So where was he?

"You're Crystal Yates," said the boy with the black-and-blue arms.

The brood of first-years went quiet.

And don't you forget it, Crys reminded herself firmly.

"Gen 3," a few wonderstruck first-years whispered.

Sometimes it still felt like a dream, but Crys did not demur. She leaned into their attention like a sapling reaching for sunlight. Lifting her chin, she smiled. "From one former orphan to another, welcome home." It was the same greeting Damon had spoken to her own inaugural class six years ago. A handful of the preteens' eyes were already swimming, salty tears of hope washing the grime clean. Crys looked away.

She decided she'd take them first to the Angels Walk, a U-shaped overlook that jutted out a hundred feet from the peak's edge. The sun's fire-gold glow hit the glass-and-steel structure in such a way that it appeared to be floating on air. It was an enchanting place to take in the world that Damon Yates had created, and to introduce the foster sibs to their new upgraded lives. They'd get a hawk's-eye view of the sprawling thousand-acre Quest Campus, an institution so complex it operated like a city. It had its own firehouse, hospital, and water tower, its own clean-energy monorail line, with podcar stations connecting everything from Adsum Academy to the sustainable parks nestled among the canyons, all the way to the Quietude, a meditation center on the northernmost peak that commanded a calming view of the Pacific.

Sixty thousand Questers, all safe and thriving within the campus gates.

A voice, bold and taunting, broke in on her thoughts. *Show them the HyperQuest portal.*

Crys's lungs suddenly locked, her mind threatening to slip into the cold terror of a memory. Before she could get lost in the darkness, trapped by the echoes of her sister's laughter cracking against the hyperloop tube walls, Crys rooted herself to the present.

The past only lives if you let it, she reassured herself, harnessing a simple coping exercise that Damon had taught her to curb incoming panic attacks. Her "fear incursions," as Zoe liked to call these sudden bouts. In the span of a blink, Crys visualized flames in her mind's eye, burning the parasitic memory until all images of her sister were reduced to ashes, cremains to be scattered in the wind.

Breathing more freely, Crys focused on the tops of the Forest, a cluster of eighteen soaring, interconnected mass timber towers, the largest carbon-neutral structure in the world. Various offices were interspersed with giant vegetable gardens, boutique retail shops, and cafés where Adsum students could use "sums" to purchase whatever they desired. Knowing that the former Unfortunates likely never had money before, Damon had created a unit of currency for his academy to encourage entrepreneurship, teaching the students to build wealth by launching their own start-up companies. Some built websites for their classmates, others helped with social-media branding or founded tech-support businesses. Crys had started her own line of premium perfume. She was flush with sums. In a little under three years, she'd become a self-made Adsum millionaire.

She hoped Damon had noticed.

Poppy broke from the first-years and strode toward Crys, smoothing her already glossy bob. Her dark eyes were narrowed on the academy. "And what brings the transients here?"

Once more, Crys's sister crashed into her thoughts. Why—*how*—did the elusive Jade Moore steal herself back inside these secured gates? The idea of seeing Jade again made the fine hairs on Crys's arms stand on end, her body charged, primed for a lightning strike. Her head snapped toward the academy's second-floor balcony, following Poppy's gaze, where she saw not Jade, but Palmer and Vance, known as Gen 1 by every Quester. The senior scions of the Yates family. Though little else but legal ties bound them to her as siblings, Crys still treasured the idea she was their true kindred. Gen 3, Damon's last, his only *chosen* Yates.

Poppy placed a hand on Crys's shoulder. "Don't worry, darling, it appears Gen 1 has come without their *nightmare* mother." She rubbed Crys's arms, attempting to erase the goose bumps she must have mistaken for fear of Liliane, Damon's first ex-wife. Liliane's last appearance on campus ended with a martini thrown in Crys's face after it was leaked that another generation of Yates was on the horizon.

That stray will not steal my *sons' shareholdings,* Liliane had screamed.

But Liliane had the wrong twin. Crys was not Jade.

She was no thief. Crys earned what she took.

"I'm fine," Crys said, casting her eyes back toward the balcony. But the brothers had vanished. An impulse, a niggling feeling in her bones, told her she should go and find them. She pulled herself free from Poppy's grasp, promising to rejoin the group for the welcome dinner in Vail Commons, then set off across the driveway and through Adsum's heavy arched doors. As was her custom each time she crossed the threshold of the academy, her home, Crys whispered Adsum's meaning aloud: "I am here." *I am present.* It was her way of pinching herself. *Still here.*

Her pulse quickening, Crys slipped back out of her platform oxfords and glided through the grand oak-paneled entrance hall and down a sun-drenched corridor in search of her brothers. The debonair duo, Damon's first generation of billion-heirs, rarely set foot on Quest Campus, a discredit to their father and his guiding principle that hard work shone a spotlight on the character of a person. Last Crys had heard, Gen 1 was off gallivanting with Europe's wayward princes somewhere in the Seychelles islands.

Had Damon summoned them? Was that why he'd been absent from the welcoming tour?

A new notion gripped hold of Crys, and she all but floated to the glass elevator that would usher her to the academy's famed "classfloors." *Because why limit a student's imagination to mere rooms?* Damon liked to say. As the elevator pod shot skyward, Crys's hopes and expectations rose with it.

Damon was full of surprises—and prone to lavish them all on Crys. The treasure hunt through the rugged hills of campus to discover an Oldenburg stallion waiting for her among the aromatic sagebrush. The fabricated company-wide assembly at the thousand-seat Summit Auditorium that turned out to be her very own private viewing of her favorite Tony-winning play. The elaborate party at the Castle in the Air, Damon's mountainside mansion, attended only by Damon and the Gens, where Crys had unwrapped the greatest gift of all: adoption papers.

The night Crys officially became a member of the family was the last time she'd seen Palmer and Vance. She fancied—no, she *knew*—what came next. Joining the family business, earning a stake in the Yates Empire. In the time before, Crys had been humble, timorous, with her desires, but over her years at Adsum, she'd learned to reach for *more*. *Semper in altioribus,* she thought, brushing the Latin words inked across her ribs. Always higher.

This was still the City of Dreams, was it not?

The second classfloor laboratory was empty and powered down, save for Alfred, the AI clean-bot that the fifth-years had created for a summer project to wipe down the lab equipment and seamless resin floor each evening. The brothers weren't in the third classfloor's world-class art studio, or the fourth's student lounge, replete with tufted leather chairs and multitiered geometric chandeliers beneath which students led weekly "Discovery Discussions" with the greatest living geniuses of the day.

When the elevator pod opened onto the fifth classfloor, Crys fell from cloud nine back to reality. No Damon, no surprise Yates family meeting, no slew of estate lawyers clutching documents so important they were printed on archival-quality paper. Just Palmer and his younger brother Vance in the cavernous, state-of-the-art fencing room.

Illuminated by cool, overhead track lights, Vance was midbout with an ultrarealistic projection of Carlo Morelli, the Italian ten-time Olympic gold medalist. The high-tech Holographic Sparring Experience program was exclusive to Adsum Academy. Were the brothers here for a bit of elite sport?

No, Crys knew something more urgent must have brought them here. A skittish tension choked the air. Marks of trouble were written like distress signals in the creases of Palmer's fine-boned face. Curiosity roused, Crys slipped unnoticed out of the elevator pod and sidled up behind a floor-to-ceiling display case crowded with crystal trophies.

"I mean, it's an institution for *strays*," Palmer said, pacing back and forth below the raised fencing strip, looking like a strutting peacock in his fitted blazer and custom-made loafers, each step a brazen slap to academy protocol.

Crys curled her bare toes, wondering how much dirt they'd dragged in. She hoped it wasn't the scandalous kind. Briefly, she thought of their vexatious brother Maxen, Gen 2. Her hand shot to her shoulder for the scar that wasn't there. *Not your trauma,* she chastised herself. *That belongs to a different stray, a stray that stayed gone.*

Palmer stopped short at the strip's warning line. He pulled on his ear, a stress habit she'd noted all Yates men displayed. "And this new batch Poppy just flew in brings the count to what?"

"Ninety-five," Vance answered with the easy confidence of a winner. He lunged with his saber, but Morelli was much too quick, the point of his holographic blade striking Vance first.

The actual number was eighty-eight. Over the last three years, seven of Adsum's originals had either run off or been expelled. They styled themselves "the Exiles," like the title was some badge of honor. But it was a disgrace, a shame that Crys couldn't quite disassociate herself from. How could she share blood, a *face*, with their leader?

A shiver skipped up Crys's spine as Jade's hard-edged features invaded her mind's eye. *Burn the memory,* Damon's voice soothed. *The past only lives if you let it.*

"*Exactly!*" Palmer huffed a nervous laugh. "These halls are teeming with those Unfortunate urchins." He shrugged, smoothing back one of his loose blonde curls. "You can't housebreak them all. Strays disappear. No one, not even our father *the Savior*, could be expected to save every one of them."

Vance geared up for another bout. "Even so, Poppy seems determined."

Palmer waved this away. "Poppy's a middle-aged divorcée with nearly *a hundred* children. She's just looking for a bit of male attention. Bleating about her sheep to recapture Father's eye. She's as predictable as any Quester here. Worships the ground he walks on, blah, blah, yawn."

Vance grinned. "Kisses the old man's feet, I bet."

"Perhaps the true reason for his *ghastly* shoes-off policy?"

Vance shook his head. "It's to slake a foot fetish. Still bet my inheritance on it." Without saluting Morelli, he bolted forward, a suicide run, and made a hard attack to the holograph's head, scoring his first point. Vance whooped, throwing his arms into the air to celebrate his cheap victory.

Crys eyed the antique sabers along the wall. She had half a mind to dust off her skills and show these men how the game was really played, more than ready to teach them a few lessons on honor and loyalty, but she needed them to keep talking.

Strays disappear. Were they referring to the Exiles?

Palmer's grin vanished. "Did you check the girl's records?"

"Zoe Reeves, a seventh-year . . ."

A gasp escaped Crys's lips. She widened the slit of her pinafore's skirt to pluck her phone from the garter around her thigh. She checked her screen. No response from her last message: you better be lying in a ditch somewhere . . .

Vance tossed his saber aside and leapt off the fencing strip. "Five point oh average, top intern at the Power Electronics Engineering Program at HyperQuest, volunteers at Unfortunate food banks with Poppy when she's not out hiking the Quest trails with her treasured foster sibs." He rolled down his sleeves, slipping on his smart Harrington jacket. "Not exactly the bio of a runaway."

Palmer tugged at his ear. "Christ, the press will have a field day." A quiet panic edged his silvery voice. "Where the hell is Father? Always making us wait."

"This is ridiculous," Vance said, tidying his flaxen hair by the camera of his smartphone. "The Yates Empire is a fortress. Some orphan girl isn't going to take us down."

"Apparently the girl had a *companion* in the city. Poppy claims his alibi is sound, and the girl never showed for their weekend frivolities. Still, our men can operate a discreet search. We can't have Father allow her to initiate the missing persons report."

Crys gritted her teeth, holding in her shock. *Missing?* Had Zoe been taken? How? *Why?* The answer, the culprit, burned bright in Crys's mind.

Jade.

This stunt sounded right up her estranged, embittered sister's alley. Jade was a thief, a hellion, no more than a crooked heart with covetous hands. *You've done nothing but take and take our entire lives,* Crys whispered to the face that threatened to re-form in her mind. *How much more can you steal from me?*

The room's bay lights flashed on. Crys whirled, jerking backward, and suddenly there she was.

Jade, wild-eyed and terrible.

Waves of inexplicable fear flowed through Crys's trembling limbs. A scream tore from her throat as her entire body juddered and swayed like the skyscrapers on the night of the quake, before they'd collapsed into rubble. *Flee,* her instincts told her. Instead, she rooted her feet. She snapped her arm back and swung, her fist striking with devastating speed.

The face before her splintered into a thousand sharp pieces.

It was a mirror. *Not Jade.*

Crys looked down. Shards of glass glittered between her knuckles. Hot blood spilled from her clenched fist as she struggled to come down from her fear incursion.

Shame eclipsed any pain.

After all these years apart, after how long she'd trained, how could Jade still wield so much power over her? How could she still be so terrorized by her own reflection?

Crys cursed her twin, and then every looking glass in existence. She wished Zoe was with her now. Zoe was the only one who knew how twisted, how dark Crys's condition had become. Her hatred of Jade was so great that she'd been unable to bear even a glimpse of her own face in nearly three years. Over time, Crys had learned to adapt, to see herself through others' eyes. She liked herself best through Zoe's. Zoe had a way of making her appear strong, even at her weakest.

"Case in point," Palmer chided beneath his breath. Gen 1 materialized beside her, their churlish smiles aimed at the smashed mirror. "Can't housebreak them all."

"Afraid that's seven years bad luck, Crystal," Vance added.

Crys covered her wrecked hand beneath her other fist, hiding her panic behind a steady grin. Though only Palmer shared their father's height, they both had Damon's eyes, a blue so pale it was almost silver, bright as polar stars. *Men accustomed to being followed,* she thought. *The Yates family trait.* And what did those eyes see, gazing at her now? Was she just a marketing stunt, a high-concept rags-to-riches story?

Or did they see her as their sister?

She hated how badly she still wanted them to.

But you're already someone's sister, Jade's raspy voice teased. *A bond tied by blood.*

Crys's body hardened. "Tell our father"—she watched the brothers flinch at her ownership of the familial word—"not to initiate the missing persons report. I'll handle it."

When she turned away, her bare feet skirting the glass that littered the floor, Crys's mind was on one thing only.

A reunion, and not the reconciliatory kind.

Jade was a misfortune that Crys had been affixed to at birth, a problem it seemed she could no longer ignore. Was Jade arrogant and reckless enough to believe she could recruit more Adsum students to her little gang of roving strays? Did she think she could lure Zoe, Crys's staunchest ally, the truest sib she'd ever known, without repercussions?

She always steals what I love, Crys realized.

Well, now it was Crys's turn to take.

She wondered if her sister could sense her coming.

Two

The dragster stuttered to a fiery halt. The racer didn't panic or scream or fear that this time she'd pushed too far. She smiled. She might have even laughed, drunk on the thrill of danger.

Men in bright yellow jackets hurtled toward the crash site at the end of the dusty claypan drag strip. As they sprayed down the long, skinny digger with pressurized extinguishers, a figure rolled out of the cockpit. Shrouded in a cloud of dark smoke, the helmeted driver rose to her booted feet, unharmed. Ignoring the shouts of concern from the Safety Safari, she took one look at the scene behind her and ran.

More men raced after her into the hot desert, except this new bunch wore the tacky white suits beloved by Sin City's highest high rollers and carried pistols in their spray-tanned hands. They had good reason to give chase. She had, after all, just broken underground racing's cardinal rule: you wreck, you pay.

The problem was, she hadn't just wrecked the unimaginably expensive dragster she'd been hired to drive. She'd wanted to win, so she'd chosen not to slow her speed by launching her parachute before the finish line, which caused her to lose control and slam into her opponent: Roboket, the first custom-made, all-electric, autonomous dragster on the circuit. The fastest-accelerating machine on the planet now looked like the world's priciest roadkill.

It's time to pull up stakes in Vegas, she thought as she slipped off her helmet and black one-piece racing suit. She discarded the gear, shedding the identity of the mysterious unnamed dragster willing to risk it all.

Where to next? she asked herself.

She made a gamble and bet on a ticket home.

Each time she set foot inside a HyperQuest portal, she thought of Damon Yates. It might have been the ubiquitous aroma of grandeur, or the simple fact that the man's face covered every ribbed-timber lobby like wallpaper. As if anyone needed reminding that he'd been named *Time*'s Person of the Year *again*. "A down-to-earth savior who reconnected a nation," the magazine's editors had lauded.

More like the archfiend who'd torn her world apart, but that was a feral subject that was better left untouched.

The man himself was inescapable. She hoped none of that had rubbed off on her. Her style was more elusive, intangible. *Slippery*, some would call it. So far it seemed she hadn't lost her touch—no gun-toting goons were among the crush of travelers.

"Fortunes change," she whispered, leaving her loss behind her.

She grabbed a backpack she'd stashed in a short-term storage locker, scanned her e-ticket on the nearest console, then let herself get sucked into the human tidal wave that pulled her deeper beneath the Las Vegas Strip. Although she loathed relinquishing her hard-won money to a Yates innovation, few experiences matched the rush of levitating through steel vacuum tubes at nearly the speed of sound. She smiled, recalling the novelty bet she'd once wagered, that she could hit every capital in the Lower 48 *and* consume an entire plate of each state's most famous dish in less than forty-nine hours. After almost losing it all on a plate of Cincinnati chili, she'd beaten the fifty-to-one odds and lived off the payout for months.

When she made it down the escalator and onto one of the scores of platforms, the black-and-electric-green passenger pod bound for Los Angeles was already standing by. Its sleek walls were dotted with circular windows, both symmetric ends shaped like the elongated tips of a two-way bullet. The design always made her think the pod looked more spaceship than train, an impression that was doubly reinforced during twilight trips when passengers favored switching the overhead display screens to imitate a serene night sky.

There will be no peace tonight, she thought miserably as she leapt through the pod door just before it sealed. The Sin City revelers were not finished raising Cain; the sixteen-seat "social cabin" felt like she'd just stepped inside a drunken disco ball. She considered sneaking into the luxury suites, maybe getting some decent coffee and shut-eye for once, but chose instead to cut right, toward the smaller, surer bet of the "quietude cabin." Best to lick her wounds and make plans without fear of being accosted by some blowhard Fortunate.

Of the eight seats in the cabin, half were taken by executive-type women with thick noise-canceling headphones, hypnotized by their screens. On one side of the aisle, sitting alone, was a ferrety-looking man who chomped away at fingernails stained the alarming color of spoiled avocado. She wondered if it was a nervous habit or if the man was making a meal of the clippings. Old encampment tales sprang to her mind, the ones about a man who survived fourteen months eating only his own dead keratin.

This reminded her of the parting words of her third sad sack of a foster father. She and her sister had sprinted from his shoddy apartment, her bottom lip so swollen it looked like she'd just come out of a gruesome encounter with a Beverly Hills Dr. Frankenstein. *You're a guttersnipe of a girl, hanging on by her fingernails,* he'd screamed. *I'll laugh when you fall.*

Perhaps it was a poor idea to return home.

Nothing for it but to wait out the twenty minutes until arrival. She plopped down opposite the nail-biter, leaned back, and stretched her weary feet across the vacant seat beside hers. She'd barely closed her eyes for a light power doze when a voice as brash as its owner spoke.

"Jade Moore, the lone common swift, always in flight."

An involuntary grin curled up her cheeks. She remembered that particular ornithology lesson about the tiny bird that could eat, mate, molt, and most likely sleep on the wing. Jade had all of those down but one.

Languidly she opened her lids to stare into the bumptious eyes of Maxen Yates. He wore a loose-fitting bespoke suit that gave him an air of importance that no eighteen-year-old had a right to possess. His dark wavy locks had grown since she'd last laid eyes on him, and his pale skin was sun-kissed from the desert sun.

Jade yawned, pretending she'd known he was on her tail all along. "Was wondering if you'd catch up."

His smile outshone the gilded watch around his wrist. "You left quite a mess back there."

How—*when*—had he realized it was her beneath that helmet? "Tidiness has never been a virtue of mine."

"I see that." Maxen dragged his eyes over her dirty boots and her pants with holes ripped in the knees. Jade wasn't surprised when he cleared her legs off the seat and sat down himself. "Some very displeased men are chasing you."

"Yeah? And are you one of them?" Maxen was the owner of Roboket, the dragster she'd just totaled. Thanks to her, he'd probably lost a small chunk of his inheritance in less than four seconds. "It was an accident," she said, a smile edging her lips as she rubbed at the scar that looked like a clump of pink candle wax stuck to her collarbone. "The scot-free nonapology you Yates men love to use, right?" Maxen glanced at her old gunshot wound, then averted his gaze.

"Besides," Jade pressed, pleased to see Maxen yield. "Papa Moneybags will be sure to swoop in and clean up your mess like he always does." Yates's army of lawyers had covered up Maxen's little outburst Jade's first year at Adsum by flying him off to a world-class therapy retreat and assuring a twelve-year-old Jade of her bright future at Quest if she stayed quiet. "So, what's the real reason for this involuntary reunion, hmm? Spit it out."

Maxen shifted his face back to its natural simper, turned to the nail-biter across from Jade, and held out a pair of tortoiseshell earphones. "Hey, you, Nervous Naily, put these on."

The man slipped his fingers from his mouth, his brow puckering like a closed fist. "Sure thing. Should I lick your boots next?"

Maxen didn't flinch, simply offered the man his Rolex Cosmograph. Jade held her tongue, biting back outrage so hard she tasted blood. The man could have been bribed for *far* less than the cost of a Quest AV, but Maxen always did have a strong penchant for power flaunts. The man's face lit up. Within seconds, he was adorned with both watch and earphones.

"And keep that tongue of yours well away from my boots," Maxen said. "Hell knows where that mouth has been." Unable to hear Maxen's barbs, the man chewed happily away at his pinky.

Jade shook her head. "The lengths you Questers will go to for privacy."

Their gazes suddenly locked, Maxen's sharp eyes searching Jade's. *What is he looking for?* Whatever it was, she was sure she wasn't going to give it to him. He leaned toward her, indecently close. Jade didn't give an inch.

"Tell her to come home," he said.

Jade sat up straighter. Did Maxen mean her sister? Had Crys come to her senses after all?

She rested her knee along the pod's solid wall, craving the vibrations, the rush of speed against her bones. She imagined the steel tube just beyond the barrier and remembered racing barefoot through Yates's hyperloop tubes outside Adsum, her sister by her side. She had been fifteen, infallible, a fearless girl about to change the world.

How devastatingly wrong she'd been.

Jade yanked back her knee. *Crys is never coming home,* she reminded herself.

"Adsum's got another escapee, I take it?" she asked, her face a cool mask of indifference.

Maxen tugged on his ear impatiently. "Come now, don't play the humble thief. Every Adsum student you lure away to your band of Exiles is like a giant middle finger to my father. And a clear smoke signal to our sister."

You mean my *sister,* Jade thought. But no, that wasn't right, either. Jade was a solitary swift—unpaired, detached, a scrappy orphan who hunted the perilous skies alone. She took great pride in needing no one. It was better that way. For everyone.

Besides, Crys had chosen her family that night in the hyperloop tube. And it wasn't Jade.

"Trust me, Gen 2," she said. "Nothing I do is for Crystal *Yates.*"

Maxen chortled. "You're exactly like her, you know. Even after all the time and distance that separates you."

"Doubt that," Jade countered, toying with the tarnished silver necklace that held the deformed bullet she'd taken from the hospital as a souvenir. In Extremis, she'd named it. *At the point of death.*

"You both chase the spotlight like you'll suddenly disappear if every eyeball isn't pointed your way," Maxen said. "Well, you've caught the notice of the high-ups now, Jade, and you'd better slow down and think. Give back Zoe Reeves, or your next uninvited guest will be far less well-mannered than I."

Threats always made Jade smile. "Is that a promise?"

Before Maxen could answer, the walls around them began to radiate sleek, overproduced images of Silicon Bay and the revitalized

Hollywood sign, the new cultural icon that had arisen from the quake's ashes. Nine pristine fifty-foot letters that now read **HARDIHOOD**. Damon Yates's voice flooded the cabin. "Welcome to Los Angeles, the tenacious City of Angels, where dreams remain unshakable."

Jade laughed, a hollow, humorless sound. "When's the last time the old Savior graced the Unfortunate streets with his presence? There are still plenty of cracks to fall into." She stood and reached out a calloused hand to muss the top of Maxen's head, the way Gen 1 did to get under his skin. His cheeks burned a satisfying red. "Tell Yates's ghouls to have fun finding me."

And with that, Jade elbowed her way down the aisle so fast, she all but flew from the pod.

The truth was, Jade had no idea where Zoe Reeves was.

Or her Exiles, for that matter.

They aren't mine anymore, she corrected herself. She'd been away too long, nearly half a year of running, thrill-seeking across the country, never once stepping foot back on her city's Unfortunate streets. She'd been warned to stay gone, but maybe enough time had passed to take the heat off her. Maybe her homecoming would even be welcomed.

I wouldn't bet on it, Jade thought as she bounded from the HyperQuest portal and strolled down Hollywood Boulevard. When she came to the Chinese Theatre, a wave of nostalgia hit her hard, stopping her in her tracks. There, at the edge of the forecourt, past the fractured hand- and footprints of celebrities, the Exiles had made their mark. Jade thought back to the night she'd stolen cement from a quake rehabilitation zone, her blood thrumming with adrenaline as she'd snuck her crew onto the cherished grounds. Together, the seven of them had immortalized their own prints into the pavement next to the Monroes and Spielbergs of history. After three years, their marks remained.

Jade grinned at their handiwork as she trekked farther down the fifteen-block stretch. The bustling sidewalk was covered with five-pointed brass stars, and she lingered over the shiny one with the name "Damon Yates" emblazoned in gold. For a moment she contemplated defacing the monument—how had he warranted a place on the Hollywood Walk of Fame?—but she mastered her brash impulse, knowing his star would only be replaced within the week.

Yates was an entertainer of sorts, Jade supposed. He entertained the 1 percent on his billion-dollar rocket ships while the rest of the world starved and melted away below. "Plaster saint," she spat.

By now Jade's nostalgia had worn off, and she scanned the streets with clear eyes. Boulevards crammed with makeshift shelters and too-thin bodies, garbage littering the sidewalks and curbs, capsized portable toilets overflowing with human waste. She sidestepped a tattered pan-handling sign that read **2040 SURVIVOR, NOT A BEGGAR, SPARE SOME PITY**.

She shook her head. Nothing much had changed. Even people who held down minimum-wage jobs still couldn't afford to live in the city, no matter how much they worked. No matter how much they sacrificed. Nowadays, it was just too damned expensive to be alive.

Suddenly impatient to find her crew, Jade headed for the eastside.

She was thankful for the dark.

If there was one thing she hated more than a smug Quester, it was a SoCal sunset. There were times when the shocking blood-orange horizon made her think the Greater LA Fire was still feasting on neighborhoods. On people. The quake was surely the beginning and the climax of the tragedy, but the flames that followed, the unquenchable inferno that swept across the city's eastside, were the closing curtain, the final bow to catastrophe and misery. Three-fourths of the city's poorer districts burned, while the well-to-do west-siders had been saved from the most grievous damage. When the ground beneath them shook, their water pipes didn't break.

How Fortunate for them.

After hours of combing the Exiles' usual destinations—the steep streets of Angelino Heights, the free all-night parking across from the dim sum place in Chinatown, the spot beneath a copse of ten-year-old trees with the view of the restored Dodger Stadium—Jade felt the first prickle of worry.

When she'd packed her pockets and left the Exiles without so much as a "so long," she had carried with her the comforting thought that she could always return, always find them.

She never stopped to think: What if they'd gone and left *her*?

It was no more than she deserved, she knew. But since when did anyone get what they deserved?

Jade found the Exiles after midnight.

She should've known they'd camp here. Echo Park Lake's famed lotus bed was in full bloom, and the curbside surrounding the thirteen-acre urban lake was plum real estate to park a motor home. She spotted the Exiles' old-model Quest camping pod along the northwest bank and set out across a patchy yellow lawn studded with lofty palms and heaps of tents.

Geese honked at Jade as she weaved through the maze of tiny, single-person pup tents, others large enough for an entire family, and more elaborate setups with wooden walls, some with microwaves and others with artwork and potted plants placed near the door flaps like makeshift entrance halls. This had been one of the city's largest and most visible encampments for generations, and officials still had no clue what to do about it. She'd heard these Unfortunate camps called "shocking," "abhorrent," and "criminal," but they were the closest thing Jade had ever had to a home.

When she reached the Exiles' battered silver-and-black camping pod, she stopped cold. The vehicle's electric charging station had been smashed to smithereens, and the large battery pack demolished, rendering the pod immobile. A cruel shiver crawled up her spine at the smell wafting out of the dark, silent camper.

Jade immediately recognized the sickly sweet odor. The scent that a days-old dead body gives off was hard to forget. She'd first encountered it the night after the quake. When she'd lost her birth parents, her only true guardians.

She and Crys had thought their parents were playing possum. *Don't move. Don't make a sound.* A bedtime game their mother and father used to play to get them to go to sleep. But by the second day, trapped beneath the steel and granite ruins of downtown's City National Plaza, the smell had emerged, settling in the back of their throats, and the taste of death had lingered on their tongues long afterward.

Jade spat on the ground, ridding herself of the scent memory.

She pulled the collar of her shirt over her nose and made for the camping pod.

It wasn't one of her own, she told herself. A rogue Unfortunate from the encampment probably broke inside and snorted too much Soot.

Just as she'd hoped, the spare key fob she'd hidden behind the license plate years ago was still there. She took a deep breath, held it, and opened the door.

All was quiet. Unnervingly still. She dared to switch on a light. The dim green glow of a battery-powered LED strip light partially illuminated the empty bunk beds, the kitchen block that was cluttered with dirty dishes.

The body that lay supine on the convertible dinette table.

Jade stood static, her mind grabbing hold of details: the long blonde hair, the sagging, discolored skin, the bloated shape beneath the soiled sundress. The young, heart-shaped face, drained of life. Quietly, as if the slightest footstep could disturb the dead, she killed the lights and sealed the door, shutting the world out.

Jade hadn't felt real fear in years, but she was sure she was now experiencing terror's close cousin. How did this girl—her sister's best pal, the one every Quester was looking for—wind up dead on Jade's old doorstep?

Peals of laughter echoed outside the camping pod like mirthful raps on the cratered steel door. The entrance burst open, the sounds of high-spirited bickering spilling into the cramped, funeral-black quarters. If Jade hadn't been standing next to the mortal remains of her former classmate, her late foster sib, she would've smiled. She'd missed those blustery voices and the rough-hewn faces that came with them.

Eli Jones saw her—*them*—first. He hit the flashlight of his smartphone fast as a gunslinger, but he stayed where he stood, his body an impenetrable tank at the head of the shadowy Exiles. A stylish jacket draped his frame, a patchwork of secondhand plaid and jean shirts expertly designed and stitched. Upcycle streetwear had always been Eli's passion. There had been nights when they'd sat on the roof of the motor home and stared out at the haze of light pollution, dreaming. Eli had boasted about how he'd have his own pop-up shop on Melrose and Fairfax, if only he'd been born a Fortunate. Was that how he had been sustaining the others? Hustling his fashions, keeping the crew fed and together while she'd been away, drifting?

They were better without her, Jade thought fleetingly.

Eli fixed her with a razor-edged glare. "What trouble did you bring with you this time?"

"The kind that requires quick feet," Jade said, even as she heard—and *felt*—the first low rumble of police copters circling the sky overhead. "We gotta clear out before their Night Sun spotlight finds us."

From experience, Jade knew once you were caught in a copter's intensely bright search beam you were as good as handcuffed, and she had no plans to be locked inside a six-by-eight-foot cell again. She had a feeling that this time they'd throw away the key.

"Is that Zoe Reeves?" Eli asked, sweat forming like a beaded crown around his temples.

"It was," Jade sighed. She took a deep breath and held it. She needed to get out of this coffin, fast.

Eli's knees gave way. He staggered, reaching out a hand to brace himself against a nearby chair. What was happening? Eli had barely spoken three words to Zoe when he was still at the academy. This was no moment to grieve. They needed to act now, feel later.

"Where's the rest of the crew?" Jade asked, noticing only two silhouettes hovering in the doorway.

"So the scapegrace thinks she's owed answers, huh?" the curly-haired outline tsked. Cole Riggs, the last of the runaway orphans to join the Exiles, stepped into the motor home, shoving his fists into the pockets of his wrinkled coveralls. His usual tanned skin was pallid, dark half-moons under his hard hazel eyes. "What, did you get bored on your little getaway and decide to come back and start killing Fortunates again? Adsum students this time?"

Jade would have to let the first accusation stand. She could only defend herself against one murder at a time. Still, she couldn't believe she had to say this aloud. "Look, I didn't kill Zoe Reeves, all right? We might not have been bosom buddies, but she was our sib. And do you really think I could've carried a hundred pounds of deadweight in here all by myself? It's obvious someone is trying to set us up."

The final shadow in the doorway scoffed. "You mean set *you* up."

Ani Agassi stepped forward, her sable hair tied back high on her head, her fingers stained with paint, just as Jade had always remembered her. Ani covered her nose and mouth with the sleeve of a beat-up moto jacket that Jade had given to her for her eighteenth birthday. *You're a bona fide adult,* Jade had told her. *The navy suits can't touch you now.* The present irony was not lost on Jade.

"Tell me," Ani pressed, her husky voice growling, "why shouldn't we throw you to the navy suits? This Adsum girl has nothing to do with us. And neither do you."

Her words cut Jade like a jab from one of Ani's many concealed knives. Anger bled from her, hot and unstoppable. "Fine, but those copters above *your* wheels tell a different story." More had arrived while they'd stood squabbling, and it wouldn't surprise Jade if Yates had ordered an entire LAPD air-support division after her.

She never should have come back here. It was a trap. *Stupid swift,* she thought cruelly. *The moment you land back on ground, the predators are always here, waiting.*

If only she could fly.

Jade lifted her hand to her brow in a salute. "Seeing how I'm not welcome, good luck on your own." She barreled through the Exiles and out the door without looking back. Just as she'd expected, navy suits had swarmed the encampment in riot gear, shaking down the tents and motor homes one by one, rounding up the scared and outraged inhabitants and forcing them into a cordoned-off area near the lake. Two detective types in bulletproof vests were already headed straight for the Exiles' clunker, pistols drawn.

Jade beelined across a dark avenue, sprinting between a pair of low-income housing complexes made from recycled shipping containers.

She was midway up a fence when a shrill yelp cut through the noise of the copters.

Eli.

He sounded hurt. Terrified. Had the navy suits started shooting?

Jade made the opposite of a smart move and turned back. When she reached the Exiles in the middle of the pocked street, she saw that Eli *had* gone down, but not from a gunshot. He feebly attempted to pull himself up off the dirty concrete, but his legs appeared powerless.

Paralyzed.

"Not again!" Eli bellowed, beating at his legs. "*Work*, damn it. *Move*."

Ani and Cole tried and failed to lift him.

"How am I supposed to fight tonight?" Eli cried. "Half the Echo Park Lake encampment is banking on me."

Jade's stomach twisted. Of course, dreams had never filled pockets. Or stomachs. Eli must've joined an underground fighting ring to scrape by.

Ani pressed her plum-stained lips to Eli's forehead. "Don't think about the money. For once, think about yourself."

Cole got low to the ground, encouraging Eli forward. "Can you crawl, brother?" When Eli made no progress, Cole grabbed him under the arms and began to pull, slow and halting.

The sound of Eli's limp legs scraping against the pavement was unbearable. Jade's body vibrated from the copter overhead, which drew closer and closer to their exposed position. They had only moments before its searchlight would find them.

Eli looked to Jade. "What's happening to me? No one's ever landed a swing on me in the ring. I knock them out cold before anyone can touch me." His voice grew thin, small. Ill-matched to his sturdy frame. "So why can't I feel anything below my waist? It's just like 2040. I'm broken all over again."

Jade had no idea why Eli's childhood paraplegia had suddenly returned. Or, for that matter, why Zoe Reeves lay dead on the kitchen table, with no obvious signs of injury or struggle.

Jade knew only that if they all got locked up, so too would any chance of finding the answers.

She looked Eli square in his wide, copper eyes. He knew they were going to leave him behind. "We'll get you back," she said. "I'll figure this all out."

Eli nodded stiffly.

"Remember," Jade added, "fortunes change."

"Fortunes change," he whispered back, without much heart.

Jade snatched Ani and Cole by the scruffs of their necks and dragged them away just as Eli was caught in the blinding beam of the Night Sun.

Cole shrugged off her grip as they ran. Ani panted like a bull ready to charge. At Jade, at the copters, or at the hard luck that awaited them ahead, Jade couldn't say.

"Tell me you know a place to lie low, at least," Cole pleaded through heavy breaths.

Jade knew dozens. But they needed to go high—up into the Quest mountaintops, to the upper crust, to the man who thought himself unreachable. With every footfall, Jade's suspicions that Yates had everything to do with this grew stronger.

"Follow me or don't," she told the others. "I'm going to Adsum."

A visit to her long-lost sister was well overdue.

THREE

Crys stood on the precipice of a world in which she swore she'd never again set foot.

She slid her gaze toward the stark white letters on a mural painted along the steep concrete bank of the LA River: **DRY RIVER CITY LIMITS, POPULATION: TOO MANY**. The former earthquake refugee encampment turned permanent homeless habitation spanned a mile up and down the flood-control channel just east of downtown. The modern Wild West, where Soot cost two dollars a hit, medieval diseases were rife, and one night spent inside its infamous limits would leave one quaking.

At least, that's what her Quake Tour ticket had promised.

Crys reached for the small vial of perfume she always carried in her front pocket. She sprayed and inhaled deeply, letting the scent expunge her foul memories in favor of more pleasant associations like Quest and its fields of wildflowers at Splendor Park.

"You smell nice."

Crys jumped. At the staircase landing, a bare-breasted woman half buried in a pile of filthy blankets extended a palm pitted with open wounds. Her skin was coated so thick with dirt that Crys could only see her by the occasional passing of an AV headlight. The woman could have been sixteen or fifty. "Spare any change?"

Fortunes change. A memory fired inside Crys's mind. A phrase, a plea, that Jade would have them cling to as young girls, when their feet were too inflamed, their shrunken stomachs too neglected to drag themselves to the bustling downtown avenues to perform gimmicky dances for a few crumpled bills.

Crys shook her head and averted her eyes.

"The right thing to do," said a paunchy older man who'd appeared behind her. "She'd only spend it on an Unfortunate vice." With his luxurious multipocketed olive jacket and embossed weekender bag, the man looked fit for a safari. The only thing missing was a pair of binoculars.

Privilege wafted off the man like the smell of raw meat. A pack of boys wearing what looked like all their clothing at once was already eyeing the Fendi bag. Ears pricked up, ready to pounce.

"This way," Crys said, and the man clung close as she picked her way down a staircase cluttered with refuse and unintelligible graffiti. She pulled her medical-grade scarf mask over the lower half of her face, both as a health precaution and concealment. The silk was raven black, a color Crystal Yates would never wear. So were the oversize T-shirt and trousers she'd found in the academy's donation bin. She'd thrown her golden locks into a careless messy bun. Nico would have never approved.

Even if Crys could stand to look in the mirror, she was certain she wouldn't recognize herself, and neither would anyone in Dry River City, the last place Jade was rumored to haunt.

At the bottom of the steps, Crys caught sight of a small, conspicuous group huddled uneasily beneath the flickering glow of a portable LED tower. A Silicon Bay couple dressed for a night in West Hollywood; a woman in a tailored suit Crys recognized as an illustrious film director and her young, skittish assistant; a handful of Chinese tourists in designer face masks, gripping expensive cameras with flashguns. Crys joined the tour group's tight circle, eyes darting across the disordered rows of innumerable emergency housing structures shaped like giant two-tiered honeycombs. Each compact hexagon pod looked fit to burst, with entire families squeezed into a space designed to accommodate a single person. There must have been thousands of inhabitants packed into this unofficial city.

A muffled voice rose above the din, rough as the streets that reared him. "I count twelve audacious souls, night-trippers, sightseers, *intruders*, who've descended into my city." A wiry, dark-haired young man materialized from the loitering mass, his almond eyes greedy, hungry, his smirking lips wrapped around a spicy rice-cake skewer. He chewed, swallowed, held out the sharpened stick like a dagger. "Afraid I can only promise half of you will leave."

Bitter words bubbled up Crys's throat. Wesley Lee—or Wily as he went by now—always had liked to agitate his betters, always reveled when he had the upper hand. Crys locked her jaw, clamping down hard on her rising irritation. *Stay invisible, blend in,* she reminded herself. Neither came naturally.

"Always with the drama." Wily's business partner, a young woman with curves that rivaled Mulholland Drive's, stepped forward. She held a large black-light flag that shone an ultraviolet purple, a beacon to tourists gone astray.

"Show me your receipts. Hold them up." Jordan Parker, who'd rechristened herself Sage, began scanning the tour group's QR codes and arranging the tourists into two straight lines, as efficient and no-nonsense as Crys remembered her. During her four years at Adsum, Sage had trained to become a memory athlete. Her ability to retain vast amounts of information was exceptional; she was a four-time world memory champion, the youngest and the greatest. She could recite seventy thousand digits of pi, and yet here she was, a cut-rate tour guide, back in the squalor she'd grown up in.

Crys assumed a genius would've been able to find their way out by now. *But that's what happens when you followed Jade Moore,* Crys thought. *She pulls you down with her.*

Every muscle in Crys's body tightened at the thought of seeing her sister again. Her bones shook with the effort to stop her trembling, to beat back a fear incursion before it started. She forced her chin high. Her eyes level.

But Jade's solemn down-turned lips and warm olive skin, those features sharp as knuckles pulled over a closed fist, never appeared.

No matter, Crys told herself. Jade was roving this misbegotten city somewhere. *She has to be.* The Exiles stuck together like magnets, their bond strong as iron, Jade their powerful lodestone. Wily and Sage would lead Crys to her soon enough. And then she would find Zoe. Long before sunrise, before she'd have to witness the grim encampment in the unforgiving daylight, she and Zoe would be back home. Safe at Quest Campus.

Crys presented her digital ticket. Neither Sage nor Wily seemed to recognize her, their former foster sib, their onetime classmate, the one who had sounded the death knell for their life on Quest Campus. Crys had never had to face them since they'd both been expelled.

She felt no lingering guilt for what she had done, only a prickling irritation at Sage's and Wily's continued ingratitude. As if trying to steal millions from Damon wasn't enough, Wily had a "Quester Defector" badge pinned to the thick belt buckle that wrapped his trim waist.

Wily shrugged his moleskin trucker jacket from his naked shoulders and tossed the luxe collar over a screw on the light tower, an ease to his roguish smile. He knew no one would dare take it. Crys noted a motley collection of scars that covered his lean muscles like tattoos. "All right, my Fortunate friends," he prompted the group. "Ready to see how the other half lives?"

The first phase of the tour took them past a community garden, a kitchen stocked with crowdfunded food, and several shaded "lounge areas" littered with gutted armchairs occupied by idlers who were charging their electronics on Juiceboxes. The solar-powered batteries, invented and donated by Adsum sixth-years, were a class project

Damon started in order to help the homeless stay connected, ensuring "all promising minds have 'outlets,' even outdoors."

"Unbelievable," the director's assistant grumbled. "They're probably just binge-watching TV. It costs these freeloaders *nothing* to live in downtown's backyard, yet I give my whole shitty paycheck to my tiny, shithole apartment just six blocks over."

Wily gestured to an upcoming bank of mobile showers and restrooms that looked, *and smelled*, like they predated the quake. "As our mayor likes to put it," Wily continued, "dignity in poverty."

Crys's fingers itched for her vial of perfume. She huffed out a laugh. Wily was an Adsum sib. He knew what true dignity looked like, though his standards seemed to have deteriorated alongside the final vestiges of his potential.

Sage threw a glare Crys's way, her long flagpole dipping as she turned, nearly beheading a man selling what looked like whole fish beside a sign that read RIVER TO TABLE. Crys affected interest, moving away from Sage's keen eye, trying to stop her stomach from turning. Were those caught *here*?

Wily led the group nearer to the thin channel of water that cut through the center of the concrete city like a dividing line, the last meager evidence this place was once a wild, free-flowing river. Crys guessed that the water came from urban runoff and wastewater treatment plants, a sad, sluggish stream on a fixed course for the ocean. Orange flood barriers lined with sandbags stood in wait at its inky edges, a safeguard against the rare occasion when rain deigned to fall from LA's immutable summery skies.

"Watch your step over the bridge," Wily warned. "If you slip and find yourself having what locals call an 'unfortunate baptism,' don't open your mouth to scream. There's enough bacteria and pollutants down there to pin you to your porcelain throne for weeks."

Crys cringed with the others, watching her steps with the concentration of a tightrope walker as the group crossed a narrow bridge of wooden planks. Ahead, she noticed the young couple holding hands, nuzzling one another like the tour was some quirky date, a gripping story for their next dinner party in the hills. Crys intended to tell *no one* of this experience, this nightmare. She shuddered, imagining what Palmer and Vance would think of her being here.

This *was where you came from?*

On the other side of the scaffolding, a thickset man stood at the end of the metal railing. A gatekeeper, Crys realized. She gazed out over the east side of the pitiable river, where the gloom of the city deepened, the shadows stretched and darkened. An old woman with swollen bare feet and a hooked spine approached the bridge. The gatekeeper shook his head, and the old woman shuffled off.

Sage shouldered up to Crys, making her flinch. "Just the natural order of things, right? Even so-called bottom-dwellers cling to their rung on the hierarchical ladder."

Crys pretended not to hear.

"Even the lowest wretch wants to be higher than *someone*," the director whispered to her assistant. "That's good, that's good, write that down."

As they passed beneath the wide arches of First Street Bridge, Crys covered her ears against the curse-laced squabbles and manic soliloquies that echoed off the underbelly of the old viaduct. Wily paused the group. "Refreshments time."

The tourists' noses wrinkled en masse at the idea of tasting the local fare.

Wily smiled when a small girl with a dirt-freckled face appeared, a tray of steaming street tacos in hand. He inhaled three without stopping to breathe. Crys always marveled at how Wily could eat so ravenously and never gain an ounce of fat. He'd come to the academy as a heavier child, but by his third year, he'd shed half his weight and hardened into a sinewy young man with the metabolism of a hummingbird.

Safari man let out an excited gasp. Crys's attention turned to two dark shapes who'd sprung out of the shadows with weapons that looked like lead pipes raised high. They skirted past the terrified tourists and jumped a man sleeping on the open ground, beating and kicking him before running off with his paltry belongings.

"Good thing you're all running with me," Wily said with a wink.

The beaten man curled into a ball, his painful moans eliciting a mixture of shocked tears and wide-eyed thrill. *Exactly what the tourists came to Dry River City to experience,* Crys thought. Danger with guardrails.

Crys was wise to this little street show: rough people up, pay the injured parties a percentage of ticket sales. But from the seething look on Sage's face, this scheme wasn't on her Quake Tour program.

The young Silicon Bay woman in high block heels drew back, cowering closer to her date. "Wasn't a body just found in one of these encampments? A dead one, I mean."

Sage shrugged her broad shoulders. "Two thousand people die per second in the world, what's your point?" But her eyes slid to Wily, a tense disquiet passing between them.

"Yeah," added Safari man, "but the *point* is the girl wasn't local, the manner of death suspicious—"

Crys found herself tripping toward the man, heartbeat hammering in her ears. *What—who—is he talking about?* Her mind raced, but then a loud bray of laughter stopped her in her tracks. She'd recognize that hearty sound of glee anywhere. *Zoe.*

Crys closed her eyes in relief. *Zoe's here. She's safe.*

Before she even opened her wing-tipped eyelids, Crys spun on her heel and slipped away from the tour group, losing herself in the fray. *Zoe chose me,* Jade jeered inside Crys's mind. She fought her way through the congested underpass toward the bright, lively voice that had suddenly died out. Unwashed bodies plowed into her from all directions, a shock to her Fortunate system, which had grown accustomed to Questers all too happy to clear a path for Damon Yates's only daughter.

Crys searched face after strange face but found no sign of Zoe. Was she hiding from Crys? Was this a sick game Jade was making Zoe play?

The last night Crys had seen her sister flashed before her mind's eye. Jumbled images burst forward before Crys could beat back the mayhem of memories: her bare feet slapping the HyperQuest tube, her bruised fists pounding at the walls, her sister grinning wildly beneath an oxygen mask as they both ran out of air, and options, and time.

Then a flicker of platinum blonde hair lured Crys from her memory. "Zoe?" she shouted. The young woman didn't turn. Crys followed the platinum hair toward a band of teens sprawled on stacks of stained cardboard, their eyes glued to a video projected from a boy's cracked phone onto the wall of a canvas tent. Crys recognized the face of a popular gossip influencer, except she wasn't wearing her trademark smirk. Instead, tears tracked down her filtered cheeks.

"One of Adsum Academy's luckiest stars was found murdered in a homeless encampment . . . brace yourselves for my exclusive footage leaked from the crime scene . . ."

Crys made herself look. An officer knelt over a black vinyl bag. The zipper had caught on Zoe's waist-length hair. Her lifeless emerald eyes were wide open, her usual upturned lips now a rigid blue line.

Bright streaks flashed at the edges of Crys's vision, all sound a confusing blur. She turned her back on the video, on the idea that Zoe was dead. *Murdered.*

Jade.

Jade.

The name and face chased after Crys, no matter how fast she ran.

Could Jade really have done this?

Dread twisted Crys's stomach as she fled for the staircase. Back to Quest Campus and Yates. *Home.* She made it all of two steps before something solid blocked her path.

A man, tall and lissome in a flashy three-piece suit. A silver goatee clung to his narrow jawline, severe as ice against his bronze skin. He radiated authority, cold and absolute.

"You've got the nerves of a Dry River rat, I'll give you that," he said, tearing away Crys's scarf mask and bearing down on her with an intensity that made her freeze beneath his glare. "Although I thought I made it plain to never come back."

Crys betrayed her instincts and opened her mind to her past, to the Unfortunate life she kept buried. She searched through the dusty cobwebs and skeletons she'd tried so hard to keep dead. But the man's weathered cheeks, his grizzled brow, his protruding granite eyes, were nowhere in her memories. Crys didn't know this man.

But then she understood. This man didn't see *her*.

He saw the woman Crys hadn't been mistaken for in years.

"Every navy suit in the metropolis searching high and low for Jade Moore," he said, "and she walks right into my reach." He took hold of Crys, his fingers tight as steel wire, and before Crys could even think to run, to shout, *You've got the wrong twin*, he dragged her away into the cramped, airless dark.

Four

Jade didn't stand a chance. As soon as she'd crossed through the gates of Quest Campus, the memories of her academy days hit her like superbly aimed bullets, like underhanded gut punches that left her reeling.

Memories were a bane that only got heavier the more years she collected and carried them. When she was a girl, when she was tired of the burden, she'd often found a way to float. Now, as Jade looked up toward Adsum Peak, spotting the graceful arches of the conservatory's giant glass-and-metal dome, a distinct recollection caught her between the eyes.

She was fifteen, a fourth-year at the academy. She was floating in the center of a glassy pond. The cool water filled her ear canals; the humid air, her lungs. She was a weightless deaf thing, buoyant in the *now*.

Something rippled the still pond.

"Get *out*!" Crys screamed.

Jade righted herself, treading water. Her sequined gown clung to her legs, weighing her down. "Get *in*," she'd countered.

"This pond is meant for our scientific studies, not your stunts," her sister replied. "Do you even *think* about others? You're messing with the ecosystem."

"Well, you're messing with my atmosphere."

Crys bent as low as her tight silk suit would allow, whispering despite the emptiness of the domed conservatory. "You just walked offstage in the middle of our annual awards ceremony. You're making us look bad."

Jade chuckled.

Crys sniveled. "*Damon Yates* is here. We can't have him see you killing his endangered green algae and water lilies."

"It's all replaceable, Crys. Just like us."

Crys rose to her full height, cheeks burning a deep crimson. "Get out and grow *up*!"

Jade obliged. She stood, sopping wet, shivering, before her sister. *Her refined better half,* as so many Questers liked to whisper in cafés at the Forest. This was back when Crys still shared their family name. When she still remembered the roots she'd grown from. When her curls were still the color of the oak tree branches they'd climbed together as kids in Griffith Park. Her eyes still a russet brown.

Back when Crys was a reflection of Jade. Before her features transformed into the sky-blue and honey-gold hues of Crystal Yates.

"Up, up, up," Jade taunted her. "Higher and higher. All you care about is ascension." With a roguish grin, she bounded for the gumwood tree that grew beside the shoreline.

Climbing the tree was more than a lark, a self-dare. There was an inexplicable pull inside of Jade, an ache that always drove her to find the ragged edge, and then pass it. Urging her up the tree's pendulous branches, to its leafy crown. She looked down at Crys, fifteen feet below.

"Don't," Crys pleaded. "You'll hurt yourself. It's too high."

"I thought, for you, there was no such thing as *too* high?" Jade shouted. "You can keep fighting to rise, Crys, but don't forget, we're all prisoners to gravity. What goes up must come down."

She jumped. Fell for a handful of seconds. In the shape of a cannonball, she crashed into the pond, carving into water that now felt hard as concrete. The bottom came up quick. *Rock bottom always did,* Jade lamented.

Jade remembered the agony as every metatarsal bone in her foot fractured. The pain of every heartstring that had snapped as she realized that the intangible bond linking her and her twin sister together was rusting over, rotting away.

When Jade had broken the surface, Crys was no longer alone. Damon Yates, in his fine, midnight-blue tuxedo, stood between them. Everything about him was irritatingly smooth, except his pale blue eyes. There was a roughness in them, like shards of splintered glass that bore into Jade as she struggled to tread water.

Yates motioned to the tree. "*This* is all you can do with what I've given to you?"

But what had he given her besides a window into a life she would never belong to? His shiny world merely provided a mirror, showing her who she was always meant to be. A scapegrace. A fly-by-night crook, unattached and untethered.

An elbow to the ribs brought Jade back from her memories. "We've got half an hour max before the navy suits turn up to search Zoe's dorm," Ani said, cleaning green and yellow paint from her nails with the tip of a tanto knife. "Whatever grand plan you think you have, I suggest you get on with it."

They stood beneath a grove of California black walnut trees tucked away on the southern border of campus. Just as Jade had wagered, one of the many "just in case" exits she'd made during her stint at the academy was still there, allowing them to slip through the Quest gates unseen. A proclivity from her early foster care days—you never knew when you'd need to cut and run.

"Crys will most likely be at Aevitas House," Jade said. "We'll start our search there." She began moving toward the tree line, but the tough, green walnut husks crunching beneath her feet sounded wrong. Unaccompanied. She turned. Threw up her arms. "What's the problem?"

"Of course you're just here for Crys," Cole snapped, holding his ground. "Everything's *always* about you and your sister. Well, you can have fun abducting Gen 3 by yourself. It really worked out for you the first time."

Jade scoffed. "I didn't *force* Crys to go into the hyperloop tubes with me—"

"Just like you didn't force that Fortunate up onto First Street Bridge with you?"

The backs of Jade's ears burned. She still wasn't used to Cole's cantankerous moods. At Adsum, he had been carefree and content. A permanent smile. Nothing had surprised Jade more than the night he'd come knocking on her motor home's dented door, looking the image of abject misery. Cole, *Crys's ex*, was the *last* person she figured would have sought shelter under her meager, ruffled wing.

But one by one, every Exile had come to Jade for refuge. She'd never asked to be strapped with the role of caretaker, and they should've known she'd disappoint them, even cheat them, and then take off, like every other guardian had in their lives.

Ani pocketed her knife and turned her back on Jade, her thick ponytail whipping across her shoulders. She hadn't met Jade's eyes once since her return.

Jade knew Ani and Cole had a right to take a stand against her. She had it coming. But this really wasn't the right hill to die on.

"Look, this isn't about me, all right?" Jade pressed, lifting her open hands in a small gesture of cease-fire. "I'm here for Eli, to find answers and get him free. All I want to do is speak to Crys. Just talk to her. See if there's a connection between Eli and Zoe."

"Okay sure, and how are we going to do that?" Cole said irritably. He held a nail-bitten hand to his temple, like he was exhausted. "Ani and I will trip the facial recognition sensors if we go any deeper into campus. All good for you, of course. You've got *her* face."

"Yeah, well, I'm saving up for a new one," Jade joked, trying to keep her tone light. One early morning, when they couldn't sleep from Eli's snoring, Jade had asked Ani to sketch a new face for her on recycled paper they'd found in the park bins. A smaller nose, fuller cheeks. If she was unrecognizable to Crys, would her sister still detest the sight of her?

The last time Jade had seen Crys was during the rare occurrence when her sister had cause to leave campus, to board Yates's superyacht on the bay. Jade had waited all morning at the marina, but Crys had recoiled—*ran* from her—when she'd approached, shrieking for her to stay away. And for three years, Jade had done just that.

Ani's gaze found Jade's. She dug into a vegan-leather pocket and handed over a pair of round oversize shades. "In case you find her."

Was that sympathy softening Ani's steely eyes? Jade bristled but took the glasses. Gripped them tight. The lenses were smudged and scratched—it would be difficult to see in the dark—but if Jade wanted an interview with Crys, maybe they would help. Maybe she'd listen.

Maybe this time she wouldn't scream.

"Cole and I will go check out Beelzebub Rock," Ani offered. "Any Questers looking to blow off steam will be up there, getting high, trading rumors and theories about Zoe. Where she was, who she was with before . . . before you found her remains on our kitchen table. *Someone* has to know something."

Damon Yates, Jade wanted to shout. *Let's snatch him.* But it was too soon, Jade knew. You couldn't swoop in and capture a lion with only suspicions for weapons. *Data,* Yates would always preach. *Gather big data before you make big moves.*

Jade shoved on the shades and turned toward Adsum Peak. "I'll meet you back at our old Husk Row retreat. Don't wait for me."

"Don't worry," Cole answered, already halfway to the trail. "We never have."

Gemini winked down on Jade as she exited the academy's podcar station.

She'd been alone inside the cozy, cube-shaped cabin, no one present to witness the sentiments that flitted across her face as more cumbersome memories sucker punched her from every direction. The ring-shaped Quietude building, the hospital, the canyons dotted with coyote brush—she'd watched the familiar settings of her past rush across the pod's floor-to-ceiling windows. Yet somehow, the new places—the timber towers of the Forest, the idyllic employee housing compounds—landed harder, dirtier, than the memories.

Quest Campus was thriving. Here, things grew, while on the wrong side of the hyperloop tracks, things only ever crumbled. "Fortunes change," she mumbled half-heartedly, then spurred her body forward.

It wasn't long before sobs reached her on the crisp night air. She crouched low to the dew-covered grass and stalked toward the sound, sticking close to the vine-covered walls. Despite the late hour, inside Aevitas House a dozen Adsum students were wide awake, pacing up and down the common room, hugging each other and weeping. The glass veranda doors were wide open, as if in some vain hope of welcoming one of their own back home.

Jade didn't bother to scan the room for her sister. She knew Crys would be alone, sequestered from the others, mourning the loss of Zoe in private. *Why shed your insides for all to see?* Crys once told her. *Tears give you nothing but pity.* And Crys loathed pity even more than Jade did.

The third window on the left, if Jade remembered correctly. She prowled closer, nearly blinded by the geometric chandelier that shone like a beacon through the glass. She shrugged, tested whether the glass would rise beneath her gentle filcher's touch. The window yawned open. *Unlocked?* Jade shook her head, amazed. Crys had grown soft. Comfortable. Stupid.

Jade crept inside.

A woman sat hunched on the four-poster bed, its long white curtains pooling languidly on the ground beside her like drooping angel wings.

"I knew you'd come," Poppy whispered. "You never could stay far from trouble."

Jade hopped from the windowsill, landing solidly on her feet. "It's the other way around, actually. Trouble can't stay away from me." Keeping on her toes, she slid off her shades and glanced around the grand room that she'd once shared with Crys.

"Oh, is that why you're trespassing on Quest Campus?" Poppy sneered. "Breaking into the dormitory of your sister, because misfortune's chasing *you*?" The svelte dean looked haggard. Mystified. Her eyes two empty wells, her natural reservoir of poise and warmth drained. "Don't play the victim, Jade. Not tonight." Her pale fingers smoothed the wrinkled sleeves of the Adsum blazer draped over her lap.

Jade recognized the bright jazzy pins that embellished its left lapel, marking the uniform as Zoe's. Something lurched inside Jade's chest. The first signs of grief? Or a rising indignation at having to defend herself for the third time tonight? "The Exiles didn't kill Zoe Reeves," she answered. "You have to know that."

The dean's voice was stripped, like she'd cried herself hoarse. "I only know that one of my daughters is in a coroner's office, and one of my sons is in jail." She stilled her hands, peered up at Jade. "That Crystal Yates is missing and now you've returned home."

"Just a stopover," Jade replied, hiding her surprise that her sister was unaccounted for. She turned from Poppy's scrupulous gaze and moved for the glossy regency-style dresser that had replaced her twin bed. She perused the photographs on its marbled top. Crys and Zoe, frolicking on the sands of Silicon Bay. Yates, Crys at his side, on the ice fields of Antarctica, the Great Wall of China, grinning like a well-dressed goon as he showed the world to his future billion-heir.

"Where's Yates?" Jade challenged. "Sealed in his mansion, hoping his PR team can quiet the alarm bells that must be clanging in the masses' minds?"

Poppy sighed. "Don't be so callous, Jade. Damon is a wreck, a man in pieces—"

"Come on, Poppy. Gods don't break. We both know *the Savior's* only goal will be to save face, to hold together the image of his favorite charity project."

"Parity isn't charity," Poppy said with a drawn-out breath. "That's a lesson you never learned in your time here. How to receive support, love—"

"Seems like those lessons did jack for Zoe."

Poppy winced. "I've failed at many things. As a dean, as a guardian. But Zoe, our brilliant, radiant girl, was only just beginning. She did not deserve this end." After a long pause, Poppy cleared her throat. When she spoke again, her voice trembled. "Especially on the anniversary."

The anniversary of what?

And then another memory hit Jade, straight to her gut.

It was Remembrance Day. The anniversary of her orphanhood.

How could she have forgotten?

Jade's head began to spin. The room was steeped in Crys's signature perfume. Just-bloomed peonies, hints of cedar and amber. Jade despised the smooth, bold fragrance, the way Crys used it to cover up the stench of who she really was. Of where she'd come from.

Before Jade could stop herself, she raked her arms across the dresser, smashing Crys's gilded junk to the floor. She breathed hard, looking for the next meaningless thing to break, when something familiar caught her eye.

She bent down and picked up a spinning top. *How in the hell did Crys find this?* The faded wooden trompo had belonged to their father and had been Jade's favorite toy from childhood. From the time before. Before the world cracked open and swallowed her whole.

Poppy spoke of equality—well, it was only fair for Jade to have it now. She slipped the top into her pocket just as red and blue strobe lights flashed across the walls. The navy suits, come to cordon off Zoe's room. And maybe search for Jade, who was likely their prime suspect.

Jade flicked her eyes to the woman who'd once claimed to be her guardian. Waited for her to speak up, to yell, *She's in here!*

But Poppy just whispered, "Go."

Jade did the opposite. Her feet led her away from the window, toward the crestfallen dean. Toward answers and truth. "Eli's paralyzed again. Did you know?"

Poppy lifted her heavy lids, tears brimming in her deep-set eyes. "Another tragedy."

"Or another crime. Eli is a victim, just like Zoe."

"Who exactly are you accusing here?"

Jade hesitated. She had no hard facts. No evidence. "Yates," she answered anyway.

Poppy sighed. The navy suits were closing in on Aevitas House. Grave voices, brisk footsteps echoed off the sandstone patio outside, where the coastal morning fog was just beginning to roll in.

Jade tugged on the wide crewneck of her sweatshirt, her fingers scratching the knot of scar tissue that stood out on her shoulder like a malefic brooch. A memory, a clue, suddenly popped into her mind. "The night Maxen shot me, he was ranting about someone called 'the Doc' . . . He said he had to get rid of her. That she was reading his mind."

Poppy eyed the bullet around Jade's neck. "Not all tragedies are linked, darling. If it gives you some peace, Maxen had just learned that his father and I were separating. He had been seeing a therapist, but he was still acting out. That night he was lost in a misguided tantrum."

The cops were in the hall now. Students called the dean's name.

Poppy set aside Zoe's wrinkled blazer and rose from the bed, gathering herself. "If the police see you, I can't save you. If you're truly innocent, then *go*." She reached out and smoothed an unruly curl behind Jade's ear, the way she used to do when she was still her guardian.

It was then that Jade knew Poppy was just another one of Yates's victims. Whatever was happening to her foster children, the dean wasn't involved. Anyone trying to pin Zoe's murder on the Exiles wouldn't simply let Jade leave.

"But please," Poppy implored. "Stop looking for Crys. It will only cause more heartbreak. If you love her, stay away."

But Jade had stayed away too long.

Someone began pounding on the door, but Jade was already out the window, moving through the tall moonlit grass, her path set for a person, a place, that she thought of only once a year.

And if Crys was not on campus, she'd be there, too.

It was Remembrance Day, after all.

FIVE

The official residence of Dry River City's unofficial mayor was palatial by the neighborhood's standards. The tent was a medieval king's pavilion boasting hardwood floors, a Carrara marble–topped kitchenette in one corner, and a private bath concealed behind an ornate screen in the other. Large, jarring neo-expressionist paintings leaned against the canvas walls, the exclusive kind that required influence, rather than money, to acquire.

The mesh tent flaps were pinned aside, the exit wide open. Nothing bound her to her seat, but Crys was under no illusions that she was free to leave.

A severe boulder of a man was posted just outside, the one she'd heard the others call the Gravestone. And then, of course, Crys could not, *would* not, clamber up and out from this dry river, this concrete *hell*hole, until she'd gotten what she wanted, what they all apparently wanted.

Jade.

"You're trespassing," the mayor said from behind a heavy desk littered with Lladró porcelain figurines. He leered down at Crys in her high-backed chair, a dangerous smile edging his lips, and rapped his knuckles against the solid wood.

Crys flinched.

"You thought you could hide beneath golden curls and a flimsy mask, in *my* city," the mayor jeered. "You thought you could squirrel away with the River Rats and I wouldn't take notice? Your guts outweighed your guile, once again, Jade Moore. Your favors, your luck, have run out."

Before Crys could gather her wits for a reply, Sage and Wily sauntered into the tent. They took their place by the mayor's side, surprising Crys.

"We knew you were the scapegrace the moment you tried to cut and run," Sage growled. "*Again.*"

They're the ones who raised the alarm, Crys quickly reasoned. They'd mistaken her for Jade when she'd abandoned the Quake Tour.

"You know what they say about payback . . ." Wily sneered, slicing into a mango with a switchblade.

Sage leaned against the desk, grinning. "Hard cash is the best kind?"

Crys nearly choked on a laugh. Jade's own crew, two of her Exiles, were willing to turn her over to the law for a reward? Fleetingly, she wondered what Jade might have done to deserve such betrayal. Whatever had happened, it wasn't a clean break; Sage's and Wily's dirty looks suggested to Crys that their wounds still festered, a lingering tenderness that left them vulnerable. Credulous.

How could they not see? It had been a long time since Crys had been confused for anything other than the heiress—the *Yates*—that she was.

An acute distaste twisted Crys's mouth. *Play along,* she urged herself, stilling her shuddering limbs. She cleared her throat, sharpening her voice, making sure to throw her words like poisoned blades, the way Jade always did. "So I take it you think I'm to blame for Zoe Reeves's death?" Her blood simmered, her bones rattled against the strain of masquerading as her sister. Of admitting for the first time that her friend was gone. Murdered.

"Doesn't matter," the mayor answered, his shrewd smile melting into a scowl. "The navy suits do, and I won't let them think I gave you protection. Not this time."

Not this time. If Crys knew what Jade had done to them, it might give her a few breadcrumbs to follow, help her pinpoint where Jade could be hiding.

Sage shook her head. "You don't exactly have the best track record."

"This makes two kills now?" Wily said. "Two and a half, if you count almost killing your sister."

Crys willed her mind to stay in the tent, not to get sucked back to the terror inside the hyperloop tubes, her sister laughing as she screamed. Crys crossed her arms, lifted her chin, absorbing the news that Zoe wasn't Jade's first victim with practiced stoicism. "I have no idea what you're talking about," she finally answered. It was just the sort of smart-ass thing Jade would have said. *Confessions are for the God-fearing. Waifs own up to nothing.*

"Typical," Sage spat. She raked her acrylic nails, long as bone-white talons, through her unbrushed auburn hair, cursing at Crys in Latin, Italian, and finally in American Sign Language, slamming four erect fingers into a kind of salute along her forehead and nose.

Wily carved and swallowed a second piece of mango, licking his juicy lips.

The mayor slid a hand inside his striped suit jacket and produced a 3D-printed semiautomatic pistol. He placed the gun on top of the cluttered desk and tilted forward, tapping his knuckles again on the wood like a metronome, as if he expected Crys to start singing like a canary. "You mean to tell me," he pressed, "that you don't remember this gun?"

Crys shook her head, truthfully.

"Or the man it belonged to?"

She gave an honest shrug.

"The Fortunate whose body you threw from the First Street Bridge, whose precious skull splattered like a damn ostrich egg on *my* concrete river?"

Wily hurled the remnants of his mango past Crys's head. It exploded with a wet bang on the canvas wall behind her. This time, she didn't flinch.

"You have a following now, did you know?" Sage asked in a mocking voice. Sage studied Crys, her large gray eyes like brewing storm clouds. "Already have your very own theme song. *When misfortune chokes the air, bet your last dollar the Adsum pariah will be there. Makes misery then makes haste, she's the slippery scapegrace who lives for the chase.*"

"Why did you come here?" Wily pushed. "Did you think we'd shelter you? Forgive you? Or did you come to take us down like Zoe? Maybe rope us in, condemn us like Eli? I bet you can't stand seeing any of us holding our own without you." He stood proud, his sleek moleskin jacket draped on his wiry shoulders.

After just the barest hesitation, Crys spoke. "I had nowhere else to go." She held her answer out like a question, like bait. She hoped it wasn't true. Not for Jade's sake, but for her own. She held tight to the belief that one or both of them knew exactly where their old cohort could be.

"Oh, what a sad little story," Sage said sardonically. "It's the day of the quake and once again, you're left with no one . . ."

Crys closed her eyes, held a ragged breath, desperate not to smell the stench of her parents, the noxious fumes of the great fire that had burned her innocence to ashes. Her fingers fumbled inside her breast pocket, her tiny vial of perfume slipping from her sweaty grasp. When her lids fluttered open, Sage was inches from her face, her eyes now a shrewd slate gray.

"Only this time," she taunted, "you're all alone because it *is* your fault."

"Even that deadbeat street bum of yours wouldn't take you in this time?" Wily scoffed.

Crys's fingers curled, and as soon as she locked hold of the perfume, she grasped the answer she'd come here for. *She knew where Jade was hiding.*

With her uncle.

The other stain on her family tree.

Mind buzzing—how could Jade have ever gone to *that* man for help?—Crys bounded to her feet, the lyrics of Jade's "theme song" looping in her head. She had to go, before the slippery scapegrace slipped away again. But the tip of a blade against her carotid artery drove her back down to her seat.

No, not a blade. Sage's knifelike talons. A trickle of blood pooled into the small recess above Crys's collarbone. "What were you fiddling with in your pocket?" she asked. "A knife? Your signature flash grenade?"

Flash grenade?

"Now, now, Jade," the mayor said, clicking his tongue. "I thought we were playing nice."

A microscale error—a tick of her eyes, a twitch of her lips, Crys wasn't exactly sure what her tell had been—and a realization flashed bright as lightning across Sage's face. She lunged and seized the crystal vial from Crys's hands.

"We have an impostor in our midst," Sage spat. She held up the vial by its rose-colored atomizer, her face screwed up in such anger that veins popped out on her pale forehead.

"*Crys?*" Wily gaped. His eyes narrowed, as if aiming a gun. He shot forward, snatched the perfume vial, and launched it out the open tent door.

Crys tried to visualize the glass smashing against the pavement outside, to imagine she could smell the woody, floral bouquet, to ground herself in the scent. But it was useless.

"I don't give a dry rat's ass about why you're here," Wily seethed, stalking closer to Crys's chair, gripping his switchblade. "Tonight, all that matters is that *we*, little snitcher heiress, have unfinished business."

"You think I wouldn't find out it was *you* who snitched and got us thrown out of Adsum?" Sage said.

Crys was on her feet, shoving up her shirt's sleeve and holding up her left bicep.

Wily released a raucous laugh. "What, are you showing us your guns?"

The mayor flattened his hands against his desk, copper eyes leveling with Crys's icy glare. She brought her thumb to the soft skin of her upper arm. Four quick jabs would activate the subcutaneous microchip. Yates's bodyguards would arrive within minutes. "Afraid this interrogation is over."

"Let her go," the mayor sighed.

Wily gasped, incredulous. Sage put her hands on her curvy hips, daring Crys to move, her whisper the force of a gale against Crys's cheek. "You Fortunate piece of—"

"I said let her pass!" the mayor barked.

Sage and Wily parted, leaving only a narrow sliver for Crys to slip through. With gritted teeth, she sucked in a breath, making certain she glided by the pair untouched. Clean. She wanted to take nothing of this place back with her.

"Oh, and Ms. *Moore* . . ." the mayor said, his gritty voice dancing with devilish delight. His minions tittered at the insult. *The insolence.* "Be sure to tell Yates what I did for you."

Crys did not stop or look back. *I will tell* no one *of this,* she thought for the second time that night. Then she thought of Palmer and Vance. Her promise to her brothers that she could handle this. *Would* handle this.

There wasn't a chance in hell she'd return home empty-handed.

When she passed the Gravestone, the sturdy guard drew back, stumbling into an enormous aluminum statue that stood beside the entrance. Crys straightened. Finally, she was getting the respect a Yates deserved.

She made for the graffitied steps, a name from her past pulling her forward. Calling her back.

It was the name of a deadbeat. A bum.

Her loathsome uncle Willis.

Four years after the quake, Crys's uncle had shown up at the latest miserable inner-city school that she and Jade were attending, announcing he was going to take them in. No more foster homes. No more pretend parents pocketing their government subsidies while their own bellies went hungry. No more secret bruises, no more persistent threat of separation from her sister, no more lies and disappointment.

He was going to make them a family. A lasting one.

Willis had made this promise many vodka-soaked times before, but this time was different. This time he had a house—no, a *mansion*, in the heart of Beverly Hills, right on the very street he'd always said he'd one day inhabit: Rodeo Drive. They were moving up in the world, he had promised, finally getting a taste of the good life, a piece of the upper-crust pie reserved exclusively for hedge fund managers and Silicon Bay millionaires.

"You gotta be your own quake sometimes," he'd said with a rotten smile. "Shake things up."

Crys had smelled the alcohol on his stale breath, and yet she'd still let hope seep into her hopeless heart.

By the end of the week, they were in Central Juvenile Hall, worse off than when he'd collected them, stolen them, from the streets. Later, it emerged that he had swiped a wealthy investment banker's identity and taken out a home loan in the man's name. When LAPD had raided their shiny new Rodeo Drive address, Willis had been too drunk to care, let alone protect them.

The fresh dawn light suddenly gleamed against a sumptuous storefront window, bringing Crys back to the present. She stood once more on Rodeo Drive, looking out on the glitzy three-block stretch of glamorous boutiques and trendy restaurants, breathing its exclusive air.

She hadn't returned here in years. Nico and his team of stylists took care of all her wardrobe needs. But there was a time, a string of years, back when Jade was still with her at Adsum, when they'd come together to spy on their uncle on Remembrance Day. They'd look on the man, their wasted flesh and blood who'd chosen spirits and oblivion over them.

Crys would come to gloat. *We're the ones who've moved up,* she'd shout, knowing that even if she woke him from his stupor, he wouldn't recognize her.

But Jade, she'd come here to remember. What, exactly, Crys had never cared to ask. Their mother was nowhere in her brother Willis, even if he did share her pale skin, her loud, uninhibited laugh, and her penchant for wearing black, even on summer afternoons.

Crys stood well away from her uncle's gaudy hovel, which stood out like a vulgar eyesore against the whitewashed walls of Chanel. He'd upgraded from a pup tent to a bright yellow lean-to, the tattered tarp held up by dented aluminum trekking poles. A faded cardboard sign taped outside the door flap read, LET'S DO LUNCH—U BUY.

A woman in an exquisite tweed skirt suit approached Chanel's entrance. She swiped her manager's key card and threw a glossy sneer down at the lurid lean-to. "It's still here, Officer," she said into her diamond-encrusted earpods. She looked toward the next block, dotted with sun-bleached tents. "It's spreading to the westside. For Savior's sake, is there *really* nothing we can do about it?"

The "homeless rules" that every streetwise kid had memorized unwound themselves from the cobwebs of Crys's memory: if the dirt, grass, or concrete was ten feet from a building, entrance, or driveway, and at least five hundred feet from a school or park, and did not impede pedestrians on walkways, then the space was safe—it was *yours*. An officer could only kick a person out if there were shelter beds available, but of course, there never were. Follow the "homeless rules," and people like Willis could occupy a space on one of the most famous streets in the world. Free of rent, free of taxes.

The only price was a person's pride.

Willis's domestic monstrosity was a tasteless performance piece, a slipshod way of achieving his lofty dream of a house on Rodeo Drive. Crys wanted to melt into the shadows for shame. How could she be connected to *that*? Her blood began to boil, and for a moment she wished the heat could cleanse her.

Across the street, she pressed herself against the blinding Swarovski facade made from thousands of thin stainless-steel mirror reliefs that reflected the sparkling products sold inside. Crys needed to spot Jade before Jade spotted her. She determined that the bright light of the "crystal forest" could provide her cover, dazzling Jade's vision. Quietly, careful not to catch a glimpse of her own reflection, Crys's eyes swept the street, but she found the road deserted of Porsches and Lamborghinis, and the sidewalks cleared of the usual throngs of tourists eager to catch a glimpse of the rich and famous.

Free of the tall, swift-moving Jade Moore.

Crys wondered if Jade was inside the hovel with Willis, commiserating or fast asleep.

Should she attempt an ambush? Or somehow smoke her out and *then* strike?

A police helicopter passed overhead. *Metal birds*, Questers liked to call them. They rarely flew over the mansion-packed hills of the metropolis's westside. *Crime don't climb,* she'd heard an officer remark once. The sonorous whirs of the metal bird vibrated the concrete beneath her feet.

"It's not a quake," she whispered, rooting herself. *And I'm not the one they're after.*

When the roar of the metal bird faded, the ground once again still, *solid,* Crys heard a live podcast spilling from a passing Quest AV. Amateur investigators already dissecting the "Adsum Atrocity," breaking down the crime scene with detailed enthusiasm.

The images that Crys had pretended not to see at Dry River City, the leaked, viral video of Zoe's dead body, flashed like a bomb inside her mind. She closed her eyes, as if this could block out the unbearable, and then her invisible flames were out, ready to set fire to the past, singe the damage, burn away the memory until it disappeared. Before it could ignite, someone spoke.

The voice was distant, blunt, yet forceful enough to cut straight through her.

"It's me," Jade said. "Don't turn around. Don't scream."

Crys turned around and screamed bloody murder.

Six

Jade imagined that most family reunions consisted of hugs, wet kisses on cheeks, heartfelt proclamations of *So good to see you* and *I've missed you.*

But Jade got a hard cross punch to the jaw that knocked her flat to the ground. Ani's ineffective shades skittered out of reach. "Okay, maybe I deserved that."

Before Jade could jump to her feet, Crys swung back her leg, landing a vicious kick to her ribs.

Jade hissed painfully. "Now *that* was a cheap move for a billion-heir."

Groaning, she got to her knees. Crys faced her with raised fists, sweat pooling on her forehead, her body trembling. She looked just above Jade's head, her eyes wild with fear.

Jade wasn't sure what she'd expected, seeing her sister for the first time in three years, but it wasn't this.

"You thought you could come for me, but I'm the one who's come for you," Crys said, and she pounced.

She must have forgotten how much Jade loved threats. A smile cut across Jade's face as she rose, adrenaline coursing through her bitter heart. "You're fighting with a serious handicap, considering you can't even stand to look at me." A weakness Jade fully intended to exploit. She whistled, drawing Crys's gaze, their eyes locking.

Goose bumps erupted up and down Crys's arms, and she let loose a piercing scream. Half-mad with fear, she attempted to shrink back, but Jade already had a viselike grip on her wrist. She drove her heel into the side of Crys's knee, cutting her down to the sidewalk. The fall took the wind out of Crys, and she lay on the pavement wheezing, still pushing out a raspy scream. Jade knew her sister despised her, had anticipated that Yates would use the trauma of their parting to turn Crys against her. But this was a whole different level.

This was terror.

Jade dove on top of Crys, pinning her hands above her head with one hand, covering her eyes with the palm of her other. If she could just get Crys to settle down, to *connect* with her, maybe she could get her to snap out of it.

Maybe she could even bring her sister back to her.

"Crys, please . . . it's just me."

Crys sank her teeth deep into the ball of Jade's thumb and bridged her hips to the sky, flipping Jade onto her back. Jade shielded her face with her elbows, preparing for a barrage of strikes. Instead, Crys pushed off her chest and *ran*, still screeching.

Not down Rodeo, escaping back where she belonged, but toward their uncle's lean-to. Instead of slamming her panic button—the safe, predictable next move—Crys surprised Jade. She yanked one of the shelter's poles free, and the right side of the fluorescent tarp caved in, a brutish growl emerging from beneath the toxic polypropylene heap.

Crys turned, lifting the pole into a fencing stance. Her anguished eyes aimed at Jade's chest, her empty hands, anywhere but her face.

"Did you kill Zoe just for the rush?" Crys seethed. "You couldn't help yourself, could you? Throwing that Fortunate man off the bridge. I went to Dry River. I know what you did."

There was no point arguing. Jade unzipped her bag.

Before Crys could charge, Jade drew her police-issue BolaWrap and fired. A Kevlar cord shot forward, its hooks wrapping around Crys's arms and legs. Jade yanked, tipping Crys onto the crumpled lean-to.

Willis's scraggly head popped out, firing off obscenities. He gaped blearily at Crys, lying tied up like a hog on top of his house, and then proceeded to pass out. Jade shook her head as she approached, her eyes sweeping over the tarnished Citizens Medal of Valor her uncle wore around his grimy, sunburned neck. Willis had single-handedly saved over a dozen people from the Greater LA Fire that had swept through his neighborhood, his legs sustaining third-degree burns in his act of courage. Then the hospital bills came, and there had been no one to save *him*.

Not everyone had a golden parachute to break their fall.

In her mad struggle to free herself, Crys's head flailed back, her wide blue eyes latching onto Jade's profile. High-pitched screams sent chills down Jade's spine as she bent low over her sister. She pulled a kerchief from her back pocket and stuffed it into Crys's mouth.

An affluent man hurried past, not bothering to stop and help a young woman in clear distress. Why would he? Crys wasn't clothed in her rich Adsum blues. She looked like just another waif, like somebody else's problem.

"Sisters, am I right?" Jade gave the man her best shit-eating grin in case more scrupulous eyes were watching, then seized the zip ties that held the trekking poles to the tarp. "I'm going to delasso your arms, okay?" she whispered, careful to stay outside of Crys's sight line. "Just promise not to punch me again."

That proved too much to ask. The moment Jade released the unbreakable cord, Crys landed a knife-hand strike to her neck.

Rebounding quickly, Jade managed to get hold of Crys's arms and fasten the zip ties around her wrists. Elbows high, left arm locked at an angle behind her head. Not comfortable, but the only position that would safeguard against Crys using her anti-abduction chip to call for backup.

Why couldn't Crys understand that Jade was trying to save her?

"I know I don't deserve it," Jade pleaded, "but can you just trust me?" Like she used to. When all they had was each other.

Crys screamed into her gag.

Jade tapped open an encrypted messaging app on her phone and typed a message. She kept the invitation—the summons—short and sweet, knowing it would disappear from the group chat after five seconds, with no way of snapping screenshots.

I have evidence. Husk Row, noon. rfa.

Red fucking alert.

The houses stood like rotted tombs, the long street a graveyard made by fire. Cracks lined the road, thick and deep, as if the earth had finally shown its age. The two-seater Quest AV slowed, idling beside the weed-infested curb, and a velvety voice issued from the speakers: "This street has been designated a rehabilitation zone. It is unsafe to proceed. Please update your desired location or exit now."

Inside the AV, Jade fiddled with the rough edges of her necklace, In Extremis, and stared out at the charred and forsaken bungalows of Husk Row, one of the numerous Unfortunate streets still left unhealed from the quake. *A fitting place to mend the fractured Exiles,* she thought wryly. As the AV's door opened, all she could see was a broken past,

68

an abandoned future. This was the *last* place to venture seeking repair and recovery.

So it was the last place Yates or the navy suits would think to look.

Jade glanced at Crys. She no longer screamed or thrashed, but her body still trembled aggressively. And she wasn't talking, even when Jade had briefly removed the gag.

"We're going to walk now," she announced, adopting the soft, neutral tone of the AV. "Just keep your eyes on my feet and you won't trip."

Crys made no indication she'd heard, but when Jade propelled her forward, Crys obeyed with minimal struggle. Jade had zip-tied herself to Crys, and it took a few steps for them to get their three-legged shuffle down. They passed six wooden husks and turned left, then halted in front of a squat stucco house with no roof, wide-open windows, and cotton candy–colored walls, at least where the paint hadn't blackened when the entire block had baked in the fires. Inside, the floor had been scorched down to the concrete foundation.

Jade grinned. Ani's mural was still there, a bit faded but unmarred. It spanned the living-room floor: a portrait of the City of Angels, of wingless mortals being swallowed up by the broken earth, reaching toward a white-suited man on a mountaintop. Wings sprouted from his sides, vast and black-tipped like a predacious archangel. *Yates.*

A poor woman's Sistine Chapel, Ani had said when it was finished. Jade told her it would be a trending geotag, a tourist destination, if she only took a snap and shared it. Neither of them did, of course. This place was theirs. Or it had been.

Judging from the scattered shoeprints and chip bags, others had come and gone. But where were the Exiles? It was a quarter past noon.

"No point in hiding," Jade yelled. "We're all ex-foster sibs here—no need to be shy!"

Crys groaned, struggling to free herself.

Jade dragged them over to an unreliable-looking lawn chair, laboring to keep up her amicable tone. "Remember when Poppy used to say we were attached at the hip?"

Crys snarled, and the tattered kerchief slipped from her mouth and fell to the mural, landing on a naked woman, who looked suspiciously like Jade, floating serenely in Echo Park Lake's filthy waters while the city fell to pieces around her. The kerchief was patterned with a brightly colored *calavera*—a skull—and was identical to the one they'd seen their father carry in old videos on his long-dead social-media accounts.

"Remind you of someone?" she asked Crys. "Your real dad?"

With her free hand, she sliced the zip ties with a pocketknife and sat Crys down on the folding chair, her eyes now sealed closed. Jade could almost have mistaken Crys for sleeping, or meditating like Yates in his Quietude, if it weren't for the clenched hands and bruised knuckles, white as bared teeth.

"Now it's my turn to trust you," Jade said, backing away slowly and pocketing her knife. "If you don't run or scream, we won't have any problems. Just sit and hear me out. I'm not the one you should fear."

She heard movement outside. Scuffling, heated whispers, then Sage filled the doorframe.

"I told you to watch your step," she said irritably, as Wily wiped his boots on the concrete beside her.

"Yeah, well, I thought that was more of a *figurative* warning, for when we got inside," Wily answered. He scratched at the rakish scar that bisected his right brow. "Not 'watch your step, there's a steaming pile of shit in your path.'" He tore into an ice cream sandwich, mumbling, "Savior save me if it's human feces again."

Sage hit him on the shoulder, drawing his attention to the back wall.

"Am I seeing double," he growled, "or do we have two Moores in the same room?"

Sage charged straight for them. "What is this? Another trick?"

Crys had her eyes open now, narrowed on the new arrivals.

"This isn't a trick." Jade stepped forward, hands up, nothing to hide. "This is an inquest."

Despite the daggered glares they were throwing her, Jade was relieved that they'd answered her summons. She was going to need Sage's mind and Wily's guile on her side again if she wanted to clear her name and boost Yates's to the top of the suspect list.

"Well, this Remembrance Day keeps getting more shocking," Wily said, his smile flashing alongside his switchblade. "'Cause there's not a chance in a million you two would align again."

"I'd *never* throw myself in with you rank lot," Crys shouted. She rose from her chair, her golden curls swinging like punches.

"Wow, sib, tell us how you really feel." Ani hovered in the back doorway, the leather of her black moto jacket crunching as she crossed her arms.

The better to reach her many knives, Jade thought, heedful.

"Looks like you did abduct her after all." Cole shouldered past Ani into the house, his face dull and chapfallen, like he hadn't slept in weeks. He clocked the bruise on Jade's jaw, the abrasions on Crys's wrists. "And you did a lot more than just talk."

Crys stiffened at Cole's appearance, suddenly fidgeting with her obviously borrowed clothes, her poor choice of disguise.

The fractured Exiles hovered on their respective sides of the ravaged house, refusing the chairs that were laid out in a circle. Everyone held a weapon; even Crys had managed to find a bone-breaking clump of concrete.

"Cole, I gotta say, you're taking the whole rough-and-rugged look to new heights," Wily said, munching on another bite of ice cream. "What's your secret, you on the antishowering trend?"

"We don't all get handouts from a shady mayor like you River Rats," Cole replied flatly.

Sage's cheeks flared redder than her auburn locks. "Seems like we made the right choice in splitting ways, considering an Adsum prefect was just found in your motor home . . ."

"We were doing fine until Jade showed up again," Ani shot back.

Jade sighed. "I didn't call everyone here for a brawl." She held up her calloused palms again. "Remember how old street chums meet, with empty hands, open minds?"

But then Jade realized that not all the Exiles had arrived. Khari was missing. "Where's your girlfriend?" she asked Ani, realizing how much she longed to see the pompous hell-raiser who'd always kept her on her toes. And Ani in stitches.

"We fell out," Ani answered, crossing her arms tighter across her chest.

"Hot and cold, per usual." Cole shrugged, his gaze sliding to Crys. "We haven't seen her in months."

It could be a coincidence. An unhoused person—especially a young woman—disappearing in LA was as common as a palm-tree sighting. Khari could have relocated or simply snubbed Jade's message. Or maybe she was dead, like Zoe, and no one knew it.

Jade turned to Ani, who glared down at her mural, at Yates and the gilded pit viper that curled above the waves of his beach-blonde hair like a venomous halo. "Did you find anything at Beelzebub Rock?" Jade asked, stepping closer.

Ani's thick brows rose. "Only more theories about you, the scapegrace—"

"You mean the scape*goat*," Jade corrected. "I seem to keep having to repeat myself. I did not kill Zoe. There's something larger going on here, and I have evidence to prove it."

At least she hoped she did.

Jade set down her bag, pulled out a thin silver whistle, and blew. In less than a minute, a stocky Labrador retriever with an extravagant ruff of yellow fur came bounding through the door and stood at Jade's side, thick tail swaying, open mouth slavering.

"What is this? Canine therapy?" Cole asked.

"Even better," Jade said, leading the dog to the center of the room. She sat on the dusty floor, legs outstretched, arms raised high above her ears. "Thoreau, go find!" she commanded. The dog immediately began sniffing Jade all over, starting with her feet. She suppressed a ticklish chuckle when Thoreau's snout got to the sensitive spot behind her knees. She'd spent years honing her razor-sharp image, and she wasn't going to lose it on a giggle. The dog moved to her face, letting out a short woof when its nose reached her temple. Jade surged to her feet, tossing Thoreau a treat. "*Very* good girl."

"Did the dog just confirm that you're cracked in the head, or . . . ?" Wily said, confused.

"Thoreau here's a tech-detection K9," Jade explained, leading the dog over to Ani and Cole. "One of my contacts who squats four blocks down from here is a technophobe. She poached Thoreau from the FBI and trained her to sniff out microchips that she's convinced the government secretly implanted inside her."

Thoreau barked frantically when she buried her muzzle in Cole's chestnut curls, then again immediately on her first whiff of Ani.

"Her specialty was sniffing out micro-SD cards brimming with child porn," Jade added. "She's bagged droves of pedophiles, haven't you, girl?" She tossed Thoreau another treat.

"While all of that superfluous information is fascinating, what does it have to do with *us*?" Sage said, eyeing the dog warily as it approached her.

Three sharp woofs. Another detection, then again with Wily.

At last Thoreau padded up to Crys. She didn't try to pull back, allowing the dog to sniff her over. Thoreau placed her paws on Crys's chest, then softly licked her forehead and let out a high-pitched whine.

"Zoe's death and disposal," Jade said. "Khari's disappearance. Eli's paralysis and arrest." *Crys's inability to see me clearly,* she wanted to add. "They're all connected. They all share a link: Yates. He's behind all of it."

Crys glared at the floor by Jade's feet, her voice preternaturally calm. "This sounds like the same kind of theories that led me down a tunnel I'm not fucking going down again."

Jade flinched, worried that the others would jump on the reason—the incident—that had made Jade leave Adsum.

Wily rushed forward, breaking the standstill. "Wait, what happened to Eli? He can't walk again?"

Cole lowered his gaze, rubbing his arms. "He went down when we ran from the navy suits . . . We couldn't carry him."

"You think Khari could really be missing?" Ani asked.

"Look, Crys is right," Jade admitted. "It's just a theory, but think about it. Yates is a tech billionaire who built an entire campus dedicated to innovation. Is it so far-fetched to think he would use his academy as a research facility?"

"So, let me get this straight," Sage chimed in, speaking slowly, like she was the only sound mind in the room. "A stolen police dog is supposed to convince me that there's some mysterious Quest tech implanted inside us?"

Jade nodded, her confidence hardening. "Whatever implant Zoe was given must have malfunctioned like Eli's, except hers was lethal. Yates had her planted in our motor home to cover his tracks. His mistakes." She flicked her eyes toward her sister, making sure she heard. "His crimes."

"I can't listen to this anymore," Crys said, fully turning her back on Jade. "You were always against Damon—my *father*—always a conspiracy theorist, but Wily was right. You're cracked." She moved for the back door.

"*I'm* the one who's cracked?" Jade sputtered.

Crys lifted her arm, fingers hovering above her panic chip. "I never want to see your face again."

Although Jade didn't want to show the others, or *herself*, how much revulsion Crys had for her, she knew it was an exclamation point to her theory about Yates. And it was a bitter point, a painful one, that had to be made. Something was seriously wrong, and Crys's violent reaction to her was indisputable, living proof.

Jade lunged in front of Crys before she could punch the code into her chip, gripping Crys's face directly in front of her own. For a moment, just a split second, they stared at each other, matching glares. Then, as expected, a gut-wrenching scream erupted from Crys's chest. She flailed in panic, sending the chunk of rubble in her left hand straight into Jade's face. A sickening *crack* told Jade her sister had hit bone, but she didn't break that easy. She held the bridge of her bloody nose, her voice tight and nasally, watching as Crys attempted to flee.

"She can't even look at me without shrieking," Jade insisted. "It's like she was *made* to hate me."

Wily and Sage gave each other a look, then not so gently grabbed hold of Crys.

"I wasn't *made* to do anything," Crys fumed. "So, I despise you, who doesn't?"

But Jade could see through the smoke screen. Crys was scared stiff, a cold sweat dripping off her. *She doesn't understand what is happening to her, either.* Jade had a sudden inclination, an urge to reach for her phone, flick open its camera. Conduct an experiment of her own. She leapt for Crys and thrust the screen—Crys's image—in front of her eyes before she could lock them shut.

Crys's cries hit Jade's wall of resentment hard enough that the screams struck pity. The Exiles looked on in horror.

"I rest my case." Jade cupped her nose, holding back a gush of blood. "The Adsum orphans are more than just a social experiment. The faster we accept this, the fewer of us die." The kerchief she'd shoved in Crys's mouth earlier lay beside her boot. Jade picked it up and blew her nose, staining the vivid calavera red. She cleared her throat. "We protected each other once, we can band together again. Fortunes *can* change."

No one echoed her rallying cry, but then again, nobody turned to leave.

Ani finally spoke. "What do we do with Gen 3?"

"We keep her," Jade answered, ignoring her sister's violent protests. *We can restore our bond, too,* she told herself. *I can fix Crys.* She just had to tear out every bit of Yates in her.

Starting with that implant.

SEVEN

Shirim. Shiririiiiim. Shiiiiririmmmm.

Damon Yates had been silently chanting his sacred mantra for hours.

A meaningless, vibrational Sanskrit sound passed down to him through a long line of teachers over thousands of years.

Shirim. Shhhiriiiim.

A focused word that cleared his mind. Brought him into a state of transcendence.

Shiiiiririmmmm.

But not this time.

His overactive mind was like a raft in a tumultuous ocean. Again and again he attempted to dive below the surface. Reach the silent depths.

Shiri—

Another wave hit him.

He heard his new mother approach from behind. In his memory, she enveloped him with her lithe body, resting her chin on the crown of his grubby head. They stood in front of a modest, pueblo-style home, a string of dried chilies hanging from its adobe walls. His new father told him the chilies gave rise to *good luck and better feasting*. His parents had made a room for him; the UV-painted stars his father had hand-drawn still drying on the low ceiling. The room, *his* room, had not one but *two* eastward-facing windows with views of the sweeping high-desert Sangre de Cristo Mountains.

"There's plenty of sun to grow here," his mother whispered to him, smiling, planting the first seeds of optimism, *ambition*, inside his mire of a heart.

Shirim. Shiririiiiim. Shiiiiririmmmm.

Damon bent all of his will, all his power of thought, on the word. Eyes sealed shut, tailbone digging into the bamboo floor.

Shhhiriiiim.

He felt his mind dip, then begin to glide into a peaceful trance.

And then a titanic underwater wave struck him, tossing his subconscious around like a bath toy.

Am I worth it?

Am I good enough?

How can I be more?

He heard his worries, his torments, echoing off the illustrious halls of Princeton. He was on the edge of manhood, and yet still he was consumed, *driven*, by the ache of being given up, handed away, discarded by those who had created him, who had brought him into this brutal, iniquitous world.

Don't be enough.

Be more. Be worthy.

Shiririiiiim—

Damon's inner voice screamed, yanking him out of the painful memory wave. But it was a waste of effort. A swell crashed into him, wave after wave of intrusive thoughts gripping him like treble hooks, pulling him to the surface.

The reporters. The vultures. How many of them were gathered outside his campus gates?

Shirim.

You weren't expected, you were selected, he'd told Zoe Reeves, on the morning he collected her from the overburdened group home she'd been surviving in. *You were chosen.* The same shot in the arm his own saviors had given to him. *Not forsaken.*

Shirim.

Be worthy. Be more.

Shirim.

And he was.

She was.

Shirim.

Then why is the young woman dead? he heard the irritating cynics squall.

Why was the LAPD rifling through his academy, his mansion?

Where was Damon hiding?

Shhhhhiriiiimmmm.

For one glorious moment Damon's mind went blank. Clear as a freshly wiped hard drive.

He heard two sets of bare feet approach. An urgent whisper: "*Father.*"

Palmer, his eldest. The boldest of his sons, who walked into any room with the confidence of a man with an army at his back.

I've taught him well, Damon thought.

And yet he remained locked inside his inner kingdom, unresponsive to the outside world. He hadn't yet found his clarity, rebalanced his body and mind for what lay ahead.

His sons could wait.

Shiri—

"Father, Crystal has gone missing."

Damon's eyes flashed open. The expansive blue of the Pacific filled his vision. Glasslike, calm, the manifestation of all he had been seeking when he came to the Quietude.

He would suck the whole ocean dry, take all of her power, her strength, for himself, if he could.

His rings carved painfully into his flesh as he clenched his fists.

Through the window's reflection, Palmer and Vance must have seen the fury that burned across their father's face. They took a step backward.

"If we'd known you'd returned, we'd have come sooner," Vance said, a touch of pleading, of shame, in his voice. *A guilty conscience needs no accuser.*

Damon sprang to life. He grabbed hold of each son's stiff collar with an unconquerable strength. "Will there ever come a day when you come to me with solutions instead of problems?"

It was then he realized how much he resented his sons, both generations. They were born with silver spoons in their mouths. *They'd never be as hungry as an orphan.*

He let go of his sons and turned to the shadow standing in the corner.

"Bring me back my daughter."

Rhett, his trusted protector, his loyal enforcer, nodded and slipped out from the room.

EIGHT

Crys was asleep when she heard her sister's whisper.

"Wake up, I have something to show you." Jade's dark curls framed her bright brown eyes, her lively smile. "It's a surprise." She tore open the dresser that divided their twin beds, tossing Crys a warm set of clothes.

It was past two a.m. Well past curfew. But Crys rose, went with Jade out of their dormitory, across campus to the HyperQuest portal.

Had Jade found the treasure? Years ago, Damon had hidden a chest somewhere within the campus's thousand acres. He aspired to encourage discovery, to entice his Questers to step away from their screens and remember that in life, there was always something new to find. Eight clues to its location were woven into a poem, the treasure rumored to be riches greater than money.

Crys wanted nothing more than to be the one who found it. To prove to Damon that she was an explorer, a budding pathfinder worthy of his notice.

The portal's platforms were empty, its tracks free of pods. Jade jumped onto the east track, heading for the hyperloop tube's entrance. Crys hesitated.

"It's safe," Jade promised. "There's no pods scheduled for Quest this late."

Drowsy and foolish, Crys hopped onto the track and disappeared after her sister.

When the entrance sealed behind them, Jade placed a sleek oxygen mask over each of their faces, and they set off down the nearly airless tube by the light of their phones.

Crys didn't want to tell Jade she was scared. To have her sister taunt, like she had so many times lately that she'd turned dull, unimaginative. Pampered.

They must have been half a mile from campus when Jade finally stopped. "It's somewhere here, I know it."

Crys's heart soared. "The treasure chest?"

"No." Jade frowned beneath her mask. "What's left of the bodies."

Crys stumbled, her bare feet slipping on the steel floor. "Bodies? Whose bodies?"

"The ones Yates wants no one to find."

"You're crazy," Crys screamed. Goose bumps invaded her arms, her fine hairs stiffening, telling her to get out.

Run.

She turned, Jade chasing after her. "Think about it, Crys! This is a perfect execution chamber. The message boards are on fire with theories, if you'd just listen—"

"You'll do anything, won't you? Even get us killed, to turn me against Damon. To get me to leave and go back to our miserable lives together."

Crys swallowed her screams. Suddenly choking on panic. She'd opened the HyperQuest app on her phone. Checked for any arrivals due for campus.

She barely whispered. "There's a pod coming."

Jade smiled. Smiled. "How long do we have?"

Crys didn't answer. Couldn't. Her mind had been taken over, a hostage to fear.

She ran, she clawed, she screamed for escape, Jade laughing at her side, like death was a game. A challenge.

A light pierced the tube's darkness behind her.

She was given only fifteen years. It wasn't enough.

It wasn't enough.

She closed her eyes.

Heard a deafening thud. Then someone calling her name.

"Crystal?"

She ripped open her lids.

Damon was sprinting toward her from a grounded hyperloop pod, its emergency exits ajar. "I received an alert from Quest's portal security. If I hadn't seen you on the cameras . . ."

. . . If he hadn't acted fast, initiated the pod's reverse thrusters, there'd be nothing left of her now.

She thought he'd be furious, but she saw tears. Damon covered her with his arms. "What would ever bring you here?"

Crys couldn't even look at her. But she spat her name. "Jade."

Crys blinked open her bleary eyes, then woke with a start. It took her a moment to realize where and when she was.

She dug through her memories, uncovering how she'd ended up here. She remembered Wily cropping up beside her at Husk Row. The smirk on his face before he'd stabbed her with a syrette laden with some kind of sedative. In the span of a skipped heartbeat, she'd lost consciousness.

She was in another Exile "retreat." A hideout, this one a family-sized tent that smelled of overheated plastic and hints of wild sagebrush. It was quiet, birdsong replacing the din of the city.

"Good," Ani said. She sat cross-legged near the tent's zipped-up door. "You're awake."

Crys rose from the half-inflated air mattress and saw a swollen bruise along her left elbow, noticing how sore her right shoulder and buttock were. How many times had they dropped her comatose body on their journey to wherever it was they were now sequestered?

"Wily should be in prison," Crys said, trying her best to avoid touching her parched tongue against her fuzzy teeth. "Cellmates with Jade."

And where was Jade now? Likely off kidnapping Adsum sibs, trying to gather more evidence for her ridiculous accusations against Crys's father. She knew Jade wouldn't stop until Crys's new family was ruined, the Yates Empire left with nothing. Like Jade had nothing.

She wouldn't stop until she'd brought Crys down with her.

"You had it coming," Ani said, nodding to Crys's sore arm. "Wily pays his grudges in full. Any chance he had, he bellowed on about how you got him and Sage thrown out of the academy. You stole their futures."

"Oh, *I* told them to hack into Damon's social-media accounts and run a cryptocurrency scam?" All her father's channels had posted the same charitable message: *I'm feeling extra generous today. I'll double any Bitcoin payments sent to my BTC address in the next hour. Send $1,000 and I'll send $2,000 back to you!* In the five minutes it took for the posts to get deleted by Quest's army of social-media managers, Wily and Sage had accumulated a queen's ransom in donations.

Ani shook her head, her high ponytail lashing back and forth like a riding crop. "If you hadn't snitched, they'd still be bathing in caviar, preparing for fall internships at a Fortune 500."

"Wily and Sage committed a federal crime," Crys pointed out. "Expulsion was an act of mercy on Damon's part. Even after global humiliation, he still protected them and used his influence to get all their charges dropped."

"Yeah, and then he dropped *them*," Ani countered. She pulled out her phone and stared at the screen, a deep scallop-shell wrinkle between her brown eyes. Crys guessed she was looking for news. For a text from Khari. Just like Crys had when she'd heard Zoe was missing.

Crys knew she should take advantage of Ani's momentary distraction, lift two fingers to her upper arm, and jab the code into her panic chip. She knew the circumstances had changed, had grown larger than Zoe's murder. More complicated than merely bringing Jade back to Quest Campus for her reckoning.

And yet Crys's hands remained firmly in her lap. She refused to be rescued, to return home a victim.

"Your sister said you'd gone soft," Ani said, plucking an acrylic paint pen from the pocket of her moto jacket. "I expected you to tap the chip in your arm the moment you woke up, but it seems you have more pluck than Jade gives you credit for." She pulled a patchwork denim jacket from a duffel bag at her feet and began to draw the profile of a woman's face along its back. "That, or you found the signal jammer Sage sewed into your shirtsleeve."

Crys stood, feigning a luxurious stretch, hoping to covertly check the seams of her sleeve. There it was, a disrupter hidden just above her elbow.

The Exiles are not to be underestimated, Crys reminded herself. They were, despite all their shortcomings and failures, Adsum raised. Adsum trained.

An adversary, now united, who would not be so easily outsmarted.

Crys needed to weaken them, divide them again, coax an Exile or two back over to Yates's—*Crystal* Yates's—side. Someone must regret leaving the high life behind.

"Is that one of Eli's pieces?" Crys asked, affecting interest.

"Yeah, he lets me put my art on them sometimes. This one's for him, for when we get him out of jail."

Crys remembered Jade telling the others that Eli's paraplegia had returned before he'd been arrested. Eli had rarely spoken to Crys at the academy, but she knew he'd suffered from a severe spinal cord injury in the 2040 Quake. The walls of his parents' mom-and-pop restaurant caved in, killing the rest of his family and leaving him paralyzed below the waist.

It was Quest, and the healing power of money, that had rehabilitated Eli and gotten him back on his feet, not some experimental—*criminal*—tech as Jade was so rashly and recklessly alleging.

Did Jade really think the snout of a stolen Labrador would pull Crys back to her side?

"Have you heard from Khari yet?" Crys gazed down at Ani's work, watching the loose contour lines begin to form the sharp, elegant edges of Khari's face and the long, thick strands of her box braids. "Have the others found her?"

"It's like my phone is a black hole. It hasn't lit up in hours." For a while Ani said nothing more, lost in the likeness, the echo, of her ex. Her eyes turned glassy as she tossed aside Eli's jacket. "I should be out there looking for her myself, but instead I got benched to stay here and play sentry to *you*."

"Do you do everything Jade tells you to do?"

"That's a bit rich, coming from you. You'd walk through a wildfire if any Yates asked you to."

"Adsum doesn't foster followers," Crys said simply.

When she reached back into her recollection, Crys found only a feeling about Ani and her time at the academy. A word: *troubled*. Not everyone could manage the pressures that came with being handpicked by Damon Yates. *No pressure, no diamonds,* Zoe liked to say. But not all could keep up. Ani couldn't handle the expectation, so she ran from it. Khari left soon after. *I'll live and die by my own rules* were Khari's parting words if Crys's memory served correctly.

But why had they gone to *Jade*? An academy runaway who brought misfortune to anything she touched with her gluttonous hands. Did the Exiles think Jade took them in out of some sense of altruism, rather than to feed her own selfish needs? Although Jade sauntered about in the guise of some enigmatic loner, Crys knew the real Jade. Stripped bare, the naked truth: Jade couldn't be on her own.

Because she'd never been alone. Not truly. Since the second day of her creation, she'd had someone by her side. First Crys, her "womb-mate," as Jade used to call her, then Ani, her malleable sidekick.

"Do you not think Jade is purposely keeping you in the dark? That she's out there covering her tracks?" Crys raised her voice, both to make certain Ani was really listening and on the off chance there might be a passerby. "What if Khari's dead like Zoe, because Jade wants you to need *her*. Want her. Trap you beside her, like she's doing to me?"

"For Savior's sake, Crys, give it a rest," Ani said. She rubbed a hand across her face, leaving paint smudges on her nose and chin. "Your sister is many, *many* things, but she's no murderer."

"I've heard otherwise. Something about a Fortunate and First Street Bridge . . ."

A shadow fluttered across Ani's eyes. "You don't know what you're talking about."

"Is that why her crew left her? Or did Jade dump the Exiles first?"

Ani's mouth puckered, like she'd suddenly swallowed something bitter. "Listen, little miss billion-heir, you might run Adsum Peak, but here in this tent you're at the bottom of the ladder, so sit down and stop talking or I'll make you face your reflection." She lifted her phone and waved the front-facing camera toward Crys.

Crys slammed her eyes shut, ducking low.

"You can't even stand to *look* at yourself. Do you honestly think that's natural? Is your fear really caused by Jade, or can you just not bear to see what Yates has made you become?"

On the back of Crys's lids, she saw Jade's face, *her* face, glaring at her through the dark.

Her hands shook, and she had to bite back a panicked cry. Zoe was the only one who'd known hints of her trauma and the fear incursions that had followed. Crys hardly admitted her shameful affliction, even to herself. What right did Ani have to interrogate her, to make her question her own mind?

"I was seconds away from becoming pink mist," Crys said. "Nothing but specks of blood, all because of Jade and her *hunches*. So yes, I think my fear of my sister is pretty damn natural. It's called PTSD. And I'm not trapped in this tent because Jade wants to help me. She's a spiteful, ruthless thing, jealous of what I've become without her."

Crys laid back on the cheap air mattress, her gaze aimed out the mesh tent ceiling.

But she knew Damon's auto-copter wasn't going to appear and rescue her. This time, she'd have to save herself.

Crys rubbed the sleep from her eyes, still staring skyward through the mesh ceiling, entranced by the red-tailed hawk that circled ten stories overhead in the golden evening light. She knew the hawk was riding a thermal, using the warm rising air to conserve energy as it haloed the sky in search of rodents below.

She visualized herself as the bird of prey, high and mighty, storing her stamina, biding her time until the right moment to swoop down and strike.

A miniature chip bag landed on Crys's stomach.

She sat up, studying the familiar neon-red packaging of her one-time favorite snack. Her eyes flicked to Cole at the entrance to the tent, and despite herself, she smiled. "Ketchup-flavored potato chips. I haven't eaten these in years."

"Figured you might be hungry." Cole hovered, his hands sunk deep into the pockets of the same shabby, hunter-green coveralls he'd worn the day before. His hair was overgrown, his hazel eyes sunken and forlorn like the poor stray dogs Crys used to compete with for scraps and sympathy outside downtown's renovated Union Station.

Cole pursed his lips but didn't shy under Crys's scrutiny. "You look terrible," she said. Even more so than on the day they first met at Adsum Peak, when he was still just a frail foundling from nowhere and everywhere, with downcast eyes and a timeworn face that told of his many bleak lives. Thirty-nine foster care homes and institutions in twelve years. She remembered being in awe of him.

"Well, you don't look so flawless yourself," Cole shot back.

Crys blanched, suddenly wishing to crawl into a corner. If the haphazard briars caught in her limp hair were any indication, she must look a far cry from the glamorous Crystal Yates that Nico masterfully molded her into each morning.

I wonder what you look like stripped of all that armor, Cole used to whisper to Crys late at night, limbs tangled around her sheets. She crossed her arms, as if this could somehow protect her from Cole's searching eyes, from the irritating smile that tugged at his lips. For an instant, a glimmer of his former charming, carefree Adsum-self shone through the shell he'd become, before his grin slipped and his face fell.

"I'm not eating that bag of diabetes," Crys said, hurling the chips at his chest.

"Guess you'll just have to starve like the rest of us," he grunted. "Or do you not remember that Unfortunate feeling?"

The truth was—no, she'd long chosen to forget, but she answered defensively. "I give back—"

Cole scoffed. "Charity galas are a chance for the rich to assuage their guilt and get drunk." He pocketed the chips and stepped into the tent. "When's the last time you came back home?"

"Adsum is my home," she said firmly. "Same as yours."

Why did you leave? she wanted to ask but never would. One day he was there with her, sharing the life, the dream they'd both been given, and the next he was gone. He'd left behind no goodbye, no reason, just another hole she'd learned to fill.

Cole gave another low grunt and threw himself down on the mattress beside her.

"Here, let me," he mumbled, then surprised her by picking a leafy twig from her hair. He shrugged, tenderly moving his fingers along her cheekbone to rub away the dirt. "Since you can't use a mirror."

Crys let the shame burn through her until she felt numb.

Cole's proximity, his disarming act of tenderness, his natural scent—musk and salt and earth and smoke—lulled Crys into a memory. She was back in the coastal mountains, the pair of them on horseback cantering up Quest Campus's ethereal trails, getting lost and losing time, blissfully, tragically content. Crys yanked herself out of the vision before she could lose herself again.

That Cole, the one she fell for, no longer existed.

They said nothing, letting their breaths blend in a silent exchange, waiting to see who would bend, who would break the wistful peace.

Crys spoke first, her words spiked with accusation. "What *happened* to you?"

Before Jade had lured him away from the academy, Cole had become a lighthearted optimist, a radiant one-man solar panel that powered the vitality of all those around him. Nothing could faze him; he never had a bad day, a bad mood, a bad anything. Now it seemed the simple effort of combing his hair or lifting his head was akin to the strain of moving mountains. "What did Jade do to you?"

Sage barged into the tent, her alabaster skin ruddy from the afternoon sun. "Jade has nothing on your father, Crys. What did *he* do to us? *That's* the looming question."

Crys's ears still throbbed from the afternoon hours when it was Sage's turn as guard, when she'd recited an article so dry it could cause nosebleeds: "How Mechanical Rubber Goods Are Made," published in 1892. Sage had then recited it backward, just to nettle Crys even more.

Cole rose from the bed just as Wily charged into the cramped tent, his rows of pearl-white teeth tearing into a crisp green apple. He pitched Crys the half-eaten fruit, looking disappointed when she caught it with her hand rather than her face. "Afraid you're going to have to take your dinner to-go. We're clearing out."

Crys peered outside and spotted Ani with Jade, packing up camp. It had been over a day since she'd last seen Jade. It seemed her sister was purposefully staying away. *Out hawking delusions,* Crys thought. Smearing Crys's immaculate last name.

Wiping sweat from her brow, Crys turned to Ani and her vacant, red-rimmed eyes. She couldn't hear from where she stood, but Ani appeared to be arguing with Jade.

"I take it you've returned empty-handed?" Crys said to Wily. "No evidence of a mass Quester conspiracy?"

"Are we really going to keep pretending Gen 3 doesn't know anything?" Wily groused. "I'm tired of lugging around this vault who won't spill her secrets."

But both Cole and Sage were occupied by their phones. "As if the spotlight wasn't already burning us . . ." Sage sighed, holding up the screen for Wily to see. "Our old photo is trending right now . . ."

Crys caught a glimpse. The picture must have been taken at a Halloween party the previous year. The gang of seven was seated or standing behind high-backed chairs, all in Adsum's tailored blazers or posh, ocean-blue pinafores, their faces intricately painted like disturbing skulls and exquisite corpses. Crys could see why the photo had gone viral. It made her stomach churn, but she forced down her rising bile, her surging panic.

Wily groaned. "Well, that's unfortunate."

Cole chewed his nails absently, avoiding Crys's eye. "Not a good look in light of Zoe's death . . ."

"It makes us out to be some kind of modern-day Manson Family," Sage sighed.

Crys blinked, and in her mind's eye, the faux corpses blended with Zoe's *very* real mortal remains. A moan escaped her lips as she struggled not to burn away the painful memory. She needed it intact. She needed to remember.

When she opened her eyes, they landed on Jade's. The effort to swallow a scream left her shaking, breathless. She concentrated on the delicate lines of her fingertips, the ends of her long golden hair, anything that showed her difference, her individuality, her *distinctness*, from Jade.

Then Wily, the scoundrel, came at her with his syrette and an impish grin.

"Is this really necessary . . . ?" Cole grumbled.

Wily waved him aside.

Crys had half a mind to knock the syrette out of his hand with a lob of her browning apple, but that would only get her to first base. She needed a home run. So she kept her voice calm. "I'll need a visit to the ladies' room before moving to your next lair."

Wily hesitated before nodding. "Fine, but make it quick."

Crys allowed Cole to take her by the arm and lead her out of the tent. The Exiles had set up camp on the slope of a dusty peak, cleverly camouflaged inside a dense thicket of chaparral scrub. In the distance, Crys could see the rugged outline of the San Gabriel Mountains, which she reasoned put her still within the city, most likely somewhere on the north side of Griffith Park, far removed from trail hikers and picnicking families admiring the Hardihood sign.

Their path led them past Jade, who was taking out her frustrations on a foldable chair, trying and failing to pound it into its thin case.

"You can't always bully things into doing what you want," Ani said.

Crys avoided looking at Jade's face, but she stopped when a familiar wooden curve caught her attention. In Jade's open bag, near Ani's feet, Crys caught sight of her childhood trompo.

Jade had been inside her dorm room. Rummaged through her things. Stolen from her, *again*.

"Could I borrow a tampon?" Crys asked Ani meekly, feigning modesty. Inwardly she was seething.

"I'll get it," Jade said, grabbing hold of her tattered bag before Ani could touch it. Jade had always been protective, *secretive*, of her belongings, safeguarding whatever was hers, even people, like the Exiles.

Like me, Crys thought bitterly.

Jade squatted, further unfastening the metallic zipper, digging through the contents of her bag. With a furtive glance, Crys glimpsed the wooden trompo, a water bottle, a flashlight, and a cheap burner phone.

And then, she spotted her way out.

As Jade reached out to hand over the tampon, Crys felt Cole's grip loosen. *He never did know when to hold me tight,* she thought, before she lurched forward, her fingers fastening around the steel cylinder case of a flash grenade.

"Crys, no!" Jade shouted.

Crys gave a rapturous smile as she removed the safety pin and tossed the grenade at the Exiles.

The blinding light and intensely loud *bang* covered her escape through the chaparral scrub. Voices called out behind her, screaming her name, angry and murderous. She sprinted, down, down, down, the only direction she knew to run.

She heard pounding steps trailing after her, then felt a strong hand wrap around her shoulder, twisting her around. But it wasn't Jade who had come after her.

It was Cole.

Crys raised her arms, ready to attack, but Cole stopped her with a word.

"Home," he said, his face softening, his eyes pleading. "I'd like to go home."

Shaky and uncertain if she should trust him, Crys nodded.

They raced the setting sun down the hill. Soon shadows helped hide their flight, and the shouts of the Exiles faded, swallowed up by the night.

NINE

Jade sat in the rideshare AV, staring mutely at what was left of the factious Exiles. Ani, Sage, and Wily had been quarreling since they'd left their Griffith Park retreat, their lips snarling, their fingers pointing, but all Jade could hear was a shrill, unrelenting ringing in her ears.

A kind of haunting, solitary scream. Like Crys's fear of her had somehow been embedded inside her mind when the flash grenade went off.

Jade shook her head to clear it to no avail. She sat up from her threadbare seat in the back, groaning. She was dizzy and mad as all hell, a debilitating combination. Each provoked the other. Though at the moment, her fury was winning. Crys had swiped the trompo, her one childhood memento, and worst of all, she'd hurled Jade's own weapon directly at her face.

Jade had been quick to shield her eyes and ears, and to jump for cover, avoiding the worst of the flash-bang. Still, her sister had aimed to hurt. Possibly even kill.

She could almost hear the long-faced therapist Yates had assigned to all the Adsum sibs ask, *And how does that make you feel?*

Like sunshine, lollipops, and rainbows, she'd reply every time, no matter which personal trauma they happened to be digging into that day.

The AV made a sharp U-turn, flinging Jade against the window. Her mind spun, and a harsh sensation of vertigo gripped her, disorienting her sense of place and time.

Suddenly she was staring down the darkness of Yates's network of hyperloop tubes, playing life-or-death chicken with a pod. She was luring a Fortunate man over the railing of the First Street Bridge, dueling on its edge, a hundred feet in the air. She was dangerously accelerating when she should have slowed down, exulting in the crash with Roboket, the autonomous dragster, at the finish line.

This *is all you can do with what I've given to you?* Yates had scolded her after jumping off the gumwood tree into his eco-pond. Risking her body, her bond with her sister, in the process.

Someone shook Jade by the elbow. She turned to Ani, reading her plum-tinted lips, *End this or I will.* Ani gripped one of her weighted blades and nodded to Wily and Sage in the front seats.

Jade gaped out the rearview window at the cone-shaped spires of Forest Lawn's many churches, its dark rolling hills peppered with flat, granite headstones retreating into the background.

"Why have we turned around?"

Everyone covered their ears like she'd set off another flash-bang.

Jade threw up her hands, exasperated.

What's the problem? she signed, putting Adsum's ASL required courses to good use. *Where are we going?*

Sage's mouth split into a smug grin. *You can't really know where you're going until you know where you've been.*

"For Savior's sake," Jade cursed. The last thing she needed right now was a riddle wrapped in a Maya Angelou quote.

For example, Wily signed. *Where have you been since the night you got that Fortunate killed and fled Dry River City? Do you know what it took for me and Sage to get the mayor to let you go?*

We cleaned up your mess without even a thank-you and goodbye, Sage signed to Jade. She turned, brandishing a dagger-like nail toward Ani. *And you and the rest of the crew just deserted us.*

Great, Ani signed, her hands hurried and clumsy. *We're out here strolling memory lane while Crys is halfway to Yates by now, about to snitch all our plans.*

Not even a thank-you and goodbye, Wily repeated.

Jade closed her eyes. Their escalating battle about what to do next, and who should take charge, was going to lead them down a dead end.

Though if Jade was honest with herself, she knew the others had a point. It'd been almost two days since she'd claimed that Yates had implanted them with some mysterious Quest tech, almost two days of searching for answers. They'd tried hacking into every campus HQ mainframe and hit wall after wall. They even broke into an animal clinic and scanned themselves with X-rays, finding nothing. All was well. *Normal.*

Jade opened her eyes in time to see Ani dive for the AV's display screen, probably aiming to stop the car. But before she could reach the glass, Wily had tackled her to the stained floormat. Jade sighed, nostalgic for the days before the Exiles were broken and scattered. Back when they'd kept each other fed, protected, and if not *happy*, at least in good company.

Now they were dropping like flies.

Khari. Eli. Cole, the turncoat.

Jade gazed out the window, momentarily glad she couldn't hear the continued squabbling. Tents and RVs cluttered the sidewalks and curbs, and she spotted a battered motor home that reminded her of their old ride, the shack on wheels, in which they had once been a family. Could she make them into one again?

Everything inside of Jade screamed no.

No, she couldn't. No, she didn't *want* to. She was no guardian. Nobody's keeper. She could barely keep herself alive and free.

Jade looked to Ani, who now had Wily pinned to his seat, one of her knives kissing his throat. "When you kids are done here, meet me in the secret gardens," she shouted.

The others knew there was no better plan. Forest Lawn was the last place on their checklist, and Jade bet Sage's undying need to cross all her t's and dot all her i's would lead them there, eventually. Khari was one of their own. They might be Exiles, but none of them had ever considered themselves lost. Khari deserved to be found.

Even if it was six feet underground.

In one swift movement, Jade unlatched the car door, the cold night air lashing against her cheeks, enlivening her spirit. A smile tugged at her lips, the familiar thrill of impending danger electrifying her veins.

This was not, after all, the first time she'd been held against her will inside a speeding vehicle. *I'm not even wearing cuffs this time.* Jade laughed as she rose to the balls of her feet.

"I'm going to find Khari," she shouted, then looked toward Wily and Sage. "Thank you and goodbye." With that, she tucked and rolled out onto the street.

Jade could see why LA's bygone elite, the crème de la crème of old Hollywood, had chosen Forest Lawn Memorial Park as their eternal resting place. The sprawling three-hundred-acre grounds were serene and beautiful, more a garden of peace and reflection than a solemn cemetery.

Pudgy guards and an inordinate number of security cameras protected its dead celebrity residents, defending against people like her. Grave hunters.

A small shiver ran through her.

She wasn't here to tattoo Elizabeth Taylor's gravestone with her lipstick or have some wild romp on top of Walt Disney's tomb, but she couldn't shake the sinister feeling that breaking into a cemetery was some kind of sacrilege. Taunting death more than she already did.

Ghostly consequences be damned, Jade used a "backdoor" command code to gain admin-level access to the CCTV system and sent a hacked feed to the surveillance displays. Then it was easy enough to slip past the lofty wrought-iron gate. One guard dozed in his chair, his head, bald as Mount San Antonio, sloped over his desk, and the other was occupied by videos of bulldogs on skateboards.

Once inside, Jade was greeted by the park's signature heron fountain, a siege of the long-legged birds spewing water into the starless sky. She felt the soft droplets cling to her skin, but the soothing sounds of the elegant water jets were muted by the stubborn ringing that had melded into Crys's screams.

I hate you, she seemed to cry. *Stay away from me. You're crazy.*

Crys wasn't the only person to call Jade crazy. Suddenly she was sucked into a memory, balancing precariously on the ledge of First Street Bridge, fist clenched around a stolen 3D-printed gun, taunting a Fortunate man to come and get it. *You're insane,* he'd seethed, reaching out to grab the gun. And then the man was slipping, falling through the air, plummeting to the concrete river. His wide eyes caught hold of hers, as if that brief connection could save him. A mischief of River Rats gathered around the broken body, pointing with shocked gasps up at the bridge. At Jade. She ran and never looked back.

Jade shook herself back to the present. She was rarely haunted by the ghosts of those she'd wronged, easily keeping the skeletons of her past buried deep inside her mind. But something about wandering around a cemetery in the moonlight brought it all back to the surface.

She began to climb the steep hill of Inspiration Slope, careful to avoid the neat lines of headstones that were flush with the trimmed emerald grass, heading for the highest point of Forest Lawn, where the "secret gardens" were located. When she reached the top, she ran into a marble statue of a mother dancing with her two young daughters. Jade's mother had rarely danced, but the statues' captured joy made her think of the hard but beautiful life she'd once shared with her family, the invisible thread that had connected her with her twin sister, before Crys's adoption had severed it like a blow from a cleaving knife.

Footsteps pulled Jade from her ruminations. Her hearing had returned. Finally.

Wily emerged into an orange pool of lamplight, a greasy burrito clutched in hand.

"Really?" Jade asked. "You had to make a pit stop at a vending machine?"

Wily flashed a grin. "All this spy work makes me hungry."

Jade shook her head. "Where the hell does all the food go?" She could hardly believe that Wily had once been known as "Fleshy Wesley" by the Adsum prigs.

He shrugged, winking as he preened. "What can I say? Good genes. I'm a walking garbage disposal."

Ani shouldered past him, moving straight for the imposing bronze door of the first garden.

"Did we make peace?" Jade asked Sage when she emerged beside the ivy walls.

"More like an armistice," Sage answered. "We both know it would take you twice as long to comb through this place without me."

This area of the cemetery was locked to the public, enhanced privacy for a higher price. Only select friends and family of the deceased had keys to these gardens. Exactly the kind of exclusivity that would attract someone like Yates, especially if he had something, some*body*, he wanted to hide.

But locks had never kept Jade out of anything.

She clasped her hands to help Ani up and over the wall. After a few moments, Ani opened the heavy door from the other side, and just like that, they were through.

Inside the private garden, soft classical music played from hidden speakers. Neatly trimmed rosebushes adorned each corner of the garden. Without a word, the four of them split up and began to search the flat memorial markers set into the walls with their phones' flashlights. Jade spotted Hollywood legends Mary Pickford and Humphrey Bogart, but no markers with the estimated birth and death dates they were looking for.

For two days they'd failed to hunt down any trace of Khari; there wasn't a record of her at any hospital, institution, prison, or shelter anywhere in the country. Not even a death record. It was like she'd up and ghosted the entire world. But earlier that morning, Ani had remembered a passing remark that Khari had made when they'd first met: *Khari Raine is my chosen name, for my chosen family.*

The Exiles had rallied around a new strategy. It was a long shot, but it was *something.* They knew Khari's true birth month—a person wouldn't tattoo a giant, fiery ram across her rib cage if she wasn't, in fact, an Aries—and Sage, with her photographic memory, had set out to memorize the names of every newborn delivered in Los Angeles County from March 20 to April 19, 2034. They'd spent the day combing the city's cemeteries, to no avail. Forest Lawn was their last best hope.

We're going to find you, Khari, Jade had promised.

She found it a strange, sickening feeling both to want to find someone, and to hope with everything she had that she never did. Not here.

"On to the next garden," Sage said, heading for the door.

Ani lagged behind, her breathing too quick, fingers curled into sledgehammers.

"I know this can't be easy," Jade said, moving cautiously toward her. She pressed the toe of her boot against Ani's, as close to a soothing touch as she dared. She wanted to give solace, not sympathy.

Ani recoiled. "How would you know? You haven't cared about anyone but yourself in years." She zipped her leather jacket up to her chin and took off after Sage.

After finding nothing in the subsequent secret gardens, Jade and the others now circled the Great Mausoleum, looking for a way into the massive granite building that towered above them like an impenetrable, cream-colored castle. As they reached a section of the structure called the Holly Terrace, Jade unsheathed her phone, ready to dismantle the high-security motion sensors, when she froze.

Security was already there.

"Wait a minute . . ." Wily whispered with a tremulous smile. "Is that . . . is that the King of Pop's *spirit*?"

Jade was aware that the world-famous singer was entombed within these storied walls, but the white-gloved, fedora-wearing figure that patrolled the unlit balcony entrance was not Michael Jackson's spirit. It was an impersonator. A very dedicated one.

"Creepy," Sage said as they crept single file beneath the balcony, keeping to the shadows.

Jade shrugged, wondering if the superfan in full stage costume stood watch like this every night. "Yates always said everyone needs to find a passion . . ."

Finally they came to a door that Jade could work with. Wooden, with antique brass levers, it took only a tension wrench, lockpick, and five seconds, and they were in.

Ani's thick brows shot up as Jade slid out from her lace-up boots. "An old Adsum habit?"

"A thieves' hack," Jade answered, heat rising behind her ears. "We can't all be light-footed elves like you."

Even in the half dark, Jade could see Ani's smug smile. "But you're the famous, slippery scapegrace."

Jade ignored Wily, who'd begun to hum her vexatious theme song, and signaled the group forward. She led the way through vast, dimly illuminated hallways that possessed all the splendor and reverential ambience of a medieval church. Opulent glass sconces hung high from layered stone columns that stretched up to vaulted ceilings, soaring above them like the fine bones of a bat wing. Rainbows of light, like frameless abstract art, bounced off the smooth walls and marble floor from the rows of backlit stained-glass windows that ornamented the cavernous space.

"Might as well start here," Sage whispered, disappearing through the first arched doorway they came across.

The columbarium had three walls stacked with white square niches that must have held hundreds of cremation urns, just in this room. And there were an untold number of rooms in the Great Mausoleum. This search could take all night.

They fanned out, Sage taking the west wall, Wily the north, Ani and Jade inspecting the east. Jade skipped the rows with photographs and flowers, knowing that Khari's niche would be bare. Just a golden plate: one name, two dates. It seemed so curt. So inadequate.

When Jade reached the end of her row, she turned her phone light on Wily. His usual sturdy posture and confident strut seemed to wane with every nameplate he passed. "She's not here," he whispered. He sighed with relief. "You?"

Jade shook her head.

"I found Poppy's favorite podcaster," Sage said, "but nothing pertinent. No dates even in the right decade. How about you, Ani?"

But Ani was already on to the next room.

After searching through what felt like an endless number of columbaria, Jade, on the verge of calling the hunt a defeat, came across a faintly lit corridor that was blocked off from the main hallway by an ornate waist-high gate. A sign declared the area off-limits to the public. Jade poked her head in and saw the famous last names etched above the entrances to small, private crypts carved into the corridor. At the end of the hallway, a dark marble wall contained a single row of niches.

There was something about the grand seclusion of the space, the *quietude*, that sent tingles across Jade's body. She motioned for the others to follow her.

A chill hung in the air, a cold that seeped into Jade's skin, nipping at her bones. She tiptoed on bare feet toward the back wall of niches. At the corner of the wall, Ani hovered, like a shadowy wraith in her black leather jacket. She sank to her knees, her hand pressed to a golden nameplate. Jade shined her phone light on the dates: March 2034 to July 2052.

"Rachel Davis," Ani read aloud, the name echoing across the emptiness.

They all looked to Sage.

Sage rested a delicate hand on Ani's slumped shoulder. "The name Rachel Davis was on the LA birth records. And the month of death is around the time she disappeared."

Ani stifled a cry.

Something sickly and sweet rose up Jade's throat. The familiar taste of death. She wanted to spit out the scent memory, to run, to throw her arms around Ani and tell her it was all going to be okay. Instead, she simply stood there. Hoping her presence was enough. Knowing that it wasn't.

Jade squinted down at the Latin phrase inscribed beneath Khari's birth name.

"Ad meliora."

"Onward to better things," Sage translated.

"This has Yates written all over it," Ani said, rising shakily to her feet, her voice a choked growl.

"You know what else has Yates written all over it?" Wily snarled.

They turned to see him emerge from a dark corner, his own knife held at his throat by a sinewy man in an expensive checkered suit. A deep malice clung to the stranger like a cloak. Wily sucked in a sharp breath when the man jabbed the knife point into the lump of his Adam's apple.

"Hands in the air," the man ordered, his words direct as a bullet. "Everybody stay calm, and no one has to die here."

Jade's eyes slid to Khari's tomb. No one *else* had to die. Slowly she reached inside the left boot that she still held, mentally thanking herself for her foresight. Her fingers wrapped around a metal canister.

"The thing is," she said to the man, "I've never been the calm type."

She pulled the steel ring, smiling as smoke and screams filled the air.

TEN

Crys narrowed her whole world to the wooden spinning top she held in perfect precession in the palm of her hand. Its conical steel tip dug into her skin as the pear-shaped trompo swirled, the black-and-white pattern becoming a hypnotizing blur.

Like most things in her childhood, it was a toy Crys had to share with Jade. She remembered standing in parking lots outside their small class-C motor home, seeing who could make the trompo spin the fastest, or the longest, their parents watching on. Cheering. Laughing. Never keeping score. Crys always had the better form, Jade the greater speed. "Work together, my precious gemstones," their mother would always say. "Your fortune is in your bond."

Fortunes change, Crys thought as the luxury AV came to a stop, the trompo falling to her feet with a dull thud. She quickly pocketed the toy, feeling for her glass vial of perfume. It wasn't there.

Cole stirred in the seat beside her. "Do you really think Yates will take me back?" His eyes strained upward, toward the peaks of Quest Campus.

Crys shrugged, watching him fidget with the dirty cuffs of his coveralls, trying unsuccessfully to tame his curls, which looked the color of Silicon Beach after a hard rain.

He'd belonged here once, just as much as she did.

But he'd become a stray, like all the Exiles. What finally made him venture home?

"Damon chose you, he'll always care for you," Crys said. "Same as Poppy. Or do you not recall it was *you* who turned your back on them?"

She left the "and me" unspoken.

"I should say thanks, I guess, for letting me tag along." Cole cast back his head, raking his curls from his eyes. They were a fiery gold in the AV's warm light, his pupils wide as moons, giving Crys the impression of a pair of solar eclipses. A coming change.

She looked away.

"I half expected you to throw me out on the freeway," he continued. "Does this mean you still care about me, or are you just trying to return your dad's investment?"

Crys covered the silence with a sigh. She had intended to return with Zoe. Then Jade, Crys's abductor. Cole was just a bonus, another thing, like the trompo, stolen back from her sister when she'd made her escape.

"You're still in this car because you chose to be," Crys said curtly, turning from Cole to lift her face toward the open window. "It has nothing to do with me." She smiled up at the security camera, and the steel East Entrance gate groaned open.

The AV wound up a series of switchbacks, and Crys took in the prodigious, otherworldly mansion that dangled off the side of a rugged cliff's edge. Damon called the architectural marvel his Castle in the Air, a jaw-dropping middle finger to those who told him his ideas had no foundations, or that his hyperloop was merely a fanciful pipe dream.

As they crossed onto the property, Crys felt all the exhaustive tension vanish from her body. She melted into the seat cushion like sugar cubes in her favorite cup of tea, which she imagined would soon be in her hands. The details of the mansion, *her second home*, came into glorious focus: the breathtaking design of what looked like ultramodern glass Lego blocks hanging almost impossibly in the seaside air; the see-through sky pool; the luminous waterfall that flowed beneath the rock foundation into a babbling creek in the canyon below.

The silhouettes of four male figures that waited for them on the gravel drive.

Yates, with his sons flanking his sides.

The AV rolled to a smooth stop, and Crys stepped out from the cabin, her heart racing. Was her father angry with her for leaving? Did Palmer and Vance already know she had failed? Was this a unified front to tell her she was no longer welcome? That she was, in fact, a poor investment, too tainted by her proximity to Jade's chaos? Her tangled, unwashed hair, her torn, dirty clothes, made her feel like she was returning a beggar. Not as the exalted daughter.

"I'm sorry," she said.

Damon rushed forward and pulled Crys into an embrace so tight and reassuring, she instantly felt sturdier. Assured. Of herself, of her place in this world.

"I'm the one who's sorry, Crystal," Damon said, holding her. "I thought they'd taken you, too. I thought I'd lost you. I should have had you better protected."

Palmer stepped forward, leisurely hooking his thumbs on the pockets of his dinner jacket. "We were worried about you."

"And who is your little friend?" Vance asked, tugging his ear and inspecting Cole like a scanner searching for concealed weapons.

Maxen stood apart from Gen 1, head buried in his phone, unmoved by the return of Crys and his old classmate. Maxen had never cared for much besides himself, Crys thought with numb indifference. Maxen's tantrums might have abated in recent years, but Crys still avoided his path, avoided calling him *brother*.

Crys reached for her collarbone, for the scar that wasn't hers, and caught Palmer watching her.

Cole loitered outside the AV. He'd never been to the Yates's private home. Even though—or *because*—Damon was one of the most famous men in the world, her father liked his privacy. Guests were limited to Quest CEOs and family. Yet when Damon released his hold of Crys, his sky-blue eyes alighted on Cole and he extended his hand.

"Everyone, let's go inside, shall we? A home-cooked meal sounds divine."

The smell of smoked green chilies permeated the mountaintop air, the comforting scent wrapping around Crys like a warm blanket. Damon's generous plates of enchiladas had long since been cleared, Cole sent off to his old dormitory. It was just the Yateses on the balcony, and a wall of muted screens, the soothing sound of the nearby waterfall masking the awkward silence.

Crys's hair was still damp from her shower, her nerves calmed by chamomile tea. She'd changed into silk pajamas, though she wasn't tired. Her father had encouraged her to sleep, but rest was unthinkable. She wanted to be with her family, not tossing and turning, alone with her thoughts.

Maxen was stretched out on a lounge chair by the railing, still absorbed in his phone. Damon sat beside Crys on the outdoor sectional, sipping tequila, silent as the half dozen screens his eyes flitted between, all of which streamed live news of Jade and the Exiles.

Crys felt the weight of Gen 1's gazes on the back of her neck, waiting for her to speak.

Confess where she had been. Admit that she had failed.

Zoe's vacant eyes and lifeless body crept out from Crys's memory, taking brutal shape inside her mind. She stared at the flames of the balcony's gas firepit, hoping they might burn away the tormenting sight.

They did not.

Damon hadn't yet questioned Crys on her misadventure, the days she went missing without a word. She was grateful. She wanted their conversation to be free of the judgments and curiosities of her brothers.

Jade was a problem. A serious and deranged one. Jade was *her* problem, and Crys needed to find a solution, a swift and easy cure-all, before Jade publicized a vile character assassination of her father.

Crys had known bad men. Evil intent. Selfish souls. But Damon was good, *great*. He sought to nurture lives, not take them.

Or conduct experiments on them.

Crys watched him now, peering at the news like he expected to see more calamity and ruin at any moment. She set down her tea and slid closer to Damon. Kept her gaze turned from the screens, looking down on her fingerprints, the one piece of herself she didn't have to share with her twin. "Dad?" she whispered. "I'm going to make this right."

That's a title meant only for one man, Crys could almost hear Jade hiss. *Your birth father. Or did you burn his memory away, like you did with our other keepers? Our failed guardians?*

"Isn't this your uncle?" Maxen said, the first he'd spoken all night. With a tap of his finger, a video from his phone took over the six screens. "He's become a viral hashtag."

A pair of vloggers investigating the "Adsum Atrocity" had found Uncle Willis and his Beverly Hills hovel. Tied him to Jade and Crys. "Tell us where your niece is hiding! Zoe deserves justice!" the vloggers shouted. Crys assumed her uncle was passed-out drunk again, but then he crawled out of the tent, slurring, "You little shits better leave—" Then something caught his eye. Made him let loose a hair-raising scream. Shaking all over, wearing nothing but his Medal of Valor, he took off down Rodeo Drive, barreling through luxury shoppers like bowling pins, without ever looking back.

Crys refused to meet Gen 1's glares. Was her uncle hallucinating? She didn't have time to process the confusion, the shame, of what she'd just seen. A photo of Jade had materialized abruptly on the screens. Her sister's solemn eyes, her satisfied grin, seized Crys's vision before it was blurred by her terrified tears.

"Crystal, are you all right—" Damon reached for her.

Swallowing her scream, Crys jolted to her feet. She didn't want her father to feel her trembling. She forced a smile, resisting the urge to run. "I'm just going to lie down," she lied, leaving the balcony. Then the mansion.

Her blood felt like fire in her veins, her mind like a bomb. As sure as she knew her last name, she was certain that standing still, *doing nothing*, would detonate it. She needed to get her body moving in order to settle her mind. To clear it.

She was midway to the Yateses' private monorail station when she realized she was still in her monogrammed house shoes and silk pajamas. Any Questers she encountered might think her a roving sleepwalker. *All the better,* she reasoned as she stepped onto the bare platform. Perhaps no one on campus would try to speak with her, console her, tell her how shocked they were about Zoe. How sorry.

The podcar arrived within minutes, saving her from her black thoughts, the sorrow that threatened to burst through her dam of stoicism like an irrepressible torrent. Crys was not ready to mourn. It felt like surrendering. She wanted to fight. To rage.

Like the rest of campus, Adsum Peak was silent. The academy, usually radiant like an incandescent glass mountain, was dark, as if it too were grieving. When she moved through the arched doors, whispering, as was her custom, "I am here," she considered visiting the dorms, seeing if Cole was still awake, but she lifted her chin and took the elevator to the fifth classfloor instead.

Crys wanted the weight of a saber in her hand.

The fencing room immediately awakened to her presence. Lines of long, raised fencing strips shone blue, casting the immense room in a light designed to boost a fencer's attention, reaction times, and mood. The main menu of the Holographic Sparring Experience program flashed on, beckoning her to select her elite opponent for a bout.

But Crys wasn't here for sport. She moved to Damon's impressive collection of antique sabers, treasured weapons displayed behind a thick wall of glass like deadly art. She was a Yates, and nothing was off-limits to her, so all she had to do was scan her thumb, and the glass slid open.

She took down Bao Teng, Soaring Precious, the most expensive sword in the world. Damon had won the sword, said to be the personal saber of eighteenth-century Chinese Emperor Qianlong, at a heated Sotheby's auction for a record-breaking ten-million-dollar bid. Crys gripped the ornate white jade handle, admired the S-shaped blade inlaid with gold and silver, and it was as if the spirit of the legendary weapon seeped into her. Not just a tool of war, but a symbol of power, skill, *strength*.

Crys closed her eyes and raised the blade. She hadn't fenced in years, but alone in the blue-dark, her blood still burning, she cared little about style or technique. She started to swing.

She leapt onto the fencing strip, slashing through the air, lunging forward and back, her opponent not a holographic Olympian but a mental projection of herself. All her bottled-up pain and anger now manifested with each heavy stroke of her blade. Each thrust of steel, each cut she made, into *herself*, somehow lightened the weight, the hidden shame, *the unworthiness*, that she always carried inside.

A memory flickered. Nine years old, falling to the ground amid an encampment sweep. Feet trampling across her body, the crack of a police baton on the back of her legs. Her uncle's rants: *When you're down, they push you deeper and deeper, like they want the earth to swallow you. Bury you like the quake.*

Crys's body dripped with sweat, her silk pajamas pasted to her skin, her breath coming in thundering waves. Still, she did not stop.

Another memory blazed. Jade and Crys's fifth foster home, locked inside a crumbling apartment above an unsavory restaurant that chronically smelled of burned cooking grease and seediness. No school, no fresh air. Only let out of their room to scrub pots and pans, their hands endlessly cracked and raw from months of forced labor. *I'm going to get us out,* she heard Jade's determined whisper.

The whole world was a jail, and together they were going to break it.

A low buzzing sound, like a swarm of bees, punctured Crys's reverie. Before she even had time to react, a blinding, fast-moving blur swooped down on her. A drone, large and terrifying as a hawk. Its spotlight intensified, backing her against a wall. She slashed at it with her saber, but she missed, disoriented by the spotlight.

At the edges of her vision, she registered Palmer and Vance emerging from the shadows before red beams of light projected from the drone, scanning her face. An AI lie detector, Crys realized, her confusion rising. Her dread.

"What is this?" she demanded.

No response. Just the cruel bright light and her rapidly accelerating heart rate.

She needed to calm down. Steady her heart. The drone would analyze her microexpressions and the tone of her voice, display the results on a holographic scorecard that floated below its belly for Gen 1 to see. She didn't want her brothers to think she could be so easily intimidated.

That she had reason to lie.

Then Palmer spoke, a disembodied voice circling her, probing her, pressing to see if she'd break.

"Were you with the Exiles?"

Crys stood her ground, lifted her chin high.

"Yes."

"Do you know who killed Zoe Reeves?"

Crys hesitated. Could the AI lie detector decipher conjectures, *a feeling*, as deception? She glanced at her heart rate: 162 beats per minute. "No," she answered. "But—"

"Are you Jade Moore?"

"*What?*" 175 bpm.

"Are you the stray, Jade Moore, pretending to be Crystal?"

Crys took several slow breaths. "No, I am *not* my sister."

"Unbutton your nightshirt."

Crys did not. 181 bpm.

Vance joined the interrogation. "Show us your collarbone," he yelled, spittle flying in her face.

Crys pulled down the neckline of her sweaty pajamas. No scar, just a red-hot flush of shame, and fury. "Satisfied?"

They were not.

The drone suddenly pounced, robotic arms emerging from its sides, reaching for her eyes. Backed against the wall, Crys had nowhere to run. No way to hide from the metal claws that fastened to her temples and latched onto her lids, spreading them and forcing her eyes open.

225.

228.

To Crys's utter horror, one of the brothers placed a mirror before her vision.

She had thought she'd known terror. Her usual fear incursions had trained her well. But nothing compared to the anguish she felt now, compelled to look at, to examine, her reflection—*Jade's* reflection—unable to shut it out. Unable to stop the screaming that tore from the very core of her being as her trembling legs gave way, her back sliding down the wall. The drone shadowed her descent, not allowing her even a blink of respite. Her mind burned. The fear response in her brain desperately urging her to flee. But she couldn't. All she could do was lie there. And scream.

Crys gasped for breath, wondering if it was possible to be scared to death. Too much adrenaline, too many chemicals, flooding into her body at once. Any second now, she felt her heart would burst.

And then, the drone released her and the mirror was gone, replaced by Palmer's fair, serene face. Crys shuddered, her body an exhausted heap on the hard floor.

With his long, ringed fingers, Palmer grabbed her by the cheeks and pulled her lips to his, sealing the terror with a kiss. When he finally let go, she still felt his hold on her. "You might not be Jade," he whispered. "But you are *not*, and never will be, our sister."

As they left her shivering, a certainty swept over Crys. They knew she feared her face, her twin's. They knew something was wrong with her. *Inside* of her.

Ani's words came back to her. *You can't even stand to* look *at yourself. Is your fear really caused by Jade, or can you just not bear to see what Yates has made you become?*

What *had* she become?

Crys wiped her tears, her lips. Straightened her disheveled shirt, smoothed her golden hair. With a shaky chin, she rose and placed the preternatural saber back into its case. All of its fabled, transcendent power used up. Wasted on her.

She found herself in the elevator, then a common room, then a hallway, knocking on Cole's door. She entered without waiting for an answer. He was awake in bed, his hazel eyes piercing the half-light. He shifted over and raised the comforter so she could slip into the warm, empty space beside him. His arm wrapped around her, and she breathed him in, his scent of earth and smoke beneath the minty top notes of his bodywash.

Close to dawn, her heartbeat finally quieted to a dull hum. She closed her eyes and fell into a fitful sleep.

ELEVEN

Jade spat a mouthful of blood onto the shiny bamboo floor. She turned to look out the HyperQuest pod's window, but it was traveling so fast the slotted circular windows of the hyperloop tube appeared to melt the walls away altogether, creating an uninterrupted panorama of America's heartland, as if she were viewing the golden landscape through a zoetrope.

Endless wheat fields, mile after mile. Not a town or a person in sight. Yates's enforcer was truly taking her into the middle of nowhere.

When the smoke had cleared inside the Great Mausoleum, the Exiles had the one-hundred-eighty-pound man pinned. Wily had him in a hammerlock, Jade had his neck in a choke hold, and Ani and Sage were piled on Jade's back, striking blows to the man's flanks.

They'd wanted him to tap out. No matter Jade's mythic reputation or what Crys chose to believe, the Exiles were not murderers.

But the man did them one better. He'd rasped, "You're right."

Jade loved hearing those two words. She'd eased her grip around his neck, allowing the man to breathe.

"Why'd you let go?" Wily had squawked. "He's Yates's cleanup crew! He's his hound!"

"No, I'm a mole," the man coughed and spluttered. "I'm here to help."

Jade had believed him. The others had not. Trust was a currency, and waifs like them were too poor to spend their savings on strangers.

They'd warned her not to leave with him. For all they knew, he was the one who'd disposed of Khari's and Zoe's bodies after Yates's tech had killed them. But Jade didn't panic. In fact, she liked the chanciness of the situation. Thrived on it, really. She was either about to find a corner piece in the complicated Yates puzzle or an early nowhere grave. The life-and-death seesaw she was riding brought a bloody smile to Jade's lips. She sat back, luxuriating in the high stakes. *Go big or go home,* she'd always believed. But without answers, there would be no home. She *had* to take this ride. This risk.

"Your singing's worse than that right hook of yours," the man croaked from the reclining seat opposite hers, a fistful of ice pressed to his five o'clock shadow.

Jade laughed, then sucked in a sharp breath, clutching her sore ribs. She hadn't realized she'd been warbling her own fallacious theme song. She would have blushed, but she was too busy spitting blood from her split lip. Anyway, she could dish out cheap shots, too. "So that welt on your jawline's just a part of your natural roguish look?"

This was the most they had spoken since they'd left the cemetery. The man's silence might have been born out of an extreme paranoia— they were, after all, passengers on a Yates-owned transport—or it could have been the lingering effects of her devastating throat punch. Jade liked to think it was the latter.

Tired of this infernal quietude, she asked, "Why Kansas City?"

The man said nothing. He looked down at the frown-shaped tear across the shoulder of his expensive checkered suit. A slash from one of Ani's knives. He was lucky she'd only grazed him.

"What does Kansas City have to do with Yates or Khari or *me?*" Jade fiddled with the oversize sunglasses that'd helped get her through LA's hyperloop portal unrecognized. She looked into the mirrored lenses and nearly gasped. Her hair stuck out at all ends like matted fur. Dark half-moons hung below her eyes. Her body was telling her to rest. But not her mind—that familiar rush, that sublime triad of dopamine and adrenaline and endorphins, thrummed through her like a superpower, keeping her wide awake. Hyperfocused. Ready for another fight.

Jade unzipped her bag, keeping her plethora of weapons close. "Or is this hour-and-a-half ride to nowhere just to entice me out of the city while more of Yates's enforcers round up all his escaped experiments? As you saw last night, it's demanding work capturing an Exile—"

"*Will you shut up?*" The man had a talent for making a whisper sound like an executioner's orders screamed through a megaphone. "I prefer your tone-deaf singing to your uninspired yapping."

"You said you had information—"

"And *you* said you'd come quietly."

Jade shrugged. "Yeah, that meant no more talking with my fists."

With the point of his elbow, the man stabbed the display screen on his armrest, and a soul-punching roar of death-metal music flooded the luxury suite. He closed his eyes and tapped his foot along. The song sounded like something a draconian military would use to torture a detainee, but it only made Jade feel more alive.

She drummed her fingers against her ripped jeans, studying the man she'd chosen to gamble all her faith on. His dirty-blonde hair was styled like a soldier's: barely there sides with a slightly longer top and a side part that made him seem older than his late twenties. He had manicured nails. Teeth as white as his flawless complexion. Alligator-skin boots that emitted a mirrorlike shine. Despite the lump on his chiseled cheek and the tear in his lightly wrinkled suit, the man was polished. Well-kept. But all the gloss in the world could never fully smooth an Unfortunate. A distinct desperation clung to him. The rough kind. The sort that belonged to a fractured breed.

"How'd someone like you end up working for Yates?" Jade yelled over the music.

The man opened his eyes. His glare cut from the pink starburst scar on her sharp collarbone to the bullet hanging from her neck.

In Extremis, Jade thought, fingers wrapping around her twisted souvenir. *At the point of death.*

Jade tapped her armrest to cut the music. The utter silence was jolting—her eardrums buzzing with relief, like a boot lifted from a windpipe. She had the man's full attention. She pulled down her collar farther. "I saw your face the night I got this scar." The man set down his dripping bag of melted ice, which leaked onto the wood floor, pooling with Jade's bloody spittle. "That was you who fell from the garden wall, wasn't it?"

He yanked up his reclining seat, brushing the back of his neck. "*Not here,*" he whispered. Again, it sounded like a death sentence.

A hostile dose of impatience began to mix with Jade's superpower high. She couldn't sit still, couldn't wait. "Here and now are as good a place and time as any," she shouted, despite the silence. "Either you tell me something, or I'm reaching into my bag of tricks and only one of us will be making the trip home."

He punched the screen on his armrest, turning the music back on. A bluegrass tune filled the suite. He leaned against his window, gazing out at a horizon that seemed to stretch forever.

"This is my trip home," he whispered.

Jade wasn't sure what that meant, but it sounded like a resignation.

The Kansas City portal looked like a low-grade clone of LA's, its ribbed-timber walls chipped and worn, the lobby's design more barren than minimalist. The man led them outside to a two-door pickup he said he'd reserved for their drive deep into rural Kansas. He gave nothing further as he got behind the wheel and started the engine. Jade slid inside the cabin and slammed the heavy door before he could take off without her.

"So . . . do you have a driver's license, *Rhett*?" Jade asked.

Earlier in the hyperloop pod, when he'd scratched the back of his neck, a dry-cleaning tag had popped out from his suit collar, and Jade had spied the name on it. She used his name as often as possible to throw it in his face that she'd stolen it despite his best efforts. "Because, *Rhett*, I wouldn't want to get pulled over and end up in a country jail with you over a traffic violation. I'm sure the cops out here are on alert for the scapegrace."

Rhett answered with more silence.

For the next half hour, their off-road path hugged the unending hyperloop track, a cylindrical steel vacuum tube built on raised pylons. Yates's marvel cut indifferently through wheat fields, prairie grass, wild sunflower meadows, and town squares that resembled deserted film sets built for twentieth-century period pieces.

What was so important, so secretive, that Rhett had to put over a thousand miles between them and Yates?

Somewhere outside of Tonganoxie, Rhett pulled the pickup to a stop beside an unremarkable patch of land covered in long grasses and purple bull thistles. He exited the truck without a word and started walking through waist-high weeds toward a capsized silo.

Jade could just make out the faded words painted on its side: WOOD FAMILY FARM.

The sun soared high in the cloudless sky, the air hot and sticky. When Jade caught up with Rhett beside the busted silo, they were both already sweating.

"Do you know what eminent domain is?" he asked.

Jade had an idea, but she shook her head, wanting to keep him talking.

"It's how the government can strangle a family with one hand and pat their own backs with the other." Rhett spat the words like they were venom.

He brushed the tips of his fingers gently across the sun-bleached words **Wood** and **Family**. If there used to be a farmhouse on this desolate land, Jade saw no sign of it.

"It's how the suits can legally steal private land for 'the greater good,'" Rhett continued. "My ma likened it to the trolley problem. Save the person tied to the train tracks? Or the train filled with people?" He jammed his smooth hands into his pockets, glowering at the wheat fields like some urban scarecrow come to discourage vultures from feeding off the carcass of his family's farm. "The two hundred acres of land my forefathers and foremothers broke their backs over, bled their hearts into for two centuries, apparently stood in the way of progress, growth . . . *the future*." He looked at Jade. "*The hyperloop was coming*," he said with mock elation.

Jade felt his scorn, his pain spreading like volunteer seeds in the faint breeze.

"But damn if it doesn't hurt when you're the poor fuck tied to the tracks."

Jade could almost hear Yates now: *There's no soufflé without a few cracked eggs*. She wanted to tell Rhett that Yates had broken her family, too, but she suspected he already knew this. Why else would he bring her here?

"The Wood Family Farm survived the Great Depression, Big Agriculture, climate change . . ." Rhett clenched his jaw, the welt beside his cleft chin seeming to redden and swell the more he divulged. Recollected. "Turns out the farm couldn't survive one man's infernal *quest*."

He hunched, staring unblinking over the unsettled land. Jade thought he was about to scream. Maybe fall to his knees. But he just stood there, out of place in his fancy checkered suit. She wondered when Rhett had been here last. Wondered when he'd made the move to Los Angeles. Did he leave to remember, or to forget?

Sweat slid down Jade's forehead, stinging her eyes. "Your parents lost it?" she asked. "The farm?"

Rhett nodded. "They had no education, no savings. The farm *was* their 401K. The lowball sum that Yates's middlemen strong-armed us into accepting lasted three years. Pops lasted four. Shotgun to his heart. I found the body."

Jade thought of her own parents, the sight, the smell, of their bodies when the firefighters finally found their motor home, entombed by the quake's wreckage. Her adrenaline skyrocketed. Her impatience burned deliriously.

She clawed the memory away and grabbed Rhett by his lapels. "Why are you telling me all this? Everyone has a sob story, but what's yours got to do with Zoe and the Exiles?" she pleaded. "How does it help me get my sister out of Adsum, or get the Quest tech out of my body, or put the Savior behind bars?" She tried to shake him out of whatever stupor he'd been lost in these past six-odd years. "How does it explain how you knew where to find Khari's niche? Or how a Kansas boy with a dead father goes on to become Yates's trained enforcer?"

Rhett glared at her, his eyes cold and expressionless. "This is as far as I'll take you." He peeled Jade's hands off and took a step back. "If you want to know more, you'll need an appointment with the Doc. Go to the Say-So for a referral."

The *Say-So*?

The *Doc*? The same one Jade had interrogated Poppy about? After her encounter with the dean, Jade had reasoned the title referred to Maxen's behavioral therapist. Did Rhett mean an *actual* doctor, or was "Doc" some kind of ironic nickname?

"I'm going to need *a lot* more than that—" Jade started, but Rhett had already turned and was hustling toward the pickup.

If he thought he could just abandon Jade Moore in the backside of beyond without a fight, he must've missed a few important chapters of his homework on her. Jade sprinted after him, drawing out the pair of knives Ani had lent her for a moment just like this. *Moles are solitary creatures,* she'd warned. *They don't play well with others.*

Jade was quick, but Rhett's legs had five inches on hers. He got to the pickup first, jumped in, and locked the doors.

"*Bastard,*" she whispered, stopping to aim a blade. Her first knife hit the truck's cargo bed. The second hit the back tire, though it didn't puncture deep enough to stop the pickup. Undiscouraged, Jade just laughed as she sprinted toward the truck, visualizing a common swift as she leapt into the air. She landed on the roof just as Rhett accelerated.

Wind whipped her hair into her face, stinging her eyes as she gripped the edges of the moonroof and crawled to the windshield, the better to look Rhett in the face. If he was shocked by her daring—*her stunt,* Crys would have called it—he didn't show it.

"Stop the truck!" Jade demanded, pounding on the windshield.

To her surprise, he did her one better. Rhett slammed the brakes, catapulting Jade to the ground. She didn't land pretty. She heard a stomach-turning *pop,* and saw her shoulder was twisted at a *very* wrong angle. Before she could vomit or even form an appropriate curse, the truck drove off.

Leaving Jade in the dust.

TWELVE

Crys sat rigid in her plush box suite, feeling as though she was watching a tragic piece of theater.

The Summit Auditorium was filled to capacity. The audience of a thousand mourners all huddled together, clutching flickering LED taper candles, their misty eyes locked on the circular stage and the magnetic leading man at its center.

Damon Yates. Her father.

Adoptive, she could almost hear Jade whisper. *Deceiver.*

Crys felt like a field after a Malibu brush fire. Scorched and empty and desperate to heal. The flames of fear had moved on, leaving behind only a blistering numbness.

Could Damon possibly be the director of the larger tragedy befalling the Adsum sibs? All these years, had she blinded herself to his darker shades? Colored them in with light, seeing the version of the man, the father, that she wanted, *needed,* to see?

All Crys knew was that the play was far from over, a niggling feeling in her gut telling her that her role in it had only just begun.

Tears tracked down her cheeks, her heartbreak leaking from her, hot and mutinous. She swiped them away before Poppy, who sat beside her in the suite, could see, smearing her painted face. She lowered the lace veil from the black fascinator hat that she'd requested from Nico and his style team.

"But no one will see your lovely face," he'd said.

"Precisely," Crys had responded. Nor would *she*, if she chanced upon mirrors, reflective windows, *Gen 1*.

Crys looked down at her lap, realizing her right knuckles were bloody, staining the tips of her dark silk sleeves. She'd been absently tearing at the scabs she acquired three days before, when she'd smashed the looking glass inside the fencing room. Back when she thought Zoe, her rock, was still breathing, laughing, dominating this life with her light.

Crys covered her hand, the blood, and looked askance at all the Questers holding their phones aloft with their blinking candles. She knew they were livestreaming the vigil, knew millions were watching, scandalized, *tantalized*, by a Fortunate's unfortunate end.

She wanted to howl, but she was so tired of screaming. Tired of contributing to the spectacle. The lie. The academy and her Adsum sibs were a trial, a test. And she couldn't help thinking that Crystal Yates was Damon's greatest invention.

She had never truly been a daughter, Gen 3, a future billion-heir.

The revelation was earthshaking.

So why wasn't she running?

Distantly, as if listening through the clangor of a collapsing world, she caught the silvery cadence of Damon's solemn speech. She'd heard the famous bereavement poem before; her uncle had chosen it when they'd laid her parents to rest.

Do not stand at my grave and weep. I am not there. I do not sleep . . .

Crys's eyes fell on the large screens that haloed the auditorium, encircling the audience with videos of Zoe atop the Eiffel Tower, a wind turbine, Yosemite's Half Dome, her blonde hair whipping across her infectious smile.

I am a thousand winds that blow, I am the diamond glints on snow . . .

She was in a world of white, dancing beneath the northern lights.

I am the sunlight on ripened grain, I am the gentle autumn rain . . .

Crys's vision blurred from unshed tears, and then all she could see was Zoe's dull eyes, her flatlined lips, her body still, her soul gone. But not at rest.

When you awaken in the morning's hush, I am the swift uplifting rush . . .

Crys swept her gaze to the far side of the theater, lingering on Cole, who stood by the exit doors, candle-less and alone. He still wore his tattered coveralls, though they'd been cleaned, along with his tidal wave of chestnut hair. He looked incongruous, disreputable, dressed more for dirty work than a vigil.

Crys felt a pull to descend the steps and stand with him.

Of quiet birds in circled flight . . .

The auditorium's roof suddenly retracted, and a thousand necks and phone screens snapped up toward the clear, star-spattered sky.

I am the soft stars that shine at night . . .

An aircraft Crys recognized as the Quest-funded Ravn X, the world's largest drone, hovered thousands of feet above campus.

Do not stand at my grave and cry. I am not there. I did not die.

With exquisite timing, a rocket shot from the drone, a chorus of astonished gasps erupting from the audience as they watched the magnificent streak of light leave Earth's atmosphere. Every Quester held a collective breath as the rocket released its payload, revealing a small satellite.

"We've just witnessed the launch of *Zoe 1*, a premiere environmental satellite, built by our own Quest aerospace engineers, in honor of our dearest luminary," Damon announced. "She is not gone, she has just ascended higher, a glowing sentinel in the heavens, watching over the family she so loved."

Crys followed *Zoe 1*'s brilliant light trail as it raced across the sky, outshining even the brightest of stars.

Semper in altioribus, she thought, brushing the Latin words inked onto her ribs like a soothing stone. *Always higher.* One of Damon's favorite phrases, it had become her own.

"A beautiful tribute," Poppy wept. "It's what Zoe deserves."

No, Crys thought, anger coiling inside her chest. *Zoe deserved to live.* "Have you seen her autopsy report?" she asked, not caring if it was tactless to ask a mother. There was no delicacy to murder; she might as well hear it straight.

Poppy grimaced and gripped Crys's hand. She frowned at the smeared blood on Crys's knuckles but didn't pull away. Crys leaned into the dean's comfort, resting her head against a padded shoulder, the way she used to when Poppy was her guardian.

"The fight to find answers isn't over, darling," Poppy consoled, "but the postmortem examination came back inconclusive. Cause of death: undetermined."

Crys ripped back her hand, jolting upright. "How is that even possible?"

Feverish whispers broke out across the auditorium, fingers pointing at a second artificial light traveling behind *Zoe 1.*

Crys's stomach dropped. Another memorial? Another fallen Adsum sib?

Khari.

Cole must have had the same black thought, because he suddenly stood alert, fists balled.

A PR Quester joined Damon on stage, holding a high-end camera poised on a Steadicam. Damon took a step forward as if hitting some imaginary mark, drew a few grounding breaths, then addressed the camera.

"Our city has been in a drought for so long," he began, "that it's easy to forget the American proverb: *when it rains, it pours.*" He closed his eyes, cleared his throat. Held the silence for ten seconds. Twenty. Was he meditating or painstakingly choosing his next words? "This morning I received news: Khari Raine, another member of our Quest family, was taken from us too soon."

A cry died on Poppy's lips.

Crys's mind spiraled. Had the Exiles found evidence of Khari's disappearance? Was Damon including Khari in Zoe's vigil so that *he* could control the headlines, and not Jade?

Damon unbuttoned his knitted sports jacket and pushed up his tailored sleeves as if preparing for a fight. "I want the world to know that I will defend and protect, with all my power, each and every one of my Quest family. Even those, *especially* those, who are estranged. The ones who call themselves the Exiles."

Crys could hardly believe what she was hearing. What Damon was acknowledging.

The lost ones. The forsaken ones.

The ones the Savior had failed.

"Come home," he pleaded to the camera. His pale blue eyes hardened to steel.

The steel of a shield or a blade? Crys thought. *Come home for protection or extermination?*

"Stop hiding from the police," Damon continued. "Stop running from the true culprit of these heinous crimes against your foster sisters. Jade, Ani, Wily, Sage—I hope you are watching and hearing this. Quest is the safest place for you right now. *Come home.*"

Crys felt the color drain from her face. The very idea that Jade could return to campus, *Crys's haven*, sent an icy panic through her veins. She looked back across the auditorium, wanting to catch Cole's eyes. If the Exiles came back to Adsum, would he stand with her, or would he realign himself with them? *With Jade?*

But she already had her answer.

Cole was gone.

Crys surged to her feet. She turned and burst out of the box suite, ignoring Poppy's calls. Instantly, a dozen Questers were on her.

"Crystal, this must be so dreadful for you—"

"Your father can't possibly let those dropouts back in—"

"When's the last time you've even seen Jade?"

"Where were you yesterday for the memorial hike to Zoe's favorite peak?"

If Crys didn't have answers for her father—she'd locked her door this morning, feigning tiredness, buying herself more time—she certainly didn't have any for the Questers.

A hand grabbed her arm, and she spun to find Maxen in his baggy suit and black Fendi sneakers. He looked elegantly loose as always; not even a vigil could constrain his frivolity. Stiffen his leisure.

"Not planning on making a break for it again, are we, sis?"

"I don't answer to you." Crys shrugged him off and kept searching for Cole's shaggy head above the crowd.

"Nor I to you," Maxen asserted, blocking her path.

"Get out of my way, Maxen."

"It's dangerous out there," he warned.

She thought of Gen 1 and their AI drone, Palmer's stolen kiss, the possible surreptitious Quest tech ticking like a time bomb somewhere inside of her. It was dangerous *in here*. It was time for *her* to become the menace.

Swift and discreet, Crys buried her fist into Maxen's stomach.

Maxen gasped, his body folding forward. Crys pulled him into a hug, pretending to take comfort in him. She squeezed tight, giving the onlookers a touching encore.

"Stay away from me," she whispered through gritted teeth. "Give your brothers the same warning."

The night air was chilly and vacant. No Questers on the benches or walkway outside the auditorium. No Cole. Just Crys and the duet of her hastening steps and heartbeat. The urge to stop and scan the sky for *Zoe 1* was almost unbearable. But she kept her head down, her veil on. Her guard up.

By the time she reached the Forest, Crys found herself whispering, panhandling for tips. *Come on, Zoe, guide me. Show me what happened to you. Point me where to go.*

Then she heard her name on the wind.

She didn't turn back. Instead she plunged into the sea of twilight shoppers and workaholics, weaving through the grove of mass timber towers, avoiding the reflective glass of the lower floors, ignoring the diners' stares.

She stumbled when she hit a wall of scent—hints of cedar and amber, her own perfume—emanating from a boutique shop ahead. It smelled like home, like comfort. *It reeked of lies.*

Holding her breath, Crys barreled ahead, nearly crashing into a woman she recognized as an algorithms engineer at HyperQuest. The tipsy woman didn't seem to recognize Crys beneath her veil. "Slow down, you inconsiderate lummox!" the woman cried after her.

But Crys felt like she was strapped to a runaway hyperloop pod and there was no getting off. Where was she headed? Where was Cole? Where could she find answers?

Think, you lummox, Crys chastised herself, echoing the engineer, spurring her feet faster.

She pulled a drone's-eye view of campus from her memory. Visualized the thousand acres. Sixty-five buildings. Eight parks. Thirty-two trailheads and seventeen mountain peaks. Crys knew them all. She'd spent the last six years exploring and memorizing, the past six months reveling in the fact that it could someday all be hers. Well, a quarter of it, at least, between the Gens. She shook away the thought, the shattered dream, concentrating on her already blistering feet from her high block heels, rooting herself to the moment. To reality.

There were no unmarked buildings, no top-secret underground bunkers, no villainous laboratories hidden inside caves. There were no restricted levels, no door even a novice Quester couldn't open.

Do you know the surest way to impede a pathfinder? Damon had preached during his recent TED Talk. *Locks.*

Crys hurried past the moon gardens, where angel's-trumpets and night phloxes were in bloom, and careened onto a wide pedestrian way. Two men sauntered arm in arm. A woman power walked alongside her Goldendoodle. All wore a respectful mourner's black. None gave her a second glance.

Except for the dog. Crys swore she saw the great beast's snout lift in her direction.

What did it smell on her?

Fear.

Death.

Tech.

Remember, Crys prodded herself. Were there any blurry gaps of time, unaccounted for? In hindsight, were any of her doctor visits suspicious or peculiar? Had she ever awakened in the middle of an unauthorized surgery, strapped to a damn gurney?

This is ridiculous, she thought.

What was she looking for?

Crys saw that her sore feet had led her to Sophia Ray Medical Center. With a glance behind her shoulder, she decided to go inside.

Inspired by the beauty and efficiency of nature, the world-class hospital was built on a podium enveloped by a hillside studded with trees. Its two glass towers were designed in the image of organic rock formations, their edges soft and rounded, their colors soothing and restorative, as if Mother Nature had sculpted them instead of human hands.

The automatic door slid open, and Crys stepped into the central atrium. The warm limestone flooring, soaring glass panels, and wooden screens instantly created a restful, healing environment. Crys felt her pulse slow. Her breathing ease.

She nodded hello to a cluster of nurses at the front desk. No one questioned her presence as she headed for the bank of elevators at the back of the grand lobby.

A pair of doctors in white coats exited the West Tower's wide elevator, too engrossed in a patient's chart to notice Crys. She entered alone, scanning the buttons. No suspicious sublevels. No restricted floors.

So she decided to start at the top. *Always higher.*

The elevator doors opened again onto the rehabilitation ward. The floor plan was circular, with a single brightly lit corridor leading to twenty separate patient rooms. The air had a pure fragrance, not sterile, just clean. Crys breathed deeply and strode onto the high-gloss wood floor, walking counterclockwise. She peered first into the physical-therapy room, her eyes lingering on state-of-the-art training stairs, hydro equipment, treadmills, and parallel bars. A rosy-cheeked man soaked inside a steel whirlpool, eyes blissfully closed, as a PT nurse massaged his hands.

Crys kept walking, finding nothing out of the ordinary. Nothing sinister. Just more rooms occupied by happy convalescents enjoying the best health care in the country.

What else had she expected?

Feeling foolish, like she'd gone off the rails, Crys started to turn around when she heard a muffled scream. She followed it, arriving at a patient's room, four doors down, that had a curtain drawn around the twin-size bed. A large silhouette lay curled in a ball behind the thin fabric, his screams melting into a terrible low moaning.

Crys hesitated, wondering if she should call the doctor. But something, a prickling feeling at the back of her neck, made her hold her tongue. She opened the door and stepped in. Cautiously, she approached the bed, and when she pulled back the curtain, she saw the last person she had expected.

An Exile. An Exile who should have been across the city, behind the stainless-steel doors of a prison cell.

Eli Jones.

Terror twisted Eli's face. His deep brown skin looked drained of blood, his tiny-pupiled eyes bulging wide with fear. He hugged himself tight, trying to stop his tremors.

"Eli, what's happened to you?" Crys asked, reaching out a hand to calm him. She noted the tray with its half-eaten dinner turned over beside him on the bed, the crumbs scattered across his chest. "How did you get here?"

But it was like Eli couldn't even register her presence. He just kept moaning, his horror-stricken stare locked onto a far corner of the room.

Crys turned to follow Eli's gaze, and a man in a sharp platinum-gray suit emerged, his features distorted by the close-fitting stocking pulled over his face. Crys didn't even have time to put her hands up before the man had wrapped the bed curtain around her throat. He pulled viciously.

Crys gasped, battling to breathe, her head feeling like it might explode. Her hands flew out wildly, trying to tear the nylon stocking from her attacker's head. She wanted, *needed*, to see his face, but her vision blurred and she began to twitch.

The man ripped off her fascinator and its veil, smiling as he seemed to recognize she was Crystal Yates. Laughing as he watched the life drain out of her. He bent close, whispering something in her ear, but all Crys could hear was the slowing of her heart.

She was slipping away.

But then, from the edges of her darkening vision, she saw the gleam of a syringe needle before it disappeared into her attacker's neck. All at once the pressure on her throat released, and she felt herself falling.

Wheezing, choking on lungfuls of beautiful, precious air, she opened her eyes to find herself in the arms of Cole. He brushed back the mangle of tears and hair stuck to her cheeks and brow.

Crys smiled, light-headed. "I thought needles were Wily's sort of thing."

"I was in a pinch." Cole shrugged, returning her grin.

Crys hauled herself upright, clutching at her tender throat, and gazed down at the suited man crumpled on the floor. She pulled off the stocking. The man was a stranger. She noted quick details: his light copper hair, high forehead and widow's peak, diamond earing, small enamel pin on his lapel, three red diagonal stripes that looked like claw marks.

"What did you inject him with?" Crys rasped.

"Nothing lethal," Cole said, grabbing the man's gloved hand and sliding him to a corner. He threw the torn curtain over the comatose heap. "At least, I think. I swiped whatever I could find."

A low moan came from the bed, and they turned to Eli. His muscular arms were still trembling, but his eyes were clear, aimed on Crys.

"She an Exile now?" he asked.

Cole rushed toward the bed. "I'll carry you this time, brother," he said, taking Eli's hand.

But Eli pulled himself up to stand, unfolding to his full, sturdy height. "I can walk."

Cole gaped, his stony cynicism rupturing into a smile so wide, it nearly took away what little air Crys had left in her lungs. "You can walk," he laughed.

"Yeah." Eli's big, bloodshot eyes flicked toward the unconscious body on the floor. "But I think we'd better run."

If Crys had been inconspicuous on her way in, she held every nurse's and doctor's attention during her exit. The threesome sprinted down the corridor, Eli in his crisp white hospital gown, winged by a veil-less Crys and a scalpel-wielding Cole.

"Is that Crystal Yates?" a bewildered nurse shouted.

"What is she doing?" another yelled as the elevator doors closed.

What *was* she doing?

"We're on the south end of campus, right?" Cole whispered feverishly. Crys didn't answer. "Right?" he asked again, hands on her shoulder, shaking her out of her shocked silence. "Crys, are you with us?"

Crys nodded as the elevator door opened onto ground level.

"Good," Cole sighed, releasing her with a brief squeeze. "We can avoid the main gate. I know a way out through the walnut groves."

As they raced from the medical center up to the tree line, the cotton ties of Eli's hospital gown slipped loose, exposing his backside, his two taut buttocks mooning the night. Crys glanced up to the sky, trying to find Zoe among the stars.

"Crystal, stop!"

She tripped as she recognized the voice of the man who she'd once called her father, a force so powerful it nearly ground her to a halt.

Crys gripped the trompo tightly in her pocket, imagining herself back in her Unfortunate neighborhood, her birth parents cheering on as the spinning top whirled faster and faster. *Don't fall, don't fall,* they told her now, as she sprinted through the trees, the fence and its three missing bars in sight.

Behind her, Damon cried out, his voice now faint and thin. "Crystal, I won't let you go."

But Crystal Yates was already gone.

THIRTEEN

The last time Jade was in Manhattan, the borough had been covered in three feet of snow. Yates had taken his Adsum students on an elaborate field trip to the city that never slept to imbue the reformed waifs with a little art and culture. Jade remembered the first few days of flashy Broadway plays, mustard-covered street hot dogs, a private Statue of Liberty helicopter tour, an exclusive inside look at high-flying Wall Street firms. Lazing in Central Park's Sheep Meadow next to Crys, back when silence between them meant comfort and ease, not the hollow sound of a broken bond.

And then Snowzilla hit. Millions of people along the Eastern Seaboard were pummeled with the biggest blizzard ever recorded, and the sun-worshipping Californians were caught smack in the middle of it. Jade was freshly fourteen and had never seen snow before, much less been buried in it. And while for most young people it was a day for sledding and lobbing snowballs and building snowmen, for Yates's Adsum sibs, it was an opportunity to be of service. Yates put them to work aiding the low-income neighborhoods whose power had gone out, delivering water and hot meals, setting up generators for those with no heat.

The consummate bicoastal Savior, Jade thought now as she hopped off the escalators that led from the HyperQuest portal into the Main

Concourse of Grand Central. It was three a.m., which meant Jade had the rare pleasure of moving through the immense transportation hub unimpeded, no tourists' camera flashes ruining the view of the celestial vaulted ceiling like the last time she was here.

She pulled the terry hooded cloak she'd filched on the pod higher over her shoulders, the better to hide the makeshift sling she wore underneath. Popping her own arm back into place was not one of the more pleasant experiences of her life, but she'd lived without health care long enough to learn how things were done. Google was her doctor. And grit was her painkiller. Suck it up and carry on: the modern can-do spirit.

Yates's voice suddenly rang across the terminal. He was calling for her by name.

Jade searched for the source, finding a young couple loitering beneath the famed opal glass clock near the information booth, watching news clips on their phones. Jade drew closer, catching a glimpse of their screens over their shoulders. Yates was on a stage, pleading into the camera, looking every bit the Savior. "I hope you are watching and hearing this. Quest is the safest place for you right now. *Come home.*"

The clip cut to two satellites rocketing across the sky, an eternal memorial for Zoe *and* Khari, then to a wide shot of the thousands of Questers packed inside Summit Auditorium, wholly ignorant to the fact that they were listening to, *believing*, the young women's murderer.

But right now, Jade only had eyes for one Quester. Rhett, near the front of the stage. When he'd returned to campus, he must have told Yates that the Exiles had found Khari's resting place. Was Rhett truly a mole? Was he now covering his tracks? Or was Jade walking into yet another trap?

She sighed and gazed up at the terminal's massive constellation ceiling, wondering how many more satellites would be added to the night sky before this was all over.

Some sixth sense told Jade to turn around. There, ambling into the grand room from the portal escalators, was the one billion-heir she was hoping to avoid tonight.

Maxen Yates wore an expertly oversize suit of fine merino wool with cocoa-brown sandals that handsomely matched his tousled mop of hair, their leather distressed in a just-so way, signaling to passersby he was sporting *fashion*, not destitution. He had on a smug, self-righteous smile, like he hadn't just come straight from the vigil of two classmates—two *experiments*—his father had, without question, put an end to. She wondered how Maxen could stand to look at himself in the mirror.

He *should be the one with Crys's affliction,* Jade thought bitterly. *It would do him—and the world—some good.*

What in Savior's name was Gen 2 doing here? Had Rhett double-crossed her already?

She found herself prowling toward him. Face hidden in her cloak, she lingered behind a custodian's forgotten mop and bucket, catching Maxen from behind.

"They let you off campus?" she remarked coolly. Her voice echoed in the vastness. "I figured Poppy would've locked you in your golden tower."

To his credit, Maxen didn't jump. He took his time before turning around. "Jade Moore, you really are slippery," he said, stalking toward her.

"As ice," Jade answered. "Watch where you step."

"Always sharp and to the point, aren't you?"

"No really, watch your step—"

Maxen's feet went flying out from under him and Jade rushed forward to intercept his fall. She slid her uninjured arm into her bag, quick as a blink. They were nose-to-nose, so close Jade could almost taste the bitter coffee lingering on his full, sneering lips. "I seemed to have made it past that stretch of floor just fine before you got here," he asserted.

A handful of soapy water will do that, Jade thought, pleased with herself.

Maxen pushed away from her, his eyes suspicious as he checked every pocket of his suit. Everything was just as it should be.

Jade smiled coyly. "I thought your do-gooder father taught you better manners than that. Not every one of us Unfortunates is out to steal from the charmed."

Maxen grunted, tugging on his ear like all the Yates men did when they were annoyed.

Jade glanced at his elbow, spying the signal disruptor she'd hidden in the bunched-up fabric of his right sleeve. Sage had given it to her in case she had an unscheduled run-in with her sister. Jade figured this billion-heir might have a panic chip or two, even if he was the bad egg rather than the golden goose of the brood like Crys.

It was no secret that Maxen was a design flaw in the streamlined Yates machine. He was a free rider, a barnacle, more fitted to squander a family fortune than to grow one, let alone make a legacy of his own. Was that why he was here in New York? Finally, for once, to give his father what he wanted? To prove his worth by handing him Jade, the renegade thief who was *this* close to robbing the Savior blind?

Imagine. The penniless vagrant, come to steal the Yates Empire, keeping none of it for herself. Her fingers itched at the prospect. She was almost at the vault. She just needed the key, *the Doc,* and she would strip Yates bare. Seize his wealth, lay waste to his power, his freedom.

Take back his experimental daughter.

Crys is mine, Jade almost growled, seeing Damon Yates in Maxen's smooth face and demeanor. Crys might have hated Jade—and she had good reason—but Damon had *made* Crys fear her.

Soon, Jade would take that away, too.

Jade threw up her fists, ready for Maxen to make a move, but when he lifted his hand, it was to check his timepiece. Another Rolex, this one Oystersteel, worth two first-class tickets to Andorra, slung casually across his wrist. Andorra had no extradition treaty; the navy suits couldn't touch her. For a second, Jade wondered if she should snatch it, and her sister, and run. Disappear. But she tossed this half-baked idea from her mind like an undercooked hunk of poultry. The notion made her sick. Besides, she was no chicken.

"As much as I'm loath to cut this delightful run-in short," Maxen said dryly, "I'm late for my rendezvous."

A three a.m. engagement? Jade almost laughed. Was Maxen really caught up in some cross-country dalliance? "Well, don't let me keep you," she said.

He lingered a moment, then with a smirk, turned and continued on his way.

Jade trailed him. She had her misgivings when he took a left on Forty-Second Street, then a right on Park Avenue. Felt disconcerted when he made another left and vanished into an alleyway. But the hairs on the back of her neck bristled when she stepped between the two unassuming buildings and caught a glimpse of Maxen's two-toned suit through arched bronze doors closing behind him.

Jade blinked at the steady green light above the entrance: she had reached the Say-So, the "millionaire's only" club, her destination. She frowned. So Maxen had a few tricks up his custom-fit sleeves. He might be more than just a spendthrift wastrel, after all.

Go to the Say-So for a referral, Rhett had told her. Was Maxen here to get an appointment with the Doc, too? The last time she had heard him looking for someone called the Doc, he was wielding a gun, screaming atop a three-tiered marble fountain in the Adsum gardens. Jade gripped the bullet around her neck and barreled forward, ramming open the metal doors.

She needed to get a referral before Maxen killed her only lead.

A person built like an iron statue stood in her way. "Why do riffraff even try?" the hard-bodied bouncer muttered. "Members only. No one enters without my say-so."

But Jade was not one to stop on the say-so of anybody. She smiled, slammed the heel of her boot into the bouncer's foot, and charged down the staircase before he could grab her.

No basement in the world was more legendary than this glitzy private social club. Jade kept her head low and stepped across the leather-paneled threshold and into a room lit by chandeliers, its walls hand-painted with rich garden murals. She instantly spotted no less than half a dozen of the world's richest scions. Waiters in tuxedos delivered martinis on silver trays to the upper crust, who danced beneath strobe lights, dripping in jewels, cigars, and privilege.

They've probably been partying for days, Jade thought, slinking across the dance floor, searching for a face she recognized. Getting wasted and being wasteful was all the million-heirs and billion-heirs were good for.

But maybe one could be of use to her tonight.

She scanned the back of the basement and saw no sign of Maxen, but she did notice Leo Benson seated at a plush corner table, surrounded by beautiful people whose overly enthusiastic energy screamed they had been paid to be there.

Benson's family money had funded everything in his entire Fortunate life. Prep school, a semester at Stanford before he dropped out to found a tech venture headquartered on the swanky, sandy arc of Silicon Bay. She'd met him in her academy days, at one of Sage's intercollegiate memory tournaments. The man didn't lose well. In the after-party that followed Adsum's swift victory, Jade had caught the million-heir standing over Aevitas House's high-priced saltwater pools, relieving himself—and his sorrows. Though the chloramines had caused the third-years to break out in inexplicable rashes, Jade never snitched. She stored up favors like cash.

And she was ready to spend.

She advanced toward Benson, mounting the carpeted steps to his table. "Ur-*ine* for a surprise—"

Just then the bouncer locked the back of her neck in an iron grip.

Benson raised a hand, cool as rain. "Jim, that's all right. Leave her with me."

The beautiful hangers-on scattered, along with the bouncer.

"What's a girl like you doing in a place like this?" Benson asked, smiling as he slouched in his chair.

Jade hated the pinstripes on his dark blue suit, the restful superiority that etched his diamond-shaped face. "I'm looking for someone who goes by 'the Doc,'" she said in an even tone. "Can you give me a referral or not?"

A prickly revulsion jabbed at her pride asking for favors from the likes of *him*, but she swallowed her ego and tried her best not to grimace.

"And why should I?" Benson simpered. His greedy green eyes combed over her breasts, her lips. "What will you do for me?"

Jade had been swindled.

She grinned, bent over the table, batted her lashes, and swung.

There was a certain dexterity to Jade's punches, and this one landed just where she wanted. Mere centimeters in front of his wide, crossed eyes. Benson winced, falling backward in his chair. Several men at nearby tables stared, mildly amused.

Jade hovered over the million-heir as he struggled to get off the floor. "How about I let you keep that pretty upturned nose intact?"

"You always knew how to sweep a guy off his feet." Maxen laughed beside her. He reached out a hand to help Benson up. "Apologies, my sister's sister can be a bit forward when she gets offered a raw deal."

Jade studied the room. The number of spectators was growing, but no bodyguards. No navy suits. Not yet.

"She with you, then?" Benson spat at Maxen.

"*She* is very much self-partnered," Jade cut in. "So do we have an understanding, or not?"

Benson sneered, tipping back a mouthful of his old-fashioned. "Tell me, what does an Adsum dropout even want with the Doc? Hoping what the Doc prescribes can help you break out of the prison cell awaiting you? Because that's the proper place for you dirty, worthless tramps. You don't belong in the Ivy League."

Jade smiled. She was getting somewhere. Though what prestigious universities had to do with Yates and his Quest tech, Jade had no idea.

Benson gazed at Jade and Maxen with the shrewd eyes of a diamond appraiser, his upper lip curling at these two pieces of hazardous coal. "I'm done humoring a pair of washout spares." He snapped his fingers twice, and the bullnecked bouncer suddenly towered at his side.

Maxen reeled on the bouncer. "Lay a hand on me or the lady, and let's see what happens."

"What lady?" Jade balked. And why was Maxen trying to help her? He was a club member and a Yates; he wasn't going anywhere, so why wouldn't he take advantage of Jade's being ousted, possibly even arrested, freeing him to find the Doc first?

Benson hoisted his hand, snapping again, this time with his haughty tongue. "Enough of this! Let no one say I'm not a giving man." He slipped a card from the inside of his blazer, holding it out to Maxen.

Jade's impatience flared. She snatched the card before Maxen could even lift a finger. She was *not* going to let Maxen get to the Doc. Whatever his reasons for a visit, his priority was the survival of his own family, and not Jade's. She glanced down at his sandals, calculating just how fast she could outrun him. A thoroughbred versus a greyhound. She buzzed at the odds.

"The referral's for Crystal's sake," Benson continued, his mouth twisting into a smarmy grin. "She looked drop-dead gorgeous at that vigil tonight. She deserves something to cheer her up."

Jade couldn't stop herself. "What does this have to do with Crys?" Did Benson know the Doc was linked to Yates?

"The poor thing must be humiliated to have *you* as a sister," Benson challenged. "I mean, you two share a *face*. She couldn't get away from you if she tried. How many times have you been mistaken for her? How many times have you mortified her with your pathetic mediocrity?"

Benson threw his insults hard enough to maim, but Jade let his words slide off her like she was made of Teflon. *Of ice.* She'd gotten what she came here for. It was time to leave. She spun on her heel without a second glance at Maxen, hastening in an attempt to shake him off.

"But know this," Benson called after her. "I wouldn't set your hopes too high. The Doc's prescription can only do so much."

A dozen red flags waved for her attention: Rhett was leading her into a trap; the Doc was working hand in glove with Damon; this was all going to end badly.

She batted away the warnings and kept moving.

Just in case Maxen had any foolish ideas about tagging along, Jade took the stairs two at a time. She burst through the exit doors and straight into Park Avenue traffic, beaming at the onslaught of angry horns and screeching tires. Maxen valued his precious body too much to follow, of that Jade was sure, and when she glanced back, she saw him pacing the alley outside the club, a shadow of a grin on his face.

"You're nuts," he shouted. "You're going to get hit!"

"*Audaces fortuna iuvat,*" Jade answered. She darted down the street, dodging the sleek, silver AVs like bullets.

Fortune favors the bold.

Jade squeezed the card tight, a piece of glossy paper with the power to change not only Yates's fortune, but the Exiles', her sister's. Her own.

She wove through the city's congested avenues until she was certain Maxen had lost her trail. Only then did she stop to scan the foil QR code—and call for the Doc.

FOURTEEN

Ten thousand wooden benches dotted Central Park, but Hema Devi only ever sat on one.

It was *their* bench, rustic and handmade, tucked along a meandering path inside the woodland gardens of the Ramble, a piece of memorialized history they'd "adopted" with a twenty-grand dedication fee. Hema's outward appearance aside—there wasn't a soul alive who could shame them into brushing their midnight-black hair or pry them out of their faded lavender sweat suit—they were a professional, and professionals required an office. As far as they were concerned, the five-by-two-inch stainless-steel plaque with their initials drilled onto the bench's backrest was as good as any nameplate hanging outside a fancy corner office.

Dawn was fast approaching; the sky awakened, turning from shades of gray into soft pinks and golds. Birds tuned up, high in the canopies, and Hema swayed to their ebullient beat while polishing off a coconut-festooned piña-colada bagel.

Hema absently began to hum along, licking cream cheese from their fingers, bright-siding themself that they were fine. They didn't mind being dragged off the couch in the dead of night for an emergency appointment. They weren't especially piqued their new VIP client was late, but who was Hema kidding? They had nowhere else to be.

Orange-chested robins flew down to gather around the bench, chirping for their breakfast, and Hema tossed scraps to the birds until the vibrational energy around the peaceful little office shifted. Someone had crept up behind them.

"What's up, Doc?" The voice was charged with a willful confidence, at odds with the deferential tone that went hand in hand with Hema's typically desperate clientele. "I'm looking for a stiff dose of the truth. Think you can give that to me?"

Hema craned their neck and saw a young woman with a nest of brunette hair, her left hand spread wide, empty, her right tucked beneath the boxy shape of her black cloak. Was she hiding a loaded gun? Or worse, a phone primed with thousands of live followers ready to raze Hema's black-market clinic to the ground? They jerked their eyes up, getting a good look at their would-be wrecking ball's face.

Shit sprang to mind. *Shit, shit, shit.*

With an artful composure that fooled even Hema's own hyperactive brain, they folded the napkin around the unfinished bagel and rose, cradling a medical cooler bag strapped to their belly like a baby carrier. The wrecking ball swung forward, blocking Hema's path.

"I went through all this trouble to book an appointment," she said, "and I don't get so much as a 'good morning'?"

But it wasn't a good morning. It was turning out to be a very *shit* morning indeed. "I'm afraid you're confusing me with someone else," Hema lied with a practiced, breezy indifference. "I have one of those faces." *A face that blends in, a face to be forgotten.* "Good day." They turned and made a single getaway step before hearing the words they'd been dreading for over six years. Even more so in the three days since the dead Adsum girls started making the news.

"And *I'm* afraid you're hemmed in. No point in running."

Hema sighed, wrapping their sticky fingers around the padded carrier. Panic gnawed at their insides, and they had to fight to keep fear from clawing up the walls of their throat, stealing into their voice. "Damon's entourage, I presume?"

"Wrong sister."

This wasn't Damon's daughter, then. She was Crys's twin, the one Damon had never been able to control, the one with a reputation so audacious, so mettlesome, that the chronic scientist in Hema found it impossible to not study her from afar. How much of Hema's work, their brainchild, was inside this ex-Adsum student? Inside all of them? But now that she was here, up close and far too personal, Hema found they didn't want to look too intently, didn't wish to meet her inquisitive eyes.

Jade Moore would see it right away, what Hema had done.

Or rather, what they *hadn't* done. Hema was aware that their silence had made them just as culpable as any supreme Quester, and that a reckoning was long overdue. And yet, Hema still wasn't ready to face it. They held tight the cooler bag, to their rebooted life, the fraying strings that held together their sanity.

"No," Hema said. "I can't help you."

They took another step, but Jade hadn't been bluffing about reinforcements. And he wasn't a mere wrecking ball, but a live, volatile explosive come to blow open Hema's world and plunder their secrets.

"Why is she still walking around free?" Maxen Yates shouted, ambushing Hema from the side and penning them in. "Bind her hands!"

Hema's sweaty palms now had a death grip on the cooler bag. Damon had taken enough from Hema already; they weren't about to allow his son to take even more from their ghostly second life. "*They*, not she. And like I already told Jade, I can't help you."

"You think I'm here for your *help*?" Maxen scoffed. "I'm here to stop you from taking any more Adsum lives."

Maxen had grown so much since Hema had been banished from LA. His features favored his mother—dark, deep-set eyes and high, sculpted cheekbones—but he'd inherited Damon's lofty height and hotheadedness. The same short fuse that burned through all evidence to reach their own conclusions.

"Wait," Jade said, "you think the *Doc* murdered Khari and Zoe?" She charged forward, an unidentifiable device in her hand. To tear Hema down, likely as not. But Jade merely stood between Hema and Maxen, her distrustful eyes locked on him. "How did you trace me here?"

The barest of smiles tugged at Maxen's lips. He peeled a clear tracker sticker off the back of her cloak. "You aren't the only one with swift moves, you know."

Jade seized the tracker and ground it into the pavement with the heel of her boot. Hema pegged her as the type who took slipups very much to heart.

"Did Poppy send you here?" Jade pressed. "I asked your mother point-blank why you were ranting about the Doc before you shot me. She insinuated the Doc was your therapist—"

Jade had been shot? Hema didn't remember that making the news, but then again, it wouldn't. And why had Maxen been ranting about Hema? How much did he know? How much did Poppy know? Damon had always kept his wives in the dark.

Maxen's smirk warped into a grimace. His attention locked onto Hema.

"They worked for my father," Maxen seethed. "*Hema Devi*, his favorite protégé. I was twelve, but I wasn't stupid. Neither was my mom. To condense the doorstopper of a saga into a logline: Drunk on power, Hema, the toast of all of Quest, chews up and spits out a marriage, tries to get a ring of their own but gets the boot instead."

Hema huffed out a laugh. "Is that the best Damon's PR team could come up with?"

Jade shook her head. "And I suppose you think *Hema* killed Yates's fosters, as some sort of 'spurned lover's revenge'?"

Maniacal laughter bubbled up from Hema's chest, spilling uncontrollably out. Their body shook with it, filling the quiet park with howling snorts. Dissolving into sobs, Hema collapsed onto the bench, letting the hysterics roll through them in cleansing waves. "You know when you're just having a bad . . . decade?"

Hema scrubbed a hand over their face to wipe their tears, peering up at a surprisingly understanding Jade. More than a decade younger than Hema, she looked as if she knew *exactly* what they'd meant. *Well,* Hema realized, *Jade's life hasn't exactly been an easy ride.* She was a quake orphan. An Adsum exile. A severed twin. A woman wanted for the murder of those she was here—risking her freedom, and possibly her life—to avenge.

Hema wondered how Jade had known to find them.

Hema wondered why they suddenly no longer cared.

"I didn't kill your sibs," they whispered, which might have been a partial lie. But holy goddess, they hoped it was the truth. "And I never had an affair with your father," they said to Maxen. "Just because, at the time, I presented as a decently attractive young woman who worked under a powerful man, it doesn't mean that I was screwing him for a step up in the world. At age twenty-three, Damon was labeled a genius. I showed the same promise, yet I got stuck with hundreds of troll accounts with handles like @HematheHarlot. Is it really so hard to believe I earned my position with my own abilities and vision?"

"So even my mother believed my father's lies?" Maxen said. "Why'd you leave Quest, then? To start peddling whatever it is in that bag of yours?" He leaned forward as if to tear the cooler away, but Jade put out a hand to stop him.

"I know the Adsum foster family was more than just a goodwill social experiment," Jade said, quick and forceful, like ripping off a bandage. "My own sister can't even look at our face without going mad with terror, Eli suddenly became paralyzed for the *second* time in his life, and Khari and Zoe wound up dead within a month of each other.

And Savior only knows what he's done to me—" She cut herself off, as if not wishing to wander too far down that shadowy line of thought. What Damon had done to her, Hema could only hypothesize.

Maxen wrenched his ear, his brow twisting. Hema had always theorized that Maxen had an unexplained aberration of his own, but that knotty secret was not theirs to unravel.

"Are you the creator, the mastermind, behind the Adsum trials?" Jade asked Hema.

"No," Hema said, the full truth. "Damon used my technology, but I never wanted or agreed to move the experiments to human trials." They closed their eyes as if they could hide from the past, just a moment longer. "No less on unsuspecting children without their consent."

The mountain of NDAs that Hema had been forced to sign, walling in Damon's secrets, binding them in silence, suddenly lost their hold on Hema. If they were sued to within an inch of their life, like the Quest lawyers had threatened, so be it.

Hema opened their eyes.

"Damon believed that for pathfinders, there should be no locks, no limitations. If one sought the elusive road to innovation, one needed to cut the red tape—all governmental roadblocks." The truth poured out of Hema like a river. But they had no life raft to offer Jade and Maxen, only more candor. "Adsum Academy was created as a cover for Damon to test Quest Bots, the revolutionary bionanotechnology that could be the high-speed shortcut to human evolution. Every foster student was given a prototype nanobot engineered to carry out a specific task inside the mind or body. What exactly the Quest Bots altered within each student is anyone's guess. I left before the subjects were selected."

"All right," Jade said slowly, horror growing in her voice. "And what exactly *is* a nanobot? Are you saying we're implanted with tiny robots?"

Hema unzipped the cooler bag, knowing it would be better to show than tell. Several colored bottles were packed inside, wrapped in trademark BRAINONUS labels designed to make them look like a sleek, top-shelf juice brand.

"Are those wellness shots?" Jade asked, touching an orange bottle of carrot juice and ginger.

Hema took out a green juice of celery and lemon they'd mixed yesterday for a silver-spooned boy who was desperate to pass a prep-school literature exam. "These are what I call my Smart Bots. Essentially, they're intelligence boosters. Each one is specially formulated, by me, to cater to the client's needs. Someone needs to learn Shakespeare in a pinch, or grasp Mandarin fast for an exam, they ingest one of these. The nanobots in the juice input information, through the bloodstream, directly to the nerves and cells of the brain, depositing excerpts of Shakespeare or Mandarin or whatever they need to keep them ahead of their peers."

Jade's lips curled back, as if she'd just tasted something sour. "You're telling me the rich are buying intelligence from you?"

Hema nodded. "Think of it as an upgrade, an enhancement—"

"Like a breast aug?" Maxen proposed.

Hema cringed. Could their life's work really be summed up as a boob job for the brain? Since they'd left Quest, they'd been playing Doc for an elite clientele willing to fork out six figures to boost their kids' chances of making it to the Ivy League. It was lucrative yet contemptible; Hema was keenly aware that with every shot, they were widening the class divide to Grand Canyon levels.

Was this how Hema envisioned changing the world? Far from it. Damon sought to use the Quest Bots, at least in theory, to build an impossible bridge for the underprivileged to cross into the upper crust. With his academy endeavoring to "uplift Unfortunates," Hema was sure Damon believed he had the moral high ground over Hema, even if Adsum's foundation was built on lies and treachery. The entire world thought him a Savior.

Hema had a name for him, too. *That two-faced bastard.*

What Hema was doing with *their* nanotech was illegal, yes, but they were no murderer. At least the Smart Bots weren't killing people. All their clients were still alive and *more* than well, sauntering about the grassy quads of Yale and the halls of the Fortune 500.

Jade pocketed whatever weapon she'd been holding beneath her cloak and sat down next to Hema. She grabbed their cheek, forcing Hema to face her.

The Exile was fearless, yet the longer Hema stared into those eyes, impenetrable as a muddy river, the more they saw the torrent of panic just beneath the surface. A fear for others, perhaps. For those she loved.

"Do you know why the Quest Bots are suddenly turning lethal?" Jade asked.

Hema shook their head. "No. But I do know how to disable them."

Jade surprised Hema by reaching out to clasp their hand. "I need you to come to Los Angeles with me."

"With *us*," Maxen added. Jade hesitated. A look passed between the two of them, some kind of an agreement, sealed with a nod.

So Hema's winding road was leading them back home to the City of Angels. They thought of Damon's parting words: *If you disappear, you better stay gone.* But Hema was tired of living as a quiet ghost. They were ready to become the disruptive poltergeist. To start throwing shit around and make some noise.

"Will you help us?" Jade pressed.

Hema packed up their shots and rose from their bench. "Yes."

FIFTEEN

Crys felt her spirit sink lower than a deep-sea trench.

Dry River City was empty.

Had the encampment finally been the target of a long-promised police sweep? Dismantled and scrubbed clean, the unhoused swept away like dirt beneath a rug. *There*, but unseen. *A bandage on an eyesore that needed major surgery,* Crys thought.

But there were no sanitation crews, no protesters, no stragglers refusing to leave their tents or hexagon pods. The unofficial city of thousands looked simply abandoned. And in a hurry, at that.

"What do we think happened here?" Cole asked. Alongside Crys and Eli, he stared down from the embankment at the grimy city, scanning the deserted housing structures, the desolate mobile showers, the vacant river market.

"Nothing good," Eli snarled, stepping forward, his body tensing. "How could an entire mischief of River Rats up and vanish overnight?"

Despite the high-noon heat, Crys pulled her threadbare sweater tighter around her chest. She'd found it at Husk Row, and the thing smelled of cigarette smoke and onions, but it got her out of her vigil suit. "Let's hope the others weren't here for the disappearing."

None of the Exiles were answering their messages, and their usual retreats were empty. They were running out of places to look.

"Why do you care?" Eli snapped, bunching up the patchwork sleeves of his denim jacket he'd discovered at their Griffith Park hideout. Crys stared at Khari's face, which Ani had painted boldly across its back. "Since when are you concerned about the welfare of your sister, or any of us castaways?"

"I'm here, am I not?" Crys said, indignant.

"Yeah, to save your own neck."

Partly true, Crys thought, caressing her sore throat. She'd almost been strangled by a mysterious man who'd only squeezed harder when he ripped off her veil and saw that she was Crystal Yates. She *had* to leave campus. Quest, her home, was no longer safe. And her father, it seemed, wanted her dead. *Yates,* she corrected herself. Add another failed foster father to her list. But she found she was beginning to care about the ex-Adsums and their precarious fate, which was now tied with hers, far more than she wanted to admit.

"Like it or not, Crys has crossed back over to the *Unfortunate* side," Cole said dramatically. "Though I like to think our luck is changing." He was aglow with optimism.

Was Cole looking at the same desolate scene that Crys was? She squinted, analyzing him closer. He'd finally changed, swapping his coveralls for one of Eli's upcycle designs. A liveliness, an irresistible light, shone in his eyes again, as if he'd somehow shed his melancholy when Crys wasn't looking. What had caused this sudden transformation?

Eli grabbed at his short curls. "I'm going to get a closer look." He pounced for the staircase, racing down the graffitied steps, heedless of the fact that he'd only been able to walk again for less than twenty-four hours.

How had Yates healed him? When Eli had been at the academy, Crys had watched in amazement as his injured body was restored, then in confusion as the stronger he became, the more he shrank from the extravagance of the pampered Quest life. Had Eli been suspicious of his first recovery? Was that why he'd originally fled Adsum?

Eli had been the third to join the Exiles.

Crys realized that she was now the last.

Her musings were interrupted by a terrible wail echoing up from the concrete river below. The same spine-chilling cry she'd heard at the Quest hospital.

Cole bolted for the stairs. "Someone's got Eli."

Crys followed close behind, but she didn't have to run far. They found Eli alone, only a few feet from the staircase, gaping at the City Limits mural painted on the embankment.

"What's wrong, talk to me," Cole huffed.

But Eli cowered, balling himself up against the concrete wall. His screams died as he sealed his eyes.

Crys couldn't believe it. It was like watching her own attacks. "I think he's having a fear incursion," she whispered.

Cole's brows shot upward. "A what?"

Eli straightened and took off. Cole charged after him, tackling him and pinning him by his broad shoulders.

"We have to leave!" Eli yelled. With an incoherent howl, he hurled Cole onto the pavement and surged back to his feet. Two glass vials fell out of the patch pocket of Cole's T-shirt. Crys snatched them, her brows knitting as she examined a silver aluminum cap with Cole's name stamped across it.

One vial was empty. *What had Cole done?*

Before Crys could question him, three figures emerged out of a honeycombed housing structure. Two seized Eli, while a ponytailed third cupped his angular face in her hands.

"Eli, it's me, Ani."

Her voice seemed to slow his breathing, soothe his all-consuming fear. His screams quieted to a low moan as she eased him down onto the bottom step of the staircase.

"Sage? Wily?" Cole exclaimed, hurrying forward.

The two local River Rats stood in front of Eli. Protecting him, *shielding* him, from Crys and Cole. Behind their hostile glares, Crys thought they looked badly shaken, shell-shocked.

Was Jade here? Fear burned through Crys's chest, but for the first time in years, it was fear *for* her sister. Not *of* her.

For the first time in years, Crys ached to see her.

"We should block his vision," she said, focusing on what she could control. Blocking him from what exactly, she wasn't yet sure. "At least, that's what helps me."

Ani slid off her leather jacket, holding it before Eli's panicked face.

"Stay away from him," Sage hissed. "Both of you."

Wily gripped a gleaming pocketknife.

Cole shuffled closer to Crys, a warm grin deflecting their cold greeting. "Empty hands, open minds, remember?"

It proved to be a disarming move. Wily lowered his blade. "Since when does 'Stone-Cole' smile?"

Sage stepped forward, her auburn hair as wild as her storm-gray eyes. She pointed at Crys with her long nails. "Were you a spy for him? Did Yates tell you to take a Quake Tour, do a bit of reconnaissance before he wiped us out in a matter of minutes?"

Dry River City had once been called Yates Haven, a temporary emergency shelter that one of his charities teamed with FEMA to erect after 2040. But why would he seek to get rid of it now, after all these years?

Damon Yates rarely gave up on anything.

Crys could almost hear his earnest, unnervingly serene voice reverberating across the vacated encampment. *Crystal, I won't let you go.* Had he ordered a sweep to find her? Was he willing to tear the entire metropolis apart to get his runaway experiments back? *His poor investments?*

"I wasn't then, nor am I now, a spy," Crys said with more than a little bite. "I was here for Jade."

Wily scoffed. "Oh right, I forgot. It's always about you and Jade."

"Guys, not now," Ani snapped, focusing on Eli. He was concealed behind her jacket, but Crys could see his hands were no longer trembling, though his feet never stopped moving, like a runner staying loose. "Eli, do you know what's making you so afraid?" Ani asked, her tone soft, coaxing him to speak.

Eli shook his head so vigorously that Ani had to cup his face again to make him stop.

Crys wondered if his fear was induced by something specific that he saw, the way Jade's face triggered Crys's own bouts of terror.

"Can you tell us how you got out of jail?" Cole asked. "How you ended up back at Quest?"

"I . . . I guess Yates bailed me out," Eli said slowly. "Or Poppy made him do it. I would've made a break for it but, you know, jail-issued wheelchairs aren't exactly prime getaway vehicles."

Crys shivered. Eli must have been terrified, traumatized, to find himself back in that chair, not knowing why.

"Then some Quester took me to the medical center," Eli continued. "I started feeling sensations in my legs last night. I didn't know they were working again until we had to run—"

"Did they give you anything?" Sage interrupted, pulling the jacket down and blocking Eli's field of vision with her body. "An IV, an injection?"

"No, nothing like that," he said. "The nurses tried to get me to eat, but I refused. I didn't trust anything Quest-made going into my body. I only risked a few sips of water."

"And did anyone come visit you?" Crys asked. "My fath—" She cut herself off, quickly correcting her former delusion. "Yates or Gen 1, maybe?"

"Only the man in the gray suit with the stocking mask," Eli said. He seemed in full control of himself again. "I was in the middle of telling that smoosh-faced bastard he was wearing his pantyhose all wrong when he started shoving a quiche down my throat."

"A *quiche*?" Wily said, with a disconcerting touch of envy. "Always fine dining at Quest, even when being force-fed."

Why would Eli be compelled to eat? Was there some ingredient, *some tech*, baked inside that had instigated his fear incursion?

"What about the trouble here?" Cole asked, addressing Wily and Sage. "There's no chance your river dwellers cleared out for better horizons?" He offered a hopeful smile, which the pair ignored.

The rattled, shell-shocked look hadn't left them. On edge, they scanned the tops of the embankment. Sage shook her head and collapsed onto the pavement next to Eli. When she gripped his hand, his feet finally stilled. "We came to wait for word from Jade," she said, staring at her acrylic nails, which Crys now noticed were chipped and caked with dried blood. "The city was already at the tail end of pandemonium. Thousands screaming their heads off, losing their minds, fighting their way up the exits." She paused. "I saw one kid try to swim the shallow channel to get away. I watched, helpless, as she drowned."

Sage's stubborn severity, which she always wore like an alabaster mask, cracked with the single tear that rolled down her cheek. Wily bent down to wipe it gently with the end of his shirt. "We moved the bodies that were trampled to death to one of the large storage tents," he said. "We didn't know who to trust to come collect them."

"The navy suits never showed up?" Cole asked.

"Figures," Eli said. "There were no Fortunate bodies here."

Sage shook her head again. "The shouting attracted the interest of a few late-night prowlers, but . . ." She shrugged. "The worst news is the mayor's gone . . . and he's *never* gone. This is *his* city, and as a point of pride, he never leaves its limits."

"Nothing short of a nuke threat would make the mayor evacuate," Wily agreed, "so where the hell did he vanish to?" He kicked at the litter along the embankment wall. A bag of unopened chips revealed itself in the melee. Wily scooped it up, squeezing it open with a *pop* before tossing the chips into his mouth like little thin slices of comfort. "And why not *us*?" he wondered aloud between swallows. "Why weren't we affected like Eli and the rest?"

A rat scurried past Crys's feet. She tracked its course, wondering whether the rodents were inflicted with the same urgent desire to flee the encampment. The rat scampered toward the thin, sluggish river and slipped into the market stall that sold whole fish, happy to devour an uninterrupted meal. But then Crys spotted something floating in the cloudy channel of water, something that made her tilt her head.

Cans of spray paint. Scores of them.

Curious.

She scanned the graffitied walls, her keen eyes halting on a symbol that looked brighter, fresher, than the washed-out tags and faded paste-ups that surrounded it. Small as a handprint, but hard to miss once it was noticed.

Three diagonal red stripes, like claw marks, like some sort of marking of territory.

It was on the sides of the honeycombed pods. The kitchen tent flaps. The seatbacks of the worn-out armchairs in the lounge. Inside the letter *D* of the City Limits mural.

It was everywhere.

She'd seen this symbol before. At the hospital, on her attacker's lapel.

Crys felt the scratchy bed curtain rope her neck, saw the man's vicious smile as he yanked tighter. She felt her lungs lock, her heart near exploding. Her mind desperate for oxygen. Answers. More time.

Suddenly Ani was at her side. "I realized I never told you that I'm sorry about Zoe."

The curtain slipped from Crys's throat; her chest heaved with violent gulps of air. An overwhelming urge to look skyward consumed her, but it was daylight. *Zoe 1* wouldn't be detectable. She held Ani's frank gaze instead. "I'm sorry about Khari."

Then a voice as coarse as rubble sounded from above. "You know what feels better than apologizing for wrongs that aren't yours?"

Crys whipped her eyes up the long staircase and saw Maxen Yates standing at the top beside a dark-haired stranger shouldering a soft-bodied cooler and numerous backpacks, the stark edges of Jade's figure hovering behind them.

Crys could almost hear Jade's smile as she answered her own question. "Getting even."

Sixteen

Jade had always been leery of Dry River's so-called mayor. Even before the night she ended up on a bridge above his city. Wound up a killer. The barrel of the Fortunate's gun jammed into her temple.

"The high-ups are like sharks," he'd told her then, just before he'd banished her, promising a bullet with her name on it if she continued her vigilante folly. "You have to let them do a few hit-and-runs, a few test bites, so they won't consume you whole."

It looked like his city was now the victim of a sneak attack. A predatory feast.

For once, Jade took no pleasure in being right.

"So, do we think the mayor was in on it?" she asked, gazing around the mayor's lord-sized tent. High-priced paintings usually cluttered the canvas walls. Collectible figurines normally crowded every surface. An invaluable, *untraceable*, 3D-printed pistol was once a fixture on his heavy oak desk. All now AWOL, like their owner.

Sage stood with Wily by the open mesh door, her thousand-yard stare aimed at fingernails stripped of acrylics and blood. "I'll let that accusation slide for the sake of the agenda. But if you say anything more against the man who took me and Wily in, *twice*, even after Yates threw us out like trash and you deserted us, I *will* displace my rage onto you."

From behind the mayor's empty desk, Hema cleared their throat. "All right, first order of business . . ." They zipped open the cooler and unrolled a plain compact bag across the top of the smooth wood. Packed inside its insulated interior pockets were shiny glass vials. Dozens of them. "I've not named these babies yet, but you can think of them as attack bots—"

"Hang on," Eli interrupted, raising his big hands. "Who said *you* get the floor?"

It had taken Jade fifteen precious minutes to persuade Eli and the rest to allow Hema, a former Quester, and Maxen, Gen 2, Yates's *son*, even to step foot in the tent.

Eli glared at them now, resting on the lip of the mayor's porcelain claw-foot tub. Ani sat beside him, monitoring him like a watchdog, on guard for signs of what Crys had called a fear incursion. They'd painted over all the mysterious symbols that had been tagged around the tent and across the encampment, but some of them had been so masterfully hidden that this was obviously much more than a rival gang attack claiming new territory.

Jade was sure the symbol had something to do with Yates, but how this new threat linked with the Exiles and their Quest Bots, she didn't yet know.

"We went to Hema for help," Ani said. "They're our guest, they should have the floor."

Eli shrugged, his jaw muscles clenching. "Guest is just another word for stranger."

Jade waited for Cole, the irritable cynic, to speak his mind. Lately, he challenged everything. But now he leaned against a bookshelf, the portrait of contentment. His normally dull, sulky eyes sparkled with vigor, his tanned skin ruddy, *glowing*, as if Ani herself had brushed color into the somber, gray sketch that had become Cole's image.

He was fixated on the opposite corner of the tent, where Crys sat stiff and cross-armed in a wishbone chair. Since Jade's arrival in the abandoned encampment with the Doc and Gen 2 in tow, she'd hardly dared to glance in Crys's direction, afraid of scaring her away.

Half of Jade was still paranoid that her sister's presence was a trick, that it wasn't real. That the Crys in the wishbone chair was a hologram, a hallucination. She'd almost searched her pockets to find something to toss at the motionless statuette. But if Jade's sister were a mere dream, she'd be looking Jade straight in the eyes.

She'd be by her side. Not across the tent, a million miles away.

"Wait, did everyone not hear the same pitch I did earlier?" Wily interjected. "Some sleeper agent who works for the archfiend we're all running from told Jade to find this 'Doc,' who wants us all to ingest *another* bot that they created in their *basement*? Hard pass."

"Why don't we just hear Hema out?" Maxen suggested, taking the words right from Jade's mouth. He paced the hardwood floor in a loose-limbed swagger, feigning an air of nonchalance.

Jade didn't know if she could trust him. Or if Maxen trusted her. All she knew was that he appeared to be as much a victim of Yates as any of them. Worse, even. Poppy had sought to keep him close, protecting him against the big bad world, but all she'd done was lock them both in with a devil with a saintly face.

"Is it really a good idea to have Gen 2 here, Jade?" Crys asked from behind her shield of golden hair. "How can we be sure he won't just run home and inform on us, either to his father or his two pricks for brothers?"

Jade couldn't believe Crys was addressing her, and slighting her cherished adoptive family, no less.

"For once I'm with the evil twin," Wily said, but his glare slid past Jade, locking onto Crys. Had he *still* not shaken off his expulsion from Adsum? Even now, after the human guinea-pig revelation? "Well, the lesser of two evils," he added, cutting his gaze back to Jade.

If the man was consistent with anything, Jade thought ruefully, it was how tight he held on to grudges. And she knew he had a festering one for Yates. She just needed to direct that glint in his malevolent eyes toward the right target.

"Listen," Jade said, rising from the sharp corner of the desk. "We don't have to be one big happy family. But everyone can agree on one thing, at least." As she looked around the room, all but Crys's pale diamond eyes were aimed on her. "We want this trial we've all been enduring, *surviving*, to end."

"Pfft, some of us," Crys scoffed, shaking her head up at Cole, who was contentedly perusing the sun-faded spines along the bookshelf, dropping a few bright-colored paperbacks into the wide patch pockets of his cargo pants.

How could Cole be so cool and collected, storing up on books while the Exiles were being chased, *hunted*, for the earthshaking tech Hema had revealed all Adsum students were hosting?

Yates wanted them home. Yates wanted them dead. But not before destroying the evidence of what made the former orphans valuable in the first place.

Who was Jade without her Quest Bot?

The question lingered in her mind like a lit grenade. She should throw it, get rid of it before it detonated. Instead, she held on with a tenacious grip. Stunned at the urgent sound of her second thoughts ticking.

Sage shook her out of it. "We've now wasted two hundred and ninety seconds on bickering and foreplay," she said. No phone or watch in her hand. Had she been casually counting the minutes in her head? "We don't have all night. I suggest we move to the main event."

Hema rolled up the sleeves of their lavender-colored sweatshirt. The air was thick with the tension and heat of nine anxious bodies trapped inside a tent. But Hema's eyes seemed more skittery than the others. Their fingers restive, searching for something to grab hold of.

Jade knew Hema must be feeling the strain of moral culpability for their part in the Adsum trials. She reached her hand out to Hema's and squeezed. "Knowledge is power, right, Doc? Set us free."

Hema straightened, smoothing back unruly bangs, their soft features settling into a steely resolve. Their eyes shone sharp as a blade, a trailblazer anyone would line up to follow. Jade could see exactly why Yates had chosen Hema as his protégé.

"Essentially, all Quest Bots are nanostructures built from engineered amino acids, which form synthetic proteins that differ from the naturally occurring proteins in the human body. The divergence in these engineered proteins is our fail-safe." Hema leaned over the vials, their body and voice animated. "I've discovered a way to identify the synthetic proteins using specifically targeted molecules, which will act like little red flags, indicating the Quest Bot's location. My attack bots will then move in and deactivate."

"Okay, I'm going to need you to repeat all of that more slowly," Wily said, rubbing his forehead.

Sage stepped forward and plucked a vial from one of the insulated pockets of Hema's bag, holding it up to stare inside. The liquid looked as innocent as water. "Hema programmed these new bots to kill the Quest Bots already inside of us."

Hema nodded, seemingly glad that at least one person understood their genius. "It could take hours, or even days for the Quest Bots to fully flush out of your systems. Outside of my lab, these attack bots have never been tested. But as with all treatments, the reaction will probably vary from person to person. And since I don't know the engineered purposes of each of your individual bots, I cannot predict the outcome of what will happen after they're disabled."

"But you do believe that Yates's bots killed Khari and Zoe?" Ani asked.

"I do," Hema said, gravely. "And I'm convinced that any one of you could be next." Hema's weighty gaze fell on each of the exiled Adsum students in turn. "Let me be very clear. Taking this vial is a deeply personal decision, one that comes with its own risks. It's a choice everyone must make for—"

Before anyone could move to stop him, Maxen swiped a vial from Hema's bag and gulped it down. Jade saw Hema's slight body tense.

Why? Hadn't Hema just told them all it was *their own* choice to make? Or did Hema know something more?

Everyone stared at Maxen like he was a high-stakes science experiment, holding their breaths, watching for any perceptible evidence of a change in him. Maxen ignored their gawking. He'd halted his pacing and now stood perfectly still, eyes closed, his breathing slow and deep, as if he'd suddenly decided to take up his father's meditation practice. Was he feeling out whether something inside him had been altered? Or was it an act, a performance to convince the Exiles that he was one of them, an unwitting victim of his father?

Jade could see similar questions written across Hema's face as they seized the bag of vials and began to pass the attack bots around.

"Don't bother with Cole," Crys said, accepting her own vial, slipping what very well might be the miracle glue that could link her and Jade back together into her sweater pocket. "He won't be terminating his bot. Not when he took all that trouble to con his way back to Adsum." She held up a second vial with Cole's name written across its silver lid, then launched it at him. He caught it with a grin. "Is this what you were creeping around the medical center for? Not to find *me*, but your Quest Bot?"

"It wasn't like that, Crys," Cole answered, the smile gone from his lips but not his eyes. "I needed the bot like Eli did—"

"Oh, so you *needed* a death wish."

"I took the bot so I could *live*, all right?" Cole paused, setting a hardcover novel back onto the shelf. "My sickness was in my mind, but it was no less fatal. My depression made me feel like I was trapped in a deep tank of water, treading the surface, struggling to stay afloat. Hoping someone would come along and pull me out. But I realized nobody was coming to save me because nobody noticed I needed help. Most drownings are silent, you know. The foster agency called it my *defect*. The reason I was in thirty-nine different foster homes. I thought Adsum had saved me. But then I found myself drowning again."

That must have been around the time he'd joined the Exiles, Jade reasoned.

The irritability, the headaches, the fatigue Cole had worn like a heavy coat. *I should have recognized the signs,* Jade scolded herself. She should have helped him. But then again, Jade could barely help herself.

"When Jade showed up on our doorstep with all her cracked Quest-tech theories," Cole said, turning to Jade, "I formed a theory of my own. Maybe whatever Yates had put inside me had expired. Like Eli's. Maybe if I could get it back, I could save myself—"

"But there are other ways," Crys pleaded. "FDA-approved medications—"

"No," Cole cut her off, shaking his head as Hema came his way. "I'm keeping my Quest Bot. It was agreed it was our own decision. And I've made my choice."

Crys sat silent. As did the others, lost in thought, contemplating their own pro-and-con checklists.

Jade wasn't surprised when Eli refused.

"But what about your fear incursion?" Ani said, eyes widening. "This bot could deactivate whatever's causing you to shrink from those symbols."

Eli stood, his sturdy frame taking up half the private bath. "I'm with Cole. I'll risk whatever might happen so that I can stay standing."

Jade couldn't deny that Eli's Quest Bot had apparently reversed his paralysis. Although she loathed shining even a *sliver* of positive light Yates's way, she had to ask, "How do we know we don't *all* have some unknown condition the Quest Bots might have 'cured'?"

"You don't," Hema said, taking their place back behind the desk. "That's the risk. It might just be that your bot was a curative for allergies. Or it might have fought off a childhood cancer you weren't aware you had . . ."

Or it might make your sister scream at the sight of your face, Jade thought. That was *one* thing Jade was certain of, at least: the purpose of

Crys's bot. For Yates to have kept Crys nice and close, and Jade good and far.

She peered at her sister, willing Crys to take the attack bot, wondering if she could force her. Maybe slip it into her water bottle, or mix it into her toothpaste. Shove it down her throat, hold her nose and mouth until she swallowed.

Ani's frustrated cry brought Jade out of her head and back into the tent.

"Or the odds-on outcome: at any second our Quest Bots could malfunction," Ani said in a forceful tone, "and we could end up dead like Khari and Zoe." Her words hit Jade with the impact of a dull blade trying to dig at her heart.

Khari should be here. Flesh and blood and whole, with *them*.

"So basically, we're all playing Russian roulette," Wily said, eyeing his vial like a loaded gun.

"If that's true, I'm going to be the one to pull the trigger," Sage said.

Wily and Sage raised their vials, clinked the rims, and drained them.

"And what about our Adsum sibs?" Maxen asked, surprising everyone. He'd always been a loner, a blue-blooded outcast among his nobody classmates. His sudden attachment was blindsiding. "They deserve to know the truth."

"We can't just abandon our Adsum family in that prison in the sky," Crys insisted. "Who knows what else Yates has planned for them."

"They're right," Ani said. "Their lives shouldn't be left to chance."

Maxen whipped out his phone. "We need to contact the dean. We need to warn my mother."

Jade shook her head firmly. "Yates will be tracking Poppy, and every Quester for that matter. Right now, we can only rely on ourselves, the people *in this tent*." She peered around at the eight Exiles, her crew, who she realized she'd be willing to bet her life on.

It had taken Jade eighteen years, but she finally understood. Family didn't always mean blood. Sometimes family was who you'd bleed for.

"Who's hungry?" Wily asked, holding up his pocketknife.

"Seriously?" Eli sighed. "Do you ever think about anything but your stomach?"

"Not hungry for food," Wily answered deviously, his scarred brow wagging. "For *retribution*."

Everyone raised their hands.

Jade's eyes crinkled with excitement. She'd always heard revenge was a dish best served cold. And she knew just the recipe.

Crys was on the other side of the woven rattan partition, fresh from a quick dunk in the claw-foot tub. The scented peppermint shampoo hit Jade's nostrils from behind the trifold screen, taking her by surprise. Crys usually went for sharp flowery smells. Mint had been their father's favorite.

"Jade?" Crys whispered. She sounded startled but not afraid.

Jade didn't answer.

"I know it's you. I can see your scuffed-up boots below the screen."

"Oh," Jade said, awkwardness clenching her voice. She thought she'd steal a moment, check up on her sister, make sure she was still here, still breathing, while the others were in the mobile showers or prepping for various field trips. She didn't anticipate a conversation.

She didn't know what to say. So, she confessed.

"You were right, I am a killer."

The slap of bare footsteps sounded from beyond the screen. Toward Jade, not away. Her sister's manicured toes only inches from her own. Jade wished she could tear aside the barrier between them. Though she supposed it was better this way. Not to see the judgment, the disappointment, in Crys's sky-blue eyes. Not earth brown, like Jade's.

"I was here, in Dry River City, the night I found out you'd officially become a Yates. *Gen 3.*" The knot in Jade's throat tightened, a long string of things unsaid, unfelt, tangled like a neglected necklace. There wasn't time to unravel, so Jade stuck to the facts. *One knot at a time.*

"I'd heard from some of the local girls about a Fortunate man in a flatcap who liked to stalk the encampment. The usual story . . . took what he wanted. Drugs, sex. Lives. The mayor tagged him as untouchable. The traitorous *sellout.*" Jade paused, cleared her throat. "That night, when I saw the Fortunate leaving the tent of a half-conscious teenager, I snapped. I went after him. Challenged him. We wound up on First Street Bridge. He slipped, and I let him fall."

"You didn't kill him." Crys's voice was soothing, like a cool washcloth pressed to Jade's fevered mind.

"Yeah, but I didn't save him."

After a few beats of silence, Jade heard the rustle of clothes, saw the back of her sister's head emerge at the end of the barrier that divided them. "I have something for you." Crys held her hand out to the side, keeping her head low, careful not to catch a glimpse of Jade.

"What's this?" Jade asked.

"A truce," Crys answered simply, revealing the trompo resting in her palm.

Jade moved to stand behind her sister. Back-to-back, crown-to-crown. The way they used to sleep, to protect and watch out for each other, back when they were young. When it was just them. When their bond was as strong and precious as gemstones.

Your fortune is in your bond, their mother used to say.

Jade grasped the trompo, then chancing a bigger risk, folded her hand over her sister's. Crys didn't pull away.

Jade smiled.

It was going to be a lucky night.

She could feel it.

SEVENTEEN

The mayor jolted awake in a shallow puddle of his own blood.

Disoriented, he lifted his head, shook it. Hissed in pain. The back of his skull throbbed like someone had thrashed it with a lead pipe.

Had someone thrashed his skull with a lead pipe?

But that question quickly became less pressing when he realized where he was.

If a person trapped inside a vacuum-sealed HyperQuest tube cried for help, and there was no one around to hear it, did he make a sound?

The mayor didn't have breath left to find out. The steel tube was nearly airless. He was going to suffocate if he didn't do something.

Fast.

He would've laughed at the beautiful savageness of it, the shrewd tidiness. If his lungs had the oxygen. Or if he had the time.

The mayor got to his feet. Which way was forward? Which was back? Back *where*? His mind told him nothing but *run!*—but his Gucci loafers slipped on the slick, curved surface of the unending tube.

He fell to his palms and knees. Got up. Scuttled four steps before he fell flat on his face again. A fresh lump on his forehead to go with the nasty gash on his crown.

His claustrophobia was setting in. A mad panic that made him think he could tear through steel with his old bare bones.

He was already dead, he knew. He might as well close his eyes. Make his peace.

He probably wouldn't even feel it.

No. *Get up and fight,* he always told his people. His city. *Never stop fighting.*

Somehow, he rose.

Again and again, he slid and lost his footing. Ended up on his knees. For a second, he thought about ripping off his shoes. He'd heard rumors Damon Yates liked to go around barefoot. Was it so he could race through his network of tubes, better able to hand-deliver poor suckers like him to their ends?

They were all just rats, he realized. Scrambling, trapped, in the Savior's twisted maze.

He got back to his feet. Kept on his shoes. Buttoned up his double-breasted jacket. No, the mayor and maker of Dry River City wouldn't go down like a beggar. He pressed his swollen fingers to the walls, feeling for signs of a levitating passenger pod rocketing toward him just a whisker shy of the sound barrier.

He wouldn't even hear it coming.

His execution would go unheard. Unseen. Unmourned. Unavenged.

The mayor lumbered faster. He needed to reach a recess, a safe haven. Or stumble on an emergency maintenance hatch. Ten more steps, and he was drained to his core. Was that all the fight left in him? His spirit roared, but his oxygen-starved body halted, sagged. Gasped for air that wasn't there.

He rested his cheek against one of the tube's slotted circular windows. The sun was setting. He supposed that was a sign. Providence telling him to put down his fists.

Dignity in poverty, he'd told his people. His city.

He would have dignity in death, too. Even if it was an unfortunate one.

The mayor turned to face the pod's path and straightened his three-piece suit. He waited with his eyes wide open.

He still didn't see it coming.

The impact of the bullet-shaped pod splintered the mayor's stout-hearted body.

He was a man. Then he was nothing.

And he didn't feel a thing.

Eighteen

Crys sat with her toes buried in the sand. The last of the evening light, a shocking neon pink, still clung fast to the clouds, casting a dreamy luster over the vibrant tech hub of Silicon Bay.

She held up her vial, pinched between two fingers. The glass was warm, the liquid clear as crystal, the cure, *her* solution, invisible to the naked eye.

She shifted her scrutiny toward Cole, who stood with Eli along the chilly shoreline, the foamy waves nipping at their heels as they watched over her. She remembered the vial Cole had taken from the medical center, his Quest Bot just as inconspicuous within it. Just as undetectable.

How could something so momentous appear so unassuming? A technological breakthrough so big it could alter all of humankind, yet each bot was roughly one thousandth the diameter of a strand of her golden hair.

Crys closed her eyes, trying to imagine her Quest Bot swimming around her brain. An invisible invader, a long-term resident, occupying the almond-shaped amygdala deep within her temporal lobe. She shivered, the fine hairs of her arms standing on end like thousands of infinitesimal knives. Her body's response to fear. A leftover trait from their animal ancestors to make her seem larger, more threatening, to potential predators. Opening her eyes, Crys glanced over her shoulder, gazing up at the mountainous peaks that cradled the Yates Empire.

How many Questers knew about the bots? How many had known Crys was nothing more than a lab rat, ignorant of her gilded cage? She had always felt her life as a Yates was a dream, but she would never have believed what an illusion it all had really been.

The truth fell on her with the weight of a crumbling skyscraper. Likely as not, Crys was a prototype, Subject Zero, the first generation of whatever fear bot was inside Eli and the Dry River City runaways. *But why? For what?* Her heart raced as she reached with sweaty palms for the trompo she'd pulled from the rubble of her childhood.

It wasn't there. Just like Jade wasn't there.

All those years.

One thousand and ninety-five days without a sister.

One hundred and fifty-six weeks living in fear. Terror. Of her reflection, her twin.

All this time she'd thought her fear incursions stemmed from memories of Jade luring her into the hyperloop tube. She'd thought it was cut-and-dry PTSD that had torn her and Jade apart. But it was Yates and his Quest Bots. She now understood he'd used her trauma as the perfect cover-up to make her believe that her fear of her sister was natural.

And what had he done to Jade? Crys had always believed it was plain old resentment that had driven Jade's daredevil need to push too far, to crave the spotlight like a drug, to risk her family, her future, *her life*, just to feel a temporary high. How much of that was Jade? Had her Quest Bot driven her to the tubes, making her so fearless, so reckless, that it had nearly killed them both?

Crys eyed the vial in her hand, knowing that their broken bond could never be magically mended with one swallow of Hema's outlaw invention.

But it could be a start.

Mere hours ago, Crys had judged Jade to be the most self-seeking maniac alive. Now she knew that title belonged to the man who had been her Savior. The man who'd saved an unseen waif sinking below the Unfortunate cracks and helped her rise to unimaginable heights.

You remind me of myself, Crystal, Damon had often told her, his pale blue eyes as nourishing as the rare summer rain. *You're going to change the world.*

She realized now he had never meant *her.*

Only her mind, and what he could do with it.

Was Crys specially chosen for Adsum solely because she was a perfect test subject? She imagined what Yates must have thought when he first laid his duplicitous eyes on her and Jade. They were by the murky water of Echo Park Lake, their tiny bodies wrapped together in an adult-sized coat. Zipped up tight against the cold, against anyone wishing to separate them.

If you can make someone fear her identical twin, her mirror, you can make her fear anything.

Crys unscrewed the lid of the vial. Did Yates ever love her? Ever truly see her as his daughter? Some small, diminishing thing inside her held tight to the fantasy that he did. That the fear bot was all a device to keep Crys close to him, to make her choose a father over a sister. Paper over blood.

She could almost hear Jade laughing all the way from the eastside.

Tipping back her head, Crys downed the clear liquid in one shot. She half expected to grimace, for it to burn like gin. But the attack bot was odorless, tasteless. Painless.

She waited for something to happen.

Eli made a move toward her, but Cole grabbed him by the shoulder, holding him back, seeming to sense she needed this moment for herself.

Was she meant to feel a tingling, a numbing, a weight lifting off her mind? She felt nothing. Normal. But what was normal anymore?

The ocean breeze picked up, crashing the waves harder onto shore. Crys turned her gaze to Hema, who'd been loitering farther up the beach, staring like a lost, disheveled pilgrim toward the heavens. Toward

Quest and Yates, Hema's late mentor and former wayward guide, who tried to lead Hema down a path they couldn't follow.

They peered fixedly at Crys now, wringing their hands. Hema wore a hood over their short hair, their long torso slumped forward from the weight of the medical cooler and two bulky backpacks, Hema's life's work, valued at untold millions, packed inside.

What did Hema see as they watched her?

Someone to be pitied or feared?

A dupe or a Yates?

Crys turned away from Hema's inspection, analyzing the half-healed scabs that pocked her right knuckles. Before she could stop herself, her sandy, shaking fingers plucked the blue contact lenses from her eyes. She was about to tear out every strand of her bottled golden curls when she saw it.

A sandcastle. Equipped with two towers, an arch, and a wall.

Just like the one she and Jade had built, the time their parents splurged on an AV to take them on their first, and only, family visit to the beach. It was Crys's favorite memory. The smell of sunscreen and salt and lighter fluid from the grill, the sound of her mother and uncle laughing in stereo, loud and unrestrained, as Jade chased the seagulls from their modest dinner. The feeling of her father's hand in her own, promising that his two precious gems would one day live in their own real castle.

I made it, Crys had whispered to her parents' memory when the Castle in the Air had become her home.

Tonight she was ready to drag it to the ground.

Down the beach, a crowd gathered around a pair of stunning influencers lying on the shoreline, dressed in glittery mermaid tails. The women writhed enticingly in the sand, pouting, flicking their jewel-studded aquamarine fins while two shirtless men in backward caps streamed the stunt to their presumed millions of social-media followers.

To Crys's horror, the mermaid with the seafoam-green hair caught her eye. Her Barbie-doll face lit up like she'd just won the content lottery.

"Oh my god, it's *her*!" she squealed. "Kyle, pick me up, pick me up, hurry!"

Kyle didn't miss a beat. He flipped his camera to selfie mode and handed it to the mermaid, then he squatted, scooping her tail and all into his muscular arms, and ran toward Crys like a lifeguard on a rescue mission.

"Hey, Cam Fam, you'll *never* guess who *this* siren just lured to the beach," the influencer said, addressing her followers with a manic energy. "Crystal Savior-lovin' Yates."

Crys lurched to her feet. Stuttered backward in the sand. She turned, pulling her tattered sweater up to hide her face, and started to jog toward the parking lot, keeping a wide berth from Cole and Eli so as not to drag them into the mermaid's net alongside her.

The Exiles were all over the news. A video capturing them out in the wild would go viral instantly. Damon would know that they were close. That *she* was close. They'd lose the element of surprise.

A pack of yapping Chihuahuas, outfitted in life jackets with fake shark fins on their backs, dashed into Crys's path, forcing her to pull up short.

"Coco, *no*!" a beachgoer shouted, reaching out to pick up a plump, grizzled shark-dog. But it was too late. The shark-dog snarled up at Crys and bit at her ankles, a signal for the rest of the pack to charge. Crys tried to break free, sidestep her diminutive attackers, but she was surrounded, and she feared crushing one of the Chihuahuas live on camera.

And then a phone was in her face.

Kyle held the shimmering mermaid over the barrage of dogs, pressing her almost cheek to cheek with Crys for a perfectly framed two-shot selfie. Crys's heart raced with familiar panic, desperate not to cause a public scene. She slammed her eyes closed before she could see her image on the phone's screen. The cacophony of barking dogs, the growing crowd of riveted tourists with Hardihood T-shirts snapping her photo, the influencer's running commentary—Had she been kidnapped? Had she run away from her castle?—all blurred into a confusing babel.

"Isn't she a dead ringer?" Cole's voice rose above the din, taking on a lighthearted peddler's tone. "The best Crystal Yates impersonator in the business, folks. If you want any more photos, you'll have to pony up some cash. Same goes for our young Chadwick Boseman here."

Eli, Crys thought, her eyes still shut, trying to calm herself, thankful for their reinforcing presence. Like most street kids, Cole was skilled at manipulating perceptions, beguiling people into seeing what he wanted them to see.

And getting a little money on the side.

"He looks *just* like him," a young girl squealed in delight. "My favorite superhero . . . Daddy, I want a photo!"

"She had us fooled, didn't she, Cam Fam?" the mermaid sighed to her online followers. "But I don't do fake Crystals."

Crys felt the influencer pull away, off to search for more juicy content for her feed. She could sense Cole's diversion working, the crowd's frenzied energy quickly dissipating.

A new body sidled up against her. "I just *love* Crystal. I've followed her story since I was a kid," said a young woman who sounded about Crys's age. "I used to dream of getting plucked from obscurity to go to Adsum, but you know"—her voice lowered to a whisper—"I wasn't *unfortunate* enough." She hooked her bracelet-laden arm around Crys's neck. "I always thought it was so tragic how she and Jade split up. Sisters forever, you know?"

Then Crys felt a row of tiny teeth sink into her ankle, and her eyelids involuntarily flashed open. The young admirer's phone was pointed directly at Crys, her cheeks sucked in, her lips pouting in a duck face as she clicked a series of selfies. Crys prepared herself for terror to burn up her sore throat at the sight of her face on the screen, for uncontrollable screams to erupt out of her, her secret shame on display for all to see.

Only, they didn't come.

The attack bot had worked.

For the first time in three years, Crys looked straight at herself and . . . *smiled*.

The young admirer held her phone before Crys, scrolling through photos. "You know, you really are a Crystal doppelgänger but . . . just a tip, she's *way* sweeter and more glam than the vibe you're giving off. You're like Crystal before the Savior, you know what I mean?"

Crys barely heard the young woman's sharp appraisal. She took the phone from the woman's hands, zooming in on the most recent photo. Tears streamed down Crys's cheeks, clouding her vision, but she could not take her eyes off the face she'd spent so much time and energy avoiding. *Loathing*.

Fearing.

She looked older, stronger, than she remembered. She looked like a Moore.

Jade was in her dark eyes. Her mom in her natural rounded brows, her dad in her oak-colored roots that were just starting to show. The family traits she'd tried to hide to fit in, to appear more like a Yates.

For years, she had truly been an impersonator, Crys realized.

But no more.

She began to weep, her overwhelming relief bursting through her once-stoic dam, cascading out of her through tears salted with undiluted joy.

Eli swept her up in his arms, playing his role of hero marvelously. Cole cleared their path across the beach toward the parking lot. "You feeling okay?" he asked, undoubtedly worried she was experiencing side effects from Hema's attack bot.

All she could do was nod.

Suddenly Eli froze midstride. "Shit."

Crys could feel his heart thudding in his chest against her ear. At first, she thought it might have been his Quest Bot malfunctioning again. His knees buckled. But from her wet peripheral, Crys spotted a patrol car pulling off the Pacific Coast Highway, rolling to a stop beside Hema.

The exiled protégé stood in the middle of the paved bike trail that bisected the parking lot and beach, only a sliver of their face visible beneath their billowing hood and bulging bags.

How? How could a navy suit clock them as Hema Devi? Crys looked upward, searching the twilight sky for a flock of metal birds. For Damon Yates.

The driver's side door of the black-and-white patrol car opened. A tall, lean officer stepped out, swinging a stun baton. Dark aviators and a black ball cap covered his features, save the stern, hard-bitten set of his jaw.

Crys's heart sank. A panic rushed over her. "If they confiscate those bags, we're done," she whispered, afraid of drawing more attention.

"Behind you!" a cyclist shouted, speeding toward Hema. Hema barely jumped forward in time, falling onto their face with a mouthful of sand. "Fucking tent people, always in the way!"

After a recent fire killed two people and their dog inside the Venice Boardwalk's swelling unhoused encampment, city officials voted to enforce an anticamping law anywhere near the famous beach. The LAPD had full authority to stop and search any persons carrying what they deemed contraband, essentially making it illegal to be homeless in this once free-spirited neighborhood.

And right now, it looked like the entirety of Hema's life was loaded onto their narrow frame. The bags. The bots. They carried the whole supply for the rest of the Adsum sibs. At all costs, Crys couldn't allow Hema to get taken into custody.

She squirmed down from Eli's arms, on the verge of rushing to grab the bags and run, cause a diversion like she was sure Jade would do, when the navy suit slid off his sunshades and grinned.

Wily.

Eli laughed. "Now *that's* a getaway vehicle . . ."

Cole beamed at Crys.

A cop car was *not* a listed ingredient to their group-approved recipe. It was highly illegal and unwise. But Crys found herself smiling back all the same.

"It's not hot, is it?" Cole asked, inspecting the light bar that trimmed the patrol car's curved roof and doors.

Hema traced a light hand along the car's flank. Their finger came up white.

Spray paint?

"Why pay for the real thing when knockoffs are just as fetching?" Wily grinned, taking a large bite out of a glazed donut.

"Gates open at eight o'clock," Sage announced from the patrol's speaker, ever the taskmaster.

"The trouble begins at nine." Wily winked, tossing Crys a uniform.

Not a navy suit but a soft blue cardigan, debossed with the Adsum coat of arms.

Crys gazed up toward the blazing lights of Quest Campus.

Gen 3 was returning.

And she was ready to dress the part, one final time.

Nineteen

Jade adjusted the focus wheel on her dented binoculars, sharpening the image of their target: the Exiles' beat-up motor home.

From the rooftop of an army-surplus warehouse, she spotted the old silver-and-black camper, parked unobstructed in the corner of the LAPD's downtown impound lot.

"Good news," she said, lowering her binoculars. "The clunker's vandalized battery has already been swapped out."

"Our girl was too big to tow," Ani said beside her. She looked as wistful as Jade felt, like she, too, longed to jump into the battered camper and drive back in time. Back to when Khari was still alive, to when the motley fellowship would gather around their tiny kitchenette each Sunday and pool the earnings they'd each scrapped together to keep them alive for the next week.

Jade squeezed Ani's shoulder. Hitching her to the future. "Looks like this will be an easy job. Like stealing candy from a baby."

"Such an idiotic idiom," Maxen noted from behind them. "Babies have no teeth. They can't even eat candy."

Jade ignored Maxen's increasing cantankerousness, turning her attention to what came next. She hadn't hijacked a vehicle in months. She took a few seconds to revel in the adrenaline that coursed through her body, to soak up the rolling jolts of excitement that lit her up from within. She felt invigorated, animated with the thrill of impending danger.

She wasn't sure if she'd ever get to feel this alive again.

Not if the attack bot stashed in her pocket, wrapped inside her calavera-patterned bandana, had its way. She shook her head, casting off the decision to rid herself of her Quest Bot for another, later hour.

"How long will this take?" Ani said, pulling a heavy-duty tablet from Jade's bag.

"I'll have control in a matter of minutes." Jade took hold of the tablet, the modern thief's lockpick, and got to work. The tips of her fingers buzzed as she remotely hijacked the camper's CAN bus system using her favorite cyberweapon: a Bluetooth connection. "These old Quest models have so many vulnerable attack surfaces, *such* a simple network structure. It's shockingly easy to allow for widespread mayhem."

"Yeah," Maxen butted in irritably, "that's why most of these models were recalled, decades ago."

"Are you seriously defending your dad's company right now?" Ani asked, incredulous.

Jade blocked out the noise.

With a few lines of Sage's brilliant code, she already had access to the motor home's entertainment system, and once you had access to *one* part of a vehicle, with a little reverse engineering, you had access to *everything*.

For instance: the autonomous driving system.

With a flourishing tap of Jade's finger, the motor home's LED headlights flashed on and off. She looked up at her coconspirators and smiled. "She's ours again."

The camper's electric motor was silent as a shadow, leaving the navy suits stationed at the impound's entrance woefully unaware that the confiscated vehicle, the crime scene in Zoe's murder investigation, had even awoken.

Ani cocked a brow, reluctantly impressed.

Now all Jade had to do was upload the software Sage had written just hours before, setting an unalterable track for the camper to follow. But a sudden, shrill chorus of police sirens rent the night air. Dozens of black-and-white patrol cars careened out of the LAPD headquarters, racing west through downtown. Toward *what*?

Had they been tipped off to the Exiles' nefarious plans?

Then a police copter powered on, the roar of the rotor blades vibrating through Jade's body, amplifying her already sky-high adrenaline level. The exhilarating rush almost made her dizzy.

"Get low!" Ani shouted when the copter's Night Sun switched on.

Jade and Ani dove for cover behind the roof's ledge, but Maxen remained on his feet.

"Maxen, get *down*." Jade pulled on the baggy hem of his pants, but it was like he couldn't hear her. His eyes were glassy, his usual haughty posture slumped, as if carrying some unseen weight.

Maxen grabbed a fistful of his hair, yanking hard. "It's happening again."

"*What?* What's happening?" A sour disquiet settled in Jade's gut. For the past hour, she'd done her damnedest to avoid every unpromising sign, dodging all the pointed glares Ani had been trying to throw her way. *You know exactly what's happening,* Ani's rusty, daggered eyes would have said, if Jade had dared to meet her gaze.

He seemed to be in the grips of a psychotic episode. Shieldless—*bot-less*—in his battle against his rare mental illness. *Childhood schizophrenia.* Jade knew the symptoms, had seen her fair share of adults struggling at the encampments without treatment or support.

"The Quake," Maxen answered, his flat, plodding voice at odds with his frenzied movements. "The real one. You thought we'd already felt the Big One, but it was only the foreshock. The Giant One, the mainshock, is happening. Can you feel it?"

He dropped onto his stomach, scraping his fine suit and face against the rocky asphalt, and pressed his left ear to the pulsating rooftop. Jade looked to the sky. "It's just the copters out in force. Just your average night in Hardihood. There's no earthquake—"

But Maxen didn't heed a word. He sprang to his feet, awkward with his new lace-up army boots, and rushed toward the railing. "I have to leave, I have to get down from here, they're trying to get rid of me."

Jade caught him by the back of his collar. "Maxen, I need you to stay with me. I need you to *listen*." For a second, he stood still. Cocked an ear. "Who is trying to get rid of you?"

"*Them*," he whispered, like someone could be eavesdropping.

"Jade," Ani hissed, crouching at her side. "We're running out of time. Which problem do you want to fix? Maxen or our captured camper?" Her eyes thinned to slits, glowering at the copter racing overhead.

"They're trying to dispose of me," he said, fighting to break Jade's hold on him. "Like they did the Doc—" He wrenched forward, wriggling free of his suit jacket and Jade's grasp. He turned to face them, his brows merging into one dark line, his voice even. "I have to warn them." Then he swung his arms, jumped from the edge, and disappeared.

Ani's mouth dropped open in a silent scream. Jade flew to the railing, verifying what she'd already guessed. Maxen was halfway down a fire escape.

The drop-down ladder whizzed past the building's three stories, landing with a rattling *clank* on the pavement. Ani cringed. "And if the navy suits didn't already know we're here . . ."

Jade swore, realizing where Maxen was heading.

Ani echoed her sentiments. "Son of a plaster saint, he's—"

Moving straight for the front doors of LAPD's headquarters.

Jade bounded onto the fire escape, shoving on a pair of gloves so she could slide down the ladder swift and painless. She had one hand on the vertical rail when Ani seized her other arm, her whip of a ponytail lashing Jade's eyes.

"Are you crazy?" Ani whispered forcibly.

"What?" Jade rebutted, trying to blink the sting from her corneas. "I can handle a few dozen navy suits."

Ani laughed at her audacity. "And what about Gen 2? Remember what happened the last time Maxen lost touch with reality?" Her thumb pressed the starburst bullet scar on Jade's shoulder, her fingers reaching for In Extremis, yanking on the silver chain that held Jade's warped souvenir.

"You think you're invincible, that you're a steel-plated brawler chasing death, but *it's the other way around*, Jade. The bot already has its claws in you."

Jade shook her head, fighting to shrug Ani off. "Maxen's going to give us away if I don't stop him. Let me go."

Ani's grip tightened. "Your Quest Bot is going to kill you, Jade. If not tonight, by making you suicidally reckless, then some other way, like it did to Khari—"

Maxen had nearly made it to the station's entrance.

Was already within range of surveillance.

Jade had to clench her jaw to keep from shouting. "The others are relying on us—"

"Exactly, and getting yourself arrested was never part of the meticulous plan. Following him will only lead to disaster."

And yet Jade craved it.

But was it the indomitable pull of the bot inside her mind, or the natural tug of sympathy that swelled in her chest, that wanted, *needed*, to save the unfortunate billion-heir?

Ani held up Hema's glass vial in one hand, Sage's drive in the other. "I won't complete the hijack unless you take the attack bot with me."

"What, *now*?" Jade demanded.

"Yes, *now*. Take it, or you're on your own."

Ani's big brown eyes reminded Jade of severed tree trunks. Desolate on the surface, but mighty beneath, a stubborn grief and determination rooting her to her purpose. Jade knew she'd never budge.

Besides, Jade was tired of being alone.

"Fine," she uttered, jostling her pockets for her bandana and the glass vial carefully stashed inside. Wasn't this what she had been fighting for? To be truly and wholly rid of Yates's hold on her? She could *die* if she didn't take this.

Yes, the brassy scapegrace in her whispered. *But if you take it, you might not fully* live.

What if she needed it?

What if she was ordinary? Mediocre? *Useless* without her Quest Bot?

Ani threaded her arm around Jade's, holding her plum-colored lips to the rim of her own vial. "Fortunes change," she toasted.

For once, Jade hoped they didn't. *To the bold,* she toasted silently. She slammed the liquid, showing her tongue so Ani would be satisfied that she'd swallowed every drop. Without another word, she slipped down the ladder, letting her adrenaline cauterize any infectious thoughts.

When Jade hit street level, she took off toward the police headquarters. She'd lost sight of Maxen during her haggling with Ani, and when she got in front of the station, she couldn't spot him among the cluster of people filing out the front doors. Just released prisoners, judging by their shifty appearances.

"They won't take it from me!" Maxen shouted, somewhere close.

Jade whirled around to find Maxen facing down none other than the gargantuan man the River Rats called the Gravestone. What was *he* doing here? Had he been arrested after fleeing Dry River City? Was that where all the encampment residents had gone? *To jail?*

But Jade didn't have time for these questions. The Gravestone had grabbed Maxen by the sides of his head and hammered his forehead into Maxen's. Maxen keeled over and sprawled on the ground, his diatribe against the inexplicable "them" unceasing.

"Shut up," the Gravestone growled, bending over him.

Whether he meant to nab Maxen's person, or the hundred grand wrapped so casually around his wrist, Jade didn't wait to find out. She ran and tackled him, pushing him away from Maxen with all her might. But the Gravestone was as hefty as his namesake, and he stood his ground. He stepped to the side and viciously struck his fist into her lower back, just below her rib cage.

Jade dropped like a stone, curling into a ball.

"Stay down," he ordered.

Jade's mind flooded, not with pain from the cheap kidney shot, but white-hot anger. This man had helped create the Dry River playground that allowed Fortunate bastards to come in and unleash their sick delights, free of consequence. And now he thought he could command her to heel like some dog?

"Here's a little down payment on your retribution," Jade wheezed, launching a ground kick straight into the Gravestone's groin.

He sank halfway to his knees, then recovering quickly, dove for Jade, snarling. But before his fingers could reach her neck, his droopy, close-set eyes locked onto hers. He cowered back, and as he did, she caught the scent of cedar and amber on his soiled shirt. Why did he smell like her sister's perfume?

Jade heard two slight pops, one after the other. The sound of blades cutting into flesh.

The Gravestone fell to the ground, staring up at Ani in shock. Two of her knives already deep in his thighs, she pointed a third at his jugular.

"I suggest you stay down."

Maxen shook his head, which seemed to muddle him further, because he attempted to crawl *toward* the navy suits who'd just charged out of the police station, taser guns raised in their direction. "They're trying to get rid of me!" he screamed.

Jade and Ani lunged for him at the same time, grabbing tight to the back of his shirt and retreating toward the street.

"Come on, *come on*," Jade said under her breath.

Bam! A few heartbeats past its scheduled jailbreak, the motor home burst through the impound's chain-link fence, powersliding onto the road.

"That's Jade Moore," the Gravestone shouted frantically to the navy suits, pointing in her direction. "She's abducting Maxen Yates, take her down!"

The Gravestone was onto something, Jade thought, wishing she'd come up with it herself. But as they say, great artists steal.

Especially the *con* type.

"I'm Jade Moore, and I'm kidnapping Maxen Yates!" Jade yelled, echoing the Gravestone's warning.

"*What the hell are you doing?*" Ani exclaimed.

Jade grabbed Ani's knife and held it to Maxen's throat. "Don't try to follow or the billion-heir will get hurt."

The navy suits loved threats as much as she did.

Then, turning to her companions, she cried, "*Run!*"

Jade dragged Maxen by his armpit toward the camper, which, using its lidar sensors, swerved around a series of AVs and sped toward them. Beside her, Ani used the tablet to open the vehicle's door remotely.

Jade's own sensors told her they were going to need more help than that. "Can you make it slow down?" she asked as they scuttled alongside the camper.

"No," Ani huffed out, "I've already uploaded Sage's route into the system controls. It's locked. Our girl can't be stopped now."

There was nothing to do but jump. Jade thrust Maxen through the door, then helped Ani catapult inside. But Jade started to lag. Her sweaty palms reached for the doorframe, for Ani's outstretched hands, but she couldn't gain purchase.

"You're going to let an AI driver beat you in a race?" Ani goaded her.

But nothing spurred a person on quite like a high-pressure air gun firing behind them.

Jade ducked, then launched herself headlong through the camper door. Through the rearview mirror, she spotted a StarChase tracker stuck to the grimy window.

The LAPD would be able to follow their every move.

Jade sprawled out on one of the swivel chairs and laughed, a euphoric high pulsing through her veins. Yes, she was still *very* much alive. "Well," she panted, "I think we've got everyone's attention."

TWENTY

Rhett had never liked heights. After his accident that foggy night on Adsum Peak six years ago, he'd manifested an extreme aversion toward any high place over two feet. For five months, stuck in a hospital bed with a broken neck, he'd been tormented with visions of climbing stairs, ascending ladders, falling from the top of the Empire State Building, all leaving him in a pool of sweaty anxiety.

Acrophobia, Yates's overpriced shrink had called it.

Which meant the very last thing Rhett should be doing right now was barreling his way into the glossy cabin of Yates's private auto-copter.

Yet here he was, doing just that.

Gen 1 was already inside. VR goggles rested on both their foreheads, their knees bouncing impatiently.

"We don't need our father's puppy dog watching over us," Palmer sneered at the sight of Rhett. "Go find another bone to chew. The strays are ours."

"Orders are orders," Rhett said, taking a seat in an empty leather chair between the brothers. He wiped the perspiration from his temples, his mind and body revolting at his cockeyed decision to place himself in a death trap flown by a semiautonomous robot with a billion-heir pilot hobbyist at the backup controls.

There were no orders.

In fact, Rhett had been instructed to remain at Adsum Academy and protect the students, by whatever means necessary. Yates had even given him an extra gun.

But Gen 1 were like two boys with a magnifying glass, ready and eager to burn the pesky ants below. Only their toys were a helicopter and the ear of the LAPD, and the ants were the Exiles, riding alone in a rust-bucket camper with death-or-glory Jade at its controls.

Rhett couldn't trust either of them without a chaperone.

The brothers slid on their VR goggles, Quest's new vision of flight control, giving the backup pilot the ability to captain the aircraft using hand motions and voice commands. Rhett elected to go goggles-free, knowing the immersive flight path would trigger a panic attack that would render him useless. He kept his gaze fixed on his feet.

Vance pounded the roof twice, and the auto-copter lifted silently into the sky.

The AI pilot steered them west, toward the coastline, where Palmer's police scanner told them the high-speed pursuit had just careened onto the Pacific Coast Highway: "Two confirmed suspects, Jade Moore and Ani Agassi, up to four more inside, all former Adsum students. One confirmed victim, Maxen Yates, and a possible second, Crystal Yates. Both VIPs. Orders are to let the vehicle run out of battery, do not engage. No risky moves. Everyone gets out of this alive."

Rhett laughed. There might be a world where that outcome existed, but it wasn't this one.

The auto-copter flew level, like a plane, rather than nose-down like a normal helicopter, which dulled aspects of Rhett's phobia, but when Palmer commanded it to increase its speed to 300 mph, Rhett's panic latched on like a nerve-sucking tick. With a few deep breaths, he grabbed his fear by its head and risked a peek down at the jammed PCH. The red taillights of stalled AVs streaked past like one endless bloody river. His head spun, his stomach flipped.

"Hey, Frankenstein," Palmer snarled. "Hey, Stein! If you throw up, I'm throwing you out."

Rhett knew the crooked snoot would make good on that promise.

Why am I here? Rhett asked himself, not for the first time. Here in this auto-copter? Here in the sun-cursed Golden State? Still under Yates's employ, tucked like a cozy chick beneath the vulture's wing?

He'd handed more than half a decade of his life, *his youth*, to a man who'd tangentially murdered his pops. Ran the Wood Family Farm into the ground. Effectively made a scraggy, country-fried Rhett a homeless orphan.

God, had it really been six years?

"Well, look what we have here," Vance laughed.

Rhett kept his eyes locked shut. Imagined himself seated in a wheat field, the crops grown tall around him.

"The northbound highway's been cleared," Palmer said. "Can't be far now."

The auto-copter dove. Judging from the piercing wails of sirens, they were zipping over the tops of several police cruisers at the heart of the high-speed chase. Rhett couldn't get his brain to settle. His half-digested foie gras dinner clogged his throat, half-remembered reflections spilling out of his mind. He was in Dubai, Hong Kong, the edge of outer space. He was shaking hands with superstars, kings. Smashing the faces of would-be Yates abductors, paparazzi, disobliging business associates.

He was richer than all his forefathers and mothers combined.

"There!" Vance proclaimed, clapping like he'd actually done something.

"I see them," Palmer said. "Now, why don't we remind those ineffective boys in blue who the real chief is here?"

Rhett peeled open his eyes to see three—no, *four*—police copters hovering above the solitary tin can of a motor home hurtling down the coastal highway, destination still unknown.

Swallowing a low groan, Rhett turned his gaze to Palmer. Then to Vance. Then to his two guns. "Hey, yacht snot," he rasped. He knew he was a touch gruel-brained from the height. Knew he was blowing his cover. But he didn't care.

He only gave a damn about the deserters. Jade and her band of Exiles. He wasn't sure if they'd found the Doc or why the hell they were leading this car chase, but they were fighting to do the job he'd been too pampered and hoodwinked to finish. They deserved his help. His admiration.

Rhett wondered if it came with getting older. Wanting comfort over unrest. Well, he was certainly uncomfortable now. And he hadn't felt this young in *years*.

"No matter how hard you try and keep them out," Rhett said, shoving his panic down with his bile, "those strays down there are going to take over your empire and shit on all your finery. Tear the veil hiding your lavish, well-kept secrets to shreds."

Rhett usually carried a few actual wheat kernels in his suit pocket, planting them in odd places around Yates's campus, seeing if they'd grow. They always died. Now he imagined the bullets in his guns as seeds, waiting to be sown into bodies.

"*Excuse me?*" Vance scoffed.

"I'm tired of forgiving and forgetting," Rhett said. His stomach dipped as he remembered his fall. His rise. He touched his fingers to the back of his sweaty neck, a motion made possible only by his Quest Bot. By the mercy and power of Damon Yates.

Damon had taken him in. Called him son. Led him to heights a boy from Kansas could never dream of climbing in a million lifetimes. No less the short, miserable one he had been destined for. Like his pops.

You're just like me, Damon had told him. Or maybe that was all just bullshit, and he'd kept Rhett close for scientific observation, like he'd done to all those Adsum students.

Rhett the mole had dug too deep. The kid who'd set out from Tonganoxie for revenge had gotten lost in his own tunnels. He'd spent too long underground.

Well, he saw the light now.

"What's this, brother?" Palmer asked, looking straight through Rhett to a smirking Vance. "Has Stein finally turned on his maker?"

"Do you really think you can get away with *octuple* homicide when every cop in the city is watching?" Rhett already knew the answer. Gen 1 didn't give a sod about Maxen, the half-genes. Crys, the adoptling.

The fewer siblings to take fat slices of their father's pie, the better. Getting rid of the feral strays with illegal Quest Bots was just the sweet, candied cherry on top.

Rhett slowly drew his second firearm from his concealed ankle holster. He'd loaded it with frangible bullets, designed to disintegrate if they struck a hard surface like the inside of an aircraft, but lethal if they hit something soft. Like a human body.

"Do you really think we'd let someone like *you*, stop us?" Vance ridiculed. He tore off his goggles, raised his phone that moonlighted as a 650,000-volt stun gun, and pressed the weapon under Rhett's armpit. The shock dropped Rhett to his knees.

Vance hooked his neck from behind with the crook of his elbow, trying to squeeze out his life without having to look Rhett in the eyes. Rhett bucked, and the back of his head slammed into Vance's nose with a satisfying crack.

Palmer screamed at the AI pilot to dive lower, ignoring the system's warning that they were cutting dangerously close to other aircraft in the crowded sky. The auto-copter suddenly dipped, just as Rhett whirled around and bashed the butt of his gun over Vance's head, accidentally discharging a bullet into the windshield. Tiny, harmless particles bloomed around the laminated glass like violent art.

Vance slumped to the cabin floor, unconscious. Rhett seized his taser, staggered to his feet, and turned to Palmer. Before he could make his move, a compartment behind the back row of seats burst open, and a drone hurtled at Rhett's face. Robotic arms locked onto his temples, two metal clasps grabbing hold of his eyelids.

How is Palmer controlling this thing? Rhett could barely hear himself think above the buzzing hum of the billion-heir's vicious toy.

A large hand smashed the side of Rhett's head against the panoramic window. Forcing his wide-open eyes to take in the dizzying heights. To see the highway whipping past as the auto-copter swooped in front of the motor home, flying backward at 100 mph.

Bile rose out of Rhett's throat and onto the glass as he watched the motor home swerve, then plow through the metal traffic barrier, all in slow motion.

He felt like he was plummeting off the cliffside. Dropping through the chilly coastal air, the auto-copter spotlighting the dramatic descent as he fell, down, down. Screaming for his life.

But it wasn't Rhett falling.

It was the Exiles.

Straight into the ocean.

TWENTY-ONE

Being held captive in the trunk of a car had always been a top-ten nightmare for Crys. Drowning was a steady top five.

Right now, the public thought Crys was sinking to the bottom of the ocean, trapped inside a stolen motor home. Really, she was crammed inside the rear storage of a counterfeit police cruiser. Although she could still hardly breathe.

"There goes the dive team," Cole announced, his wiry frame folded and compressed like a veteran contortionist beside Crys's as they waited in the dark. He held up his phone so she and Hema could see the muted livestream of rescue boats and Jet Skis swarming the black waves where the Exiles had come crashing down.

At least that's what Yates's auto-copter pilot was hoping, Crys was certain. Why else would they run the motor home off a cliff?

"Can you believe our luck?" Cole smiled, a touch too cheery given that Yates just tried to have them killed. Again. "This buys us way more time than a high-speed chase."

"As long as this Trojan horse can make it through the gates," Hema reasoned.

Cole scrolled the news feed on his phone, the stream of articles showing frenzied reporters choking the entrances outside Quest Campus, held back by an army of navy suits.

Eli grumbled from beneath the altered back seats, which had been hollowed out and stuffed with his large frame. "Why are we stalling? My legs have gone numb, and I think we all know how my psyche is handling *that*."

"Wily's probably finishing up a box of bear claws first," Cole hypothesized.

Crys could feel Hema's head shake beside her, their arms taut around the medical bag. "Does that guy take anything as seriously as his food?" Hema chided.

"Maybe teas," Cole quipped. "He's surprisingly picky about the source of his herbs."

A warm sweat dripped down Crys's sides. She hated tight, dark spaces. They reminded her of the rubble, the tubes. Of the nights she lost her parents, her sister. She tried to reach for her perfume, her trompo, anything to tamp down the panic, but they were gone. She felt Cole grip her hand, and as he continued chattering brightly, the way he used to do to silence her gloomy memories, the car's electric motor switched on, and the wheels began to turn.

Crys counted the seconds it took for their fake police cruiser to reach the North Entrance gate. Sighed in relief when she saw the car pop up on the livestream of an amateur gawker with the handle @neal_before_the_news. Held her breath as a square-jawed officer approached the passenger-side door.

Sage rolled down her window, hidden behind a false toothy smile and phony police cap. The wails of sirens and buzzing reporters drowned out the exchange, but Crys knew that Sage was rattling off the memorized names of their superiors, probably even their badge numbers, just to show off.

The officer stepped back, the wrought-iron gate swung open, and the car pulled forward. Crys started to breathe again as their cruiser left the horde of cameras and phone lenses, vanishing from the internet.

An anonymous number popped up on Cole's screen, then Wily's impish voice cut through the speaker. "Looks like Yates ordered a campus lockdown. The mountains are crawling with navy suits. So sit tight, and keep doing nothing."

Eli grumbled again from the back seat.

As Wily ended the call, Crys heard Sage muttering obsessively from the front of the cruiser. She'd been like this since she'd taken her attack bot, reciting every pop-rock album and track order from the past two decades, desperate to prove her memory was her own, a born ability, not engineered by Yates.

Crys's free hand began to shake. She still needed to take hold of something. And she now knew exactly what it was. "We need to get to the hospital." The words were out before Crys understood her true meaning.

"What's wrong?" Hema asked, reaching for Crys's wrist, checking her pulse. Her temple. "I told you to tell me the second you felt something might be off."

"You're not an *actual* doc, you know . . ." Crys answered, suddenly flustered, shrugging all the prodding hands from her body.

"Tell that to my doctorate in biochemistry," Hema answered calmly. "But first, tell me why you want to go to the medical center."

"It's for the bots, isn't it?" Cole guessed.

Crys didn't answer.

Of course she wanted the Quest Bots.

For proof.

For answers.

For reasons she did not yet dare to expound on—

"Crys, talk to me," Cole urged, gripping her hand. "Don't go dark."

Her chest suddenly felt heavy, crushed, as if the full weight of her city, her world, were pushing down on her. She closed her eyes, six years old again, listening for whispers of her parents . . .

She needed to break out from the confines of this trunk. *Now.*

Crys reached over Cole and pulled the trunk's release latch. The lid flew open, and when she stood up to leap out, Hema lunged for her, grabbing hold of her elbow. Crys saw her opening and took it. In one fluid move, she wrenched herself free, swiped the medical cooler over Hema's head, and rolled out onto the street.

The cruiser skidded to a stop.

"Okay, did we somehow swap Crys for Jade, and no one bothered to tell me?" Wily said from the driver's seat.

"They aren't there," Hema said before Crys could get her bearings.

They were outside Summit Auditorium, only five blocks from the medical center. Campus was empty, all Questers locked away safe inside their apartments. Even the sky was empty of metal birds, the restricted airspace above Yates's mountains extending to the LAPD as well as the prying eyes of the press.

There was no one around to witness their movements. Their raid.

Crys's grand larceny.

She was going to get her hands on the Quest Bots, whether the others helped her or not.

She backed away. Turned for the hospital. Was brought up short by a fleet-footed Hema.

"If you're after the Quest Bots, they won't be at the hospital. Not now." Hema brandished a stiff finger at the medical bag that Crys held rigidly against her side. Like she was back on the streets and this was her last possession. She knew how to fight for what she needed. To survive. She hoped it wouldn't come to that.

"If you hand over my bag," Hema continued, "I'll tell you where Asclepius is."

"Who?" Cole said, inching his way toward Crys.

"Not *who*," Sage corrected, freeing her auburn mane from her police cap. "But *what*." Her slate-gray eyes fell on Hema. "I assume it's the lab you helped build with our dearly despised benefactor?"

Hema nodded, toying with the elbow patches on their blue Adsum cardigan.

Eli spoke up from the back seat of the cruiser. "Is it really a good idea to sneak into the secret lair of a cracked billionaire who wants us all either dead or screaming out of our minds?"

"He's right, Crys," Cole said with a winsome grin, holding out his hand, luring her back to the car, the trunk. The plan. "We have to get to Adsum before the navy suits know we're here."

"Everyone thinks we're at the bottom of the Pacific," Wily pointed out. "Right now, we're ghosts."

"Exactly," Crys urged, jamming up her sleeves. "We should take full advantage and find the cache of bots before Yates destroys the evidence."

No one nodded an endorsement, yet no one shook their heads or unsheathed weapons, dragging her back kicking and screaming to the car.

The Exiles were *listening* to her.

"I need to know what Zoe's bot was for," Crys added with such conviction, even she believed that was her sole motivation for seeking out Yates's lab. "I need to know the reason she died." After two pounding heartbeats of hesitation, she handed the medical cooler back to Hema.

After two more, Hema made good on her trade.

"Asclepius is behind the waterfall. Beneath the Castle in the Air."

"Turn here," Hema instructed from the center of the cruiser's front seat. They pointed to a prominent coastal live oak standing alone along a canyon backroad, a quarter mile from Quest Motors.

Crys had made it her business to know the campus, her future empire, inside and out, yet she had no knowledge of this route. It was unpaved, unmarked, leading up the western ridge of the mountain that held Damon's gravity-defying private residence and its duplicitously beautiful waterfall. Crys had believed the East Entrance was the only way in.

But as with so much else she thought she knew, she'd been wrong.

Wily, now donning a collared white shirt with a loose blue-striped tie, drove the single-track path laden with high grass and sagebrush, weaving up the lush canyon without protest.

"Cut the headlights," Sage said, tucking her own tie into the waistband of her culottes.

"There's no need," Hema noted. "Unless Damon has changed—which men like him never do—there are no security cameras beyond his private gates."

"Didn't want to run the risk of someone hacking in and exposing all the sneaky goings-on in his shady mountain?" Wily suggested, eyeing Sage conspiratorially.

Perhaps that was why Damon had come down so hard on the pair, expelling Wily and Sage from the academy with no second chance. They'd hacked him once. They could do it again, with bigger consequences.

Crys felt the guilt for her role in their exile all the heavier.

"Damon always said the surveillance-free zone was a sanctuary," Crys said. And it was, she supposed. Just not for his family. It was a sanctuary for Asclepius.

Halfway to the peak, the cruiser rounded a switchback, revealing a sweeping view of the bay. Hema directed Wily to park beside a clump of large arroyo willows. "The lab's not far from here. Just a short hike."

Eli slouched beside Crys, awkward in an undersized cardigan that hugged his muscle-bound arms like a second skin. "I'll stay back as lookout. Sound the siren if I see trouble coming."

Hema led the way up the ridge, clasping tight to their medical bags, Wily and Sage close behind, with Cole and Crys making up the rearguard.

"How'd it feel?" Cole asked her as they helped each other over the slippery rocks. In his prim blazer and trousers, he looked like his old Fortunate self.

"How'd what feel?"

"Losing your bot and your fear. Seeing your face."

Crys shrugged, still nettled at his treacherous choice to reingest his Quest Bot.

Cole smiled. "I imagine it was like when I got mine back. Suddenly, just like that, I was myself again. At home in my own mind." He paused. "It wasn't me who left you, by the way. Not really."

So it was only Bot Cole who wanted to stay? she wanted to ask. Instead, she let the burbling music of the waterfall fill the silence.

"Nice eyes, by the way," he added, leaping across a shallow stream to land beside Crys with a laugh. "Tough, like a tiger's-eye stone. It suits you. Always has."

"Here," Hema whispered, moving to the waterfall's sheet of inky water and disappearing.

Droplets from the torrent tickled Crys's nose, danced atop Cole's waves of chestnut hair, making them frizz. She could barely see in the dark as she stumbled between two skull-shaped sandstone boulders that looked from the outside to form a dead-end cave.

Only, there was a door underneath the rock tunnel.

A door that was already open.

Hema hesitated, turning back. "Something's not right—"

Crys stormed past them, charging into pure darkness.

Someone had cut the power. But why? Crys drew out her phone and switched on its flashlight. Scanned the lab, searching for where the Quest Bots were stored. Instead, she found a slender man in a white coat sprawled on the floor beside the medical refrigerators.

A gunshot wound to his chest.

"Peter!" Hema cried. Coming up beside Crys, they shined a light on the bloodstained body. "This is—was—Dr. Rourke, my number two."

Hema's chest heaved with stifled sobs. "He replaced me, running the clinical study after I left. How could Damon—"

A loud *boom* swallowed up the rest of Hema's sentence. The ground shook, the laboratory equipment rattling violently, glass shattering all around them.

"We have to go, *now*," Cole said, tearing off his blazer and hoisting it over his head. He reached out for Crys, but she pulled away.

Another *boom*, and the far side of the rectangular room lit up in flames.

Was Damon trying to kill them yet again? Crys's mind raced. Burn all the evidence, the lab, the unused Quest Bots, *the Exiles* housing his clandestine experiments?

Crys shielded her mouth with her sleeve and pushed farther into the fiery lab. Coughing, her eyes stinging from the smoke, Crys ran for the wall lined with giant biosafety cabinets, pressing her phone's flashlight against the clear doors, scouring the wire shelves for glass vials. Silver aluminum caps. Tags marked with academy students' names.

Her name.

The medical refrigerators suddenly toppled with a third jolting *boom*, the fire's hungry flames licking ever closer. Crys ducked, the shriek of Eli's siren reaching her above Cole's desperate shouts, calling out for her, pleading for her to come back.

But she couldn't go back. Not without getting what she'd come here for. Not without the bots.

Finally, in the last cabinet, she found them. There was no time to be meticulous. Grabbing all that she could hold, she stuffed the vials into every pocket of her uniform. Found a messenger bag on a counter, shoved in fistfuls more.

Then a fourth *boom*, bigger this time.

The reinforced concrete floor and walls shuddered, shaking around her like a plastic dollhouse in the grips of a child's wild tantrum. Crys flew backward, slamming her head against a steel counter. Unmarked storage boxes rained down around her. The sound of exploding glass overtook Hema's and Sage's piercing cries to abandon the bots and run.

Crys sat there, dazed, confused whether the scent she smelled through the smoke was real or the blow to her head had muddled her senses.

Freshly bloomed peonies.

Cedar.

Amber.

My signature perfume.

Crys took a rattling breath and held it, crawling toward the nearest unmarked box on the floor. Small, clear crystal vials with rose-colored atomizers were stacked inside. Some were smashed, a tendril of the fragrant liquid reaching for her like an outstretched hand.

Was her fear bot hidden in her perfume vials? The fragrance Yates knew Crys always had on hand? Ever since her fourth year at the academy, after Jade left, she'd sprayed her pulse points religiously, inhaling the scent like a tonic to forget the stench of her past, to ground her to the present.

Unknowingly fettering her to Adsum, she now realized. *To him.*

"Crys!" Cole screamed. "The roof's going to cave!"

Running out of air, she seized a fistful of the unbroken vials and staggered toward Cole, leaning on him as they raced the flames for the exit. Once outside, Crys stood reeling beneath the waterfall, washing away the soot, coughing out smoke.

Freeing herself of her shackles.

Knowing *she* now held the keys.

TWENTY-TWO

Crys and the others were late.

Jade leaned against the opulent pillar of one of the many palm trees lining the grounds behind Adsum Academy, unable to stop fidgeting. She fiddled with the buttons of the tailored blazer and too-tight pleated pants she'd been saddled with from the picked-over box of uniforms Sage had hidden for her on campus, staring out at the empty road.

Jade had been late, too. She and her crew had managed to hop off their getaway camper covertly, somewhere in Little Tokyo, before the car chase hit the 101, their detour delaying them by half an hour. When she'd arrived at Adsum Peak after splitting with Ani and Maxen, who'd set off for the campus HyperQuest portal where Ani would safeguard a still unpredictable Maxen until Phase Two of the evacuation, Jade had thought Sage would have her head. Not much came between that woman and her schedules.

Which meant they'd found trouble.

The ground suddenly shook, and a deep rumbling *boom* echoed off the mountains.

Jade shot to her feet, unsure where the explosion had come from, the reverb playing tricks on her hearing. But something, or some*one*, had most definitely just been blown up. Would Yates really *bomb* his students, his dirty little secrets, out of existence?

The answer to that question spurred her to start running.

Body bent low, she swept her eyes over the dark glass curves of the academy. She dashed for the stone garden wall, searching for damage and signs of Crys and the Exiles. Instead, she found a figure staring down at her from the second classfloor window.

Yates.

Jade dropped flat. Her heart thudded in her ears, and for more shaky breaths than she cared to count, she lay there, forehead pressed to the thick grass, convinced she'd just made herself his next target.

A foolish, sitting duck who'd stumbled right into his trap.

The ground shook again, but remained firm, whole, around her. The blasts were coming from a different part of the mountain range.

Jade looked up. The tightness in her chest deflated like a popped tire.

It wasn't Yates looming down on her, but the AI clean-bot.

Really, Jade? she scolded herself. *You let* Alfred *make you jump?*

She needed to pull herself together. Fast.

She scrambled upright and heard an urgent dispatch from a police scanner over the garden wall. "Code 10-35, all available officers to Damon Yates's residence. Be advised, active fire at the scene."

Maxen. Had he gotten loose, went after the inexplicable "them" he'd been ranting about?

"Copy," the navy suit said. Jade watched him abandon his post at Aevitas House's back entrance, racing through an arched door in the stone wall toward the front driveway packed with police cruisers.

Crouching, Jade slinked into the lush garden full of rare, extravagant plants and herbs, gifts from highfliers around the world to a man who already owned everything. She wasn't worried about the security cameras nestled in the centuries-old olive trees—that's what her uniform was for, and the suits' attention had been fortuitously diverted elsewhere—it was the sight of the three-tiered marble fountain that gave her pause.

Made her chest tighten again.

Made the scar on her shoulder itch, like her wound had for weeks after surgery.

What was going on with her? Jade's fingers brushed In Extremis at her neck. She had already faced death. She'd already seen the worst and come back from it. She squeezed the cold bullet against her palm and made for her old dormitory.

When she had last seen her inaugural-class chums, she'd been skinny-dipping in the conservatory pond, drunk on gin and rancor, telling them they had only been chosen by Yates for their common trait of being feeble followers.

And yet seconds from now, she was going to ask them to follow *her*. The defector, the slippery thief, come to steal their dreams, to pop their mansion-sized bubbles. To tear them from their fool's paradise.

Will even one *come willingly?*

For once, Jade hoped they would accept her as their sib. Their kindred. She knew she had no right. Knew she'd have to earn it, to get them to see her as an honest liberator and not a crooked kidnapper. And she was willing to put in the work. Her blood. Her life, if it came down to it. *Family is who you'll bleed for.*

The bright orange bracts of the bougainvillea vines were in full bloom, enveloping Aevitas House like a lush cloak of flowers. She had gasped the first time she'd reached out to touch the sunset-hued petals— not from the beauty, but from the pain.

Thorns, she'd cried, sucking the blood from her pricked fingers. Crys had only smiled. *Beauty with claws,* she'd replied, her twelve-year-old dirt-colored eyes soaking up the Adsum splendor, already imagining how high she was destined to grow.

Jade avoided the vines and slipped into the dark entryway of the common room. Met a minor hiccup. The door was locked.

Had Yates known Jade was bound to make it here? Had he foreseen the trouble she was cooking up? She shrugged off a shiver and got out her tools. When the door's lever finally gave beneath her touch, she clamped her jaw tight, steeled her body. Prepared for the shriek of a siren.

But there was only silence.

Besides the alarm bells in her head.

She drowned them out with her theme song. *She's as silent as the bullet you didn't see coming, takes what she wants with her grit and cunning . . .*

The enormous glass-domed room was empty, lit only by the waxen moon above. Keeping on her soiled boots, she cut across the shadows and edged into the hallway.

When misfortune chokes the air, bet your last dollar the Adsum pariah will be there . . .

She knocked on the first dormitory door before shoving it open. Nobody home.

Makes misery then makes haste, she's the slippery scapegrace who lives for the chase.

She tried four more rooms. Same luck.

This was just the sort of hurdle that would usually make Jade's spirit soar. Make her smile in the face of a challenge. Laugh with the thrill of danger. But she felt no rush of adrenaline, no stunning surge of power that anesthetized all fear, all vulnerability, all scruples and hesitation. She felt raw, on her own. A tidal wave of dread yanking her ever closer to an unpleasant emotion she hadn't encountered in years.

Fear.

No, Jade chastised herself as she ran for the other two dormitories. *This is all in your head. Paranoia, self-sabotage, a nasty case of manifesting your nightmare.*

All dorm rooms were vacant. Bedsheets in jumbles, like the students had left in a hurry.

Just like the residents of Dry River City.

Had her Adsum sibs been driven away, or hidden away? Jade could not—would not—leave until she found out. *You are more than your bot,* she prodded herself. Her gutsy confidence was her own. Her bold nerve a thing she'd earned. Her one and only fortune, apart from Crys.

Yates had not *made* her fearless.

Then why was her chest heavy, her hands so sweaty she could barely keep hold of her smoke bombs? Jade shook her whole body, willing boldness back into her veins. *Fake it until you feel it,* she told herself, heading into the academy's main building, striding up to the glass elevator shaft that led to the classfloors.

Only the elevator pod seemed to be locked down, too. Jade pressed the call button again and again, but the doors remained sealed. She pivoted, making her way to the emergency staircase across the entrance hall. More bolted doors. Which, Jade noted, both went against Yates's campus-wide "open doors, open minds" policy *and* presented a serious fire hazard.

Someone didn't want anyone going *up*.

Jade seized on the idea, visualizing each lock as a big middle finger that screamed at her, *You'll never reach the top*. On her way back to the elevator, she pulled a small crowbar out from her bag. She was going to pry the damn thing open.

With the right angle, a little force, and a lot of grunting, the elevator doors gave way. She stepped inside the empty shaft, craning her neck up to see the bottom of the pod docked on the top classfloor.

Nothing for it but to climb. She dropped low, as if sitting in an imaginary chair, ready to launch herself up onto the shaft's thin ladder. But a reproachful voice stilled her legs.

"You always choose the hard way, don't you?"

Jade whipped around to find Poppy, harried and disheveled in a torn silk caftan that stopped just short of her bare, earth-stained feet. She padded closer, separating herself from the shadows, the gleam of a pistol hidden in the billowy folds of her skirts.

Jade stalked out of the elevator shaft, holding up her hands. No daggers. No tricks. She nodded toward the dean's gun. "Who are you protecting your family from? Yates, or me?"

Poppy shook her head. Her bob, usually smooth like obsidian glass, was as tangled as her words. "The quake alarms sounded . . . police scanners said it was explosions . . . the Castle in the Air is crumbling . . . tell me it wasn't you."

"No," Jade admitted. "But I can't say the same for Maxen."

Jade had no evidence, but she got the reaction she wanted. Poppy's eyes stretched wide, searching behind Jade. "Maxen's with you? *Here?* He's not answering any of my calls." She placed a shaky hand on her temple. "I've been worried out of my mind."

"Funny you should mention that . . ."

Poppy's pale face went ashen. "Maxen . . . tell me he's all right."

So his mother had *known something was off with him.* What else had she known? Jade gripped the bullet that had smashed into her collarbone. "We found the Doc all the Questers claimed had torn your marriage apart. Not *exactly* the kind of head doc you'd implied."

Poppy's hands shook, her grip on the gun clumsy, amateur. "Hema did sever my marriage to Damon."

Jade cocked her head. "So you're aware of Adsum's true purpose?"

"It was Damon's scheme," Poppy said, her voice suddenly biting. "And I learned of his next business venture a bit too late, I'm afraid. Adsum at its purest was *my* ambition, *my* academy. He never could let me have anything, trying to one-up me, every time. He thought he could keep me ignorant—"

"Well, you've certainly kept silent."

"What was I supposed to do, confront him and end up like Hema? Hunted and ostracized? Tell the media, just to have them peg me as a crazed vulture trying to take half the Yates fortune? I chose to stay for Maxen, and every one of my sons and daughters. I watched over them the best I knew how."

Could Jade have done any better? She'd always sensed there was a darker, sinister side to the Savior—that's why she'd led her sister into the HyperQuest tubes—and yet she'd run, leaving the sibs to fend for themselves. At least Poppy had stayed. Placed herself between the fosters and Yates, however she could.

Jade nodded, forceful and determined. "Tonight we can right our mistakes. Where's Yates?"

Poppy's gaze jerked to the ceiling—*Jade's sibs were up there*—then to the exit doors, then back to Jade. "I haven't seen Damon since the vigil . . . since Crys left. But he's ordered the entire police force to occupy campus. He said it was to protect the children, of course."

"But really it's to safeguard his Quest Bots. Not their hosts."

Poppy's arms suddenly wrapped around Jade, strong as a safety net. "My darling, please don't call yourself that."

Jade shrugged. "We found a way to disable the bots."

"What? How?" Poppy gasped, pulling away. "Tell me you didn't do anything reckless. Is your bot still in your system?"

Jade shook her head. It was a confession. An acceptance.

Her Quest Bot was gone. But a defiant courage still remained.

And that was better than being fearless, anyway, Jade thought. Being scared witless, and yet racing into the flames nonetheless.

"Did Maxen disable his?" Poppy demanded, her hand shaking again.

Jade thought of the damage his attack bot might have unleashed, but she shoved this concern to the bottom of her list of misgivings, thrusting her focus back to priority number one.

"We have to get to the HyperQuest portal," Jade said, plunging her hand into the pocket of her pleated pants, gripping tight to her trompo. Crys's unfortunate keepsake, now her lucky token. "I'm getting my Adsum sibs out of here. Maxen and the others should already be at the portal. Will you help us?"

Poppy stared at Jade so hard, Jade thought she was attempting to gauge her soul.

Finally, she touched an app icon on her smartwatch, and the elevator pod lowered to the ground floor. "Not all of them will want to come," Poppy warned. "Not everyone will forsake Damon and the high life on a split-second decision."

"Good thing I have a speech ready." That was a lie. Jade hated public speaking. Hated others looking to her for answers. Trust. Love.

But tonight's about facing fears, she thought as she stepped into the elevator. With her foster mother at her side, Jade hit the button for the top floor. The doors closed.

And they went up, into the flames.

TWENTY-THREE

Five phones buzzed at once. Crys lifted hers from her back pocket. The encrypted messaging app was open and waiting, bearing an update from Jade.

> Got 'em. Quest portal, now.

> You all better still be alive, or I'll kill you.

"It's good to know the attack bot didn't terminate her winning charisma," Sage said, rolling her eyes.

Crys was stunned. Her sister had persuaded the Adsum sibs to abandon their Fortunate lives without Crys there to pad the blow. An odd jealousy burned inside her belly. Was a famous scapegrace a better leader than a cast-off billion-heir?

She shook off the useless feelings. "Past the Forest, take a left," she directed from behind the driver's seat. "We can cut across Splendor Park as a shortcut to the hyperloop portal."

Wily grinned as he sped away from the mass timber towers toward the ten-acre wildflower sanctuary that lay just half a mile ahead. The conservation park was designed by Damon to foster a kinship between his Questers and nature, a place to stop and smell the marigolds in the middle of the workday, to remember the importance of preserving and nurturing the natural beauty around them. Endangered California jewelflowers, Baker's larkspurs, western lilies. Crys had carefully tended to them all.

A memory came back to her, of Jade floating in Damon's eco-pond, ruining his prized water lilies. *It's all replaceable,* she'd told Crys. *Just like us.* Who knew then how right Jade had been?

Wily idled the car outside the park's boundary line. "There's no road."

"Drive straight through it," Crys said, voice sharp as a scythe.

Wily slammed the accelerator, and the cruiser rocketed into the rainbow-colored field, the tires pulverizing Damon's cherished flowers, reaping what he had sown. Crys smiled. But the grin was quickly torn from her face.

"Uh, what's that?" Eli said, pointing up to a red flashing light soaring toward them from above. "I thought campus was still a no-fly zone."

It was. There was only one person who was the exception to his own rule.

"Damon might open fire," Hema shouted.

"Aren't cop cars bulletproof?" Cole asked beside Crys, his voice hopeful. Unworried.

"We're not in a real cop car, buddy," Wily reminded him, exasperated.

"We can't outrun an auto-copter," Sage reasoned, shaking her head. "Especially *his.*"

"We should split up," Crys suggested, thinking quick, remembering her once-father's promise never to let her go. "He's after me, I can draw him away—"

Bam! An AV rammed into the cruiser's broadside.

The front tires lifted into the air, and they spun like a trompo, round and round, Crys keeping enough of her wits to tighten her grip on her bag of vials before the car skidded to a halt.

The ringing in her ears deadened all other sound: Cole's cries as he wiped the blood trickling into Crys's eyes from a gash on her forehead, the blare of the car horn against Wily's inert body, the shattering of glass as the window beside her suddenly exploded.

Crys blinked, and a bullet-sized hole appeared in the headrest in front of her, inches from her nose. She swung her unsteady gaze to the window, and her head stopped spinning long enough to register that the copter had landed. That the face sprinting toward her, behind a gun, was not Damon's but that of his eldest son, Palmer, who looked apoplectic as he registered that the Exiles were still alive.

"I thought we'd already put you strays down!" He stopped thirty yards from the cruiser, his lips curling into a smirk. "No matter, one shot should do it." He adjusted his aim and squeezed the trigger. Once, twice, then rapid fire.

At least it was all out in the open now, Crys thought, mad on adrenaline. At least their intentions were obvious. Gen 1 wanted her and her sibs dead, just like Yates, their father. She wondered how she could have ever been so fooled, thinking she could have become one of them.

Cole grabbed Crys by the shoulders and slammed them both across the bucket seats. Her jaw knocked against Eli's knees as the second rear window cracked above her like a frozen bolt of lightning.

Crys opened her mouth. She felt her larynx tremble with the power of her yell. But she couldn't hear what she was saying. Barely knew what she was screaming. *Drive! Run! Help!*

Then survival mode cried back. *Fight.*

Finally, Crys's ears popped, and the full din of the chaos hit her like a second AV from her blind side. The rumbling of the idled auto-copter, countless gunshots splintering the night air, Hema howling for Wily to open his eyes, Sage moaning from behind the passenger airbags that mushroomed out like suffocating clouds. Eli grunting as he gave everything he had trying to bulldoze open his smashed-in door.

"We'll get out of this," Cole kept repeating. "We always do."

Crys spotted Wily's knife on the floorboard. She reached for it as a bullet struck the driver's window. This one didn't crack or burst the laminated glass. Instead, the projectile disintegrated on impact. Keeping her head low, Crys flung herself to the front of the cruiser. Two clean jabs and the airbags deflated with a hiss. Sage gasped lungfuls of air. From behind the wheel, Wily jolted back to life with a groan. He cradled his right eye, already swollen and bruised beneath his scarred brow. "I feel like I've just been hit by a dump truck."

"It was Palmer's AV Rover, but close," Crys grunted, peeking above a blown-out window to find Palmer, with Vance tramping after him, his own pistol raised, now less than twenty yards away. "Though the garbage is still coming."

Together, Hema and Sage kicked open the passenger door, and in a violent echo, Eli managed to ram his mangled door free from its hinges. It fell with a heavy clang onto a bed of fragrant flowers, sending a soft sweetness into the crisp air.

Everyone piled out of the cruiser but Wily, who kept up a fruitless battle to restart the engine. "If the car's dead, *we're* dead."

Bullets pierced the roof of the car, the front tire. Crys dove back into the cruiser, her hand outstretched toward Wily. "Don't make me have to stab you with your syrette to drag you out of here."

An impish grin cut across his face. "Well, I've always said that if I'm going to die, it's going to be on my feet."

Cole helped Crys pull Wily out from the wreckage, and they joined the others huddled behind the crushed cruiser, protecting Hema and the attack bots. The auto-copter's lights switched off. The sound of racing footsteps, of gunfire, quieted. Crys waited for the scream of sirens. Surely the commotion of their encounter had caught the attention of the navy suits. But there was only the ragged breathing of the wounded crew, the harsh, muffled whispers of her fiendish ex-brothers, somewhere out there in the dark field.

They were debating their next move, Crys realized.

She knew for certain it wouldn't be a 911 call. The last thing Yates's scions wanted was for the LAPD to arrive and put a stop to their fratricide. Gen 1 had as much to lose as Crys did—no, *more*. They'd also lost the advantage of surprise.

And we have the numbers, Crys thought. The upper hand.

"There's fifteen rounds in a clip," Hema said, breathless but sure. "I've counted eighteen so far. With two guns, that's twelve bullets remaining, if the cartridges were fully loaded. We need them to empty their clips."

"On it," Wily answered. He tore off his tattered, bloody shirt, raising it above his head like a flag that said, *Come and get me.* Crys eyed the scars that covered his arms and lean torso like tattoos. *He's used to being a target,* she thought.

"Wily, wait—" Sage urged, but he'd already taken off, sprinting in a zigzag pattern toward the auto-copter.

Vance took the bait. He raced after Wily, firing wildly into the night. One wasted bullet, two. A third burst into dust against the copter's panoramic window.

Eli held the torn-off door by its exposed side-impact beam like a shield. Sage fell in beside him, and they pushed forward, advancing toward where Vance had bolted from, giving away Palmer's position.

A spray of bullets pelted into the aluminum shield. Once again, Crys plunged back into the car, searching for something, *anything*, that she could use to help. She found Wily's stolen police stun baton and her bag of personal Quest Bots. She grabbed both and pulled out of the car, catching a glimpse of her fractured reflection in the shattered glass, a bullet hole superimposed over her forehead like a deadly third eye.

Her nonreaction, her total lack of fear, bolstered her more than any weapon.

She was no longer afraid.

Another shot went off, followed by a yelp. Eli clutched his arm. He faltered, the car door falling with him to the ground. Sage dropped flat to her stomach, covering her head with her hands. Palmer's misplaced bullets shredded flower petals all around her.

"That's twenty-nine total," Hema called out. "But I don't know which gun . . ."

Only one shot left. And Crys was going to take hers. She clamped her left fingers tight to the baton. Balled her right fist around a crystal vial in her pocket. And charged.

She made it four steps before Palmer saw her coming. Six before he trained his barrel onto her. Seven before he smiled, his fine-boned face a sculpture of self-assured calm. He took his time aiming.

She gained two more strides before he pulled the trigger.

The single *click* sounded hollow. Feeble.

Click. Click. Click.

Crys made it two more strides before she registered what that beautiful noise meant. And then she was the one smiling. Laughing. "Looks like you've run out of bullets," she taunted, lifting the baton in front of her like a saber. "How unfortunate for you."

Palmer stood his ground. Shoved his gun into the waistband of his trim linen pants. Held his fists up confidently in front of him, as if he knew the first thing about fighting his own battles.

Crys slowed for a heartbeat, positioned her feet into a fencer's stance. Made her advance, then lunged. Her stab was too quick for Palmer to block. The tip of the heavy-duty baton jammed into his chest, and with a twist of the handle, Crys unleashed nine million volts of electricity.

Palmer crumpled to the ground in a heap of designer clothes. He rolled onto his back, his golden hair a mess of mud and sweat. And, she hoped, a few tears.

He tried to speak, but Crys shouted as she knelt over him. "I might never have had your love. But I will have your fear."

Palmer's laugh was mocking. Maniacal. His ice-blue eyes met her wooden glare, then he grabbed a fistful of her golden curls, yanking hard, as if to rip off all evidence of a family resemblance.

Crys saw stars. Blood flooded her eyes from the gash on her forehead, but she was ready. She held her breath. And with a guttural grunt, she thrust her vial deep into Palmer's flared nostrils . . . and sprayed.

Perfume mist puffed out around him. He started sneezing, gagging. He dropped his hold on her and climbed to his feet, stumbling away. "*What the hell is this?*" he yelled.

Crys moved toward him. And when Palmer looked at her, he screamed.

The delicate blue veins on his neck and temples bulged as he squeezed his eyes closed against Crys's face. His cries were cut short, like an abrupt end to a song, as Cole tackled him from behind.

Crys finally let go of her breath, pocketing her perfume before Cole could see. But he was busy wrestling handcuffs onto a writhing, cursing Palmer. Cole hauled him to his feet, and Crys saw Palmer's skin crawl with uncontrollable shivers, the terror of seeing her face still racking his mind and body.

Good, Crys thought, *it's his turn to be afraid.*

She stepped back from Palmer's eyeline, careful not to elicit another fear incursion in Cole's presence, and helped drag Palmer toward the auto-copter.

Wily leaned against the cockpit window, Vance gagged and cuffed at his feet, and suddenly bent over, gripping his stomach. His face twisted in pain.

Sage rushed out of the darkness toward him, swatting away Wily's hand to see the damage. "What is it? Have you been shot? Stabbed?"

"Worse," Wily moaned, his complexion waxy. "Indigestion. All those donuts aren't sitting too well . . ."

Sage sighed and shoved his shoulder, knocking him into Vance, who began to thrash about, venom in his eyes, unable to accept being bested a second time by a pack of strays. When he caught sight of his brother, head lolling, avoiding Crys's face, he spat muffled curses that no one bothered to hear. The Exiles' attention had shifted to the unconscious man in a checkered suit, who was folded in the corner of the auto-copter's cabin.

"Who's this guy?" Eli asked, joining the group alongside Hema. The bullet had only grazed his shoulder, Crys saw. A flesh wound, already wrapped in a makeshift bandage from the leg of Hema's pant.

"Isn't that Rhett?" Sage said. "The mole?"

Hema was already at his side, scanning his body for wounds with their practiced hands. There was a days-old bruise along his jawline, an angry welt on his forehead, and deep gashes around his eyes, as if they'd been clawed by a hawk. *Or a drone.*

"Rhett," Hema whispered, slapping the man's cheeks. "Can you hear me?"

"Unfortunately," came a raspy whisper.

Wily chuckled. "Yeah, that sounds like our guy."

Hema rose, turning to Eli and Wily. "He'll need to be carried."

They both nodded, grabbing hold of Rhett's arms while Cole and Sage loaded Gen 1 into the auto-copter.

"Where should we send them?" Sage asked from the cockpit's flight controls.

"I hear Death Valley's nice this time of year," Cole offered with a grin.

The brothers roared.

Crys made sure she was the last to leave, lingering as the others took off into the field of wildflowers. She pulled open the cabin door, slipped out her vial and held her breath, spraying her fear bot straight into Vance's face.

Vance reared back, eyes wide as full blood moons. But he didn't scream like his brother. He whimpered. Begged her to make it stop.

"No," Crys said, a word that men like him seldom heard and even more rarely accepted. She forced them to look at her, opening each of their left eyes, gentler than the metal drone claws they had used on her. "You both better hope you never see my face again."

She slammed the door, caught her breath, and pocketed her perfume. As the auto-copter took flight, Crys turned to find Cole standing in a wild bouquet of purple nightshade.

"What are you doing?" he asked, a line like a question mark creasing his brow.

Crys shoved past him.

"Making my own path."

She made sure to stomp on every flower as she went.

TWENTY-FOUR

Jade felt the weight of a gaze on the back of her neck like a sixth sense. She turned from the bullet-shaped pod she was busy loading with panicked, pajama-clad first-years, and her heart caught in her throat.

Crys.

In a singed Adsum uniform, caked in blood and dirt, sprinting down the portal's escalator. Staring Jade full in the face.

Her mouth opened not in a scream but a smile. A nervous laugh. *Crys's eyes are brown again,* she thought, and then arms the same shape as her own wrapped around her, pulling her into a tight embrace. Jade instantly felt studier, like a deeply rooted tree. A grand oak from their childhood, made from twin trunks, a shared canopy protecting each other from any storm.

Did she have her sister back at last?

"The pod's full," Ani announced, slamming the rear cabin's door closed. "We'll have to order another one for the rest of us."

Jade let Crys go, hearkening to her own rule—*act now, feel later*—and saw Poppy studying them like oil and water had just miraculously mixed. "Did we all make it?" Jade asked, scanning the platform and escalators for a missing face. She found an addition to their ranks instead.

Semiconscious, carried between a battered Eli and a shirtless Wily, was Rhett Wood. So the enforcer finally had become the defector. Dried blood rimmed his eyelids. A slanted smile that might have been a snarl aimed her way. "What do you say we call it even?" he asked.

"Yeah, we're straight," Jade answered with a grin, massaging the sore shoulder she'd dislocated after she'd been hurtled from his truck. "But we *have* to get you out of that suit. Eli can whip you up something, right?"

"Make him look like a proper Exile," Eli said, patting Rhett on the back enthusiastically.

Poppy hurried toward the new arrivals. She seemed unsure what to do with her hands now that her pistol was hidden in her skirts. "Were you followed? Did you see any gray suits?"

Hema glared at Poppy, but Maxen filled the space that separated them. "Don't you mean navy suits?" he asked, scrubbing a hand over his haggard face. He stared at his mother with big, lucid eyes. Whatever episode he was in the throes of before had thankfully passed.

For now, Jade thought anxiously.

"Cole and I barricaded the portal doors," Sage said, breathing hard. "We shouldn't have any visits from Yates or the navy suits." Fresh burn marks striped her neck and cheeks. Had she been in a car crash?

"And Gen 1 must be halfway to Death Valley by now," Wily panted. He clutched at his stomach, like he'd eaten something disagreeable, but he was still beaming.

"Seems like I missed out on quite the fight," Jade said, impressed.

"What's happening?" a third-year year cried from a cabin door. "Billy said we're all going to end up like Zoe Reeves."

"Are we going to die?" another whimpered, causing a domino of panicked shouts from the students.

"No one's going to die," Crys promised, but her steady voice was suddenly overpowered by jubilant laughter echoing from inside the hyperloop tube.

The rounded entrance opened, and three elegant figures ambled out. All wore two-piece platinum-gray suits. Shiny pins on their sharp lapels. Clear, sleek oxygen masks over their noses and mouths. Beige stockings pulled over their eyes.

Jade remembered the rumors she'd once believed, of bodies being left in the HyperQuest tubes, all traces of murder erased by the speed of sound. The true magic of the hyperloop. Poof—and they're gone.

She caught eyes with Crys. *You were right,* hers seemed to say. Jade felt no swell of vindication. No surge of pride.

The arrivals moved in a V formation, the man at the tip of the arrow holding what looked like a ceremonial saber in his grip. The hilt was of white jade, the long steel blade ornamented with inlaid gold and silver. And something red . . .

Not rubies.

Blood.

"That's the Soaring Precious," Crys seethed beside Jade.

Jade nodded to the 3D-printed semiautomatic in the left suit's hand. "That's the mayor's pistol."

Poppy stiffened like a plate of armor. "Maxen," she whispered, "stay back."

"Is that . . ." Maxen mumbled, stepping forward. "*Hariri?*"

The sword-bearer slid away both masks, revealing not the hard blue eyes and wavy blonde hair of Damon Yates, but a hatchet-faced man, his thick mane and beard patterned silver and gray, giving him the illusion of a wolf.

Then the others shed their masks, unveiling a younger redheaded man with a diamond earring and a woman with a knife-edge smile.

"These your father's playmates?" Jade asked, elbowing Maxen.

He shook his head. "They used to be . . ."

Crys rubbed at her throat as Cole stepped in front of her. "That's the guy who tried to kill you at the hospital."

"Poppy, darling," Hariri shouted with delight. "You've joined the festivities."

"What the hell's happening?" Maxen asked his mother. "Since when are you chums with dad's old billionaire blowhards?"

The hair on the back of Jade's neck stood on end. Like little ancient antennae trying to give her a signal.

Rfa.

Red fucking alert.

Poppy turned toward Jade. "Quickly," she whispered through a tremulous smile. "Get the pod out of here." Then she threw out her arms, not in the stance of protection for the Exiles behind her, but in greeting to the strange trio who'd strolled out of the low-pressure tube as if it was their own private playground. "Hariri, I didn't know explosives were on the agenda tonight."

"I'll go with the students," Hema said quickly. They adjusted their cumbersome bags and moved for the closest cabin, but Crys stopped them, grabbing Hema's hand.

"Promise me you'll make sure every sib gets their attack bot."

Hema nodded, the door sliding closed behind them.

"The pod won't move," Sage whisper-yelled, kicking at the side of an electric blue door as if that would get the static escape pod going. "Those Fortunates must've commandeered the campus hyperloop."

Hariri helped the woman from the track up onto the platform. She looked well-off in her tailored linen suit and layered jewels, clenching a small leather handbag, contents unknown. Jade was too sensible to believe she was merely carrying powder for her nose.

"Jade," Ani said, low and steady, hands on her knives. "Name the trick." The strategy, the stunt. Jade always had one on hand for any jam or tight corner.

Crys grabbed Maxen's arm. At first, Jade thought she meant to throw him to the wolves, but she saw them both back slowly to the rear of the pack, toward a sleek digital kiosk. Two antithetical heirs of HyperQuest, finally collaborating.

How many ex-Yateses did it take to regain control of a Yates-made transport? Jade hoped they knew all the ins and outs of the family business, because the arrowhead was back in formation, sauntering ever closer.

Yet Jade's bag remained untouched. The rush of adrenaline, the tried-and-true power that she relied upon like a friend, her sharpest weapon, her fiercest strength, would not show up to help her.

She'd been stripped of her shield. Her armor.

She felt naked. Exposed. Like fragile flesh and bones.

Eli let loose a heart-stopping wail. His tanklike frame crumpled to the hard floor with a shuddering *bang*.

"Their pins!" Cole shouted. "It's the symbol, do you see?"

Jade saw. Three red slashes, like bloody claw marks. Who *were* these hyperloop walkers? And where was Yates? Leading from the shadows?

The woman with the handbag traded pointed looks with Hema through the pod door's window. Her long lashes fluttered when she spotted the medical cooler. Was that what the woman herself was carrying? Yates's latest generation of fear bots?

Hariri scanned the ragged group behind Poppy, scrutinizing Jade, then Cole and Rhett, the pair barely holding back a lethal Wily and Sage.

"What did you do with our mayor?" Wily growled.

Hariri reared back his head and howled in laughter. "I believe the official police statement is that the Dry River agitator seems to have simply disappeared."

"Did you kill him?" Sage yelled.

Hariri wiped tears of amusement from his eyes. "Oh, not directly. Damon took care of that bit."

Wily groaned. "What does that mean?"

"He means Yates's HyperQuest pod," Jade answered quietly.

Wily's and Sage's screams outmatched Eli's. Cole grunted with the effort to keep them in line. The Exiles were falling apart. Jade needed to make a move. She jolted out of her one-person pity party. Gritted her teeth. Held tight to her counterfeit courage and stealthily unzipped her bag.

The redhead with the mayor's gun snickered down at Eli, who'd balled himself up against the pod. His muscular arms trembled as he covered his eyes from the trio of Fortunates. From the violently red symbol on their lapels.

"I'm sure there's a good reason, Poppy darling," Hariri said, wiping who knew whose blood from his blade onto Poppy's silk skirts. "But why, may I ask, are the vermin still breathing?"

"That's a great question," Jade said, throwing Ani a sharp look and nodding toward Poppy. "Let us rectify that for you."

Jade deftly reached into her bag. Her fingers quick and furtive, she unlatched the safety pin of a rubber crowd-control grenade. She lobbed it at the Fortunate threesome just as Ani grabbed the dean, *darling Poppy*, yanking her toward the other side of the platform.

The grenade burst, releasing a cloud of tear gas, then detonated with a loud *boom*. The chemical attacked their throats, their eyes, causing them to choke, their vision to blur. Hariri wasn't laughing now. His cries were guttural as he lifted the most expensive sword in the world and charged, slashing the empty air around him with a terrible force.

"Crys?" Jade shouted over the ruckus. "I don't want to rush you, but we've said our goodbyes, and it's time to *go!*"

In answer, the HyperQuest pod packed with Adsum students took off; one second it was in the portal, the next it had disappeared. A melodious ringing, soothing as birdsong, signaled the arrival of a second pod on the opposite track. Just as the cabin doors slid open, a gunshot went off, piercing Jade's eardrums, her nerve.

She flinched. Fear flooded her mind for the first time in years, debilitating her body. Her mind.

"Jade, come *on*," Ani shouted, pushing a whey-faced Poppy into the cabin after the rest of the Exiles.

Ani reached out her hand, but this time the thrill of danger did not, *could* not, spur Jade on. She just stood there, immobilized, as Hariri heedlessly swung his sword closer and closer.

And then Crys and Maxen were there, each taking her by an arm, carrying her, becoming her wings. *Jade Moore, the lone common swift, always in flight,* she remembered Maxen saying as she collapsed inside the pod. The double doors began to close. Jade started to smile in relief, when something caught between the steel-frame doors just before they could seal.

The barrel of a gun.

"Everyone down!" Wily screamed.

In the hundredth of a second of hesitation before Jade sprang forward, Ani moved first. Two of her tanto-point knives in her grip. She sliced at the hand, its trigger finger dropping to the floor in a puddle of blood beside the pistol.

The redhead teetered backward. Hariri and the Soaring Precious took his place. Only a sliver was left in the way of safety. Escape. *But if you give a Fortunate man an inch, he takes a mile,* Jade thought.

Hariri's thin saber gleamed maliciously in the electric blue light as it drove into Ani's side like a searing blade of ice. In a blurred flash, the saber was gone. The doors closed.

Ani was on her knees. Her leather jacket was ripped below her rib cage, showing a deep gash in her abdomen. She dropped her knives, pressing her paint-stained fingers to her skin as if she could somehow hold in the life spilling out of her. She fell back into Jade's arms.

A surge of adrenaline kicked in. Jade felt the rush of energy, the shallow breaths. The pounding heart. The swell of natural terror. "Hema!" she yelled. Hema was a doctor, they could fix this. Hema could save her.

Crys slid on the slippery floor, her hands and knees covered in Ani's blood. "Hema went with the Adsum sibs."

Jade turned to Sage, her voice sharp as Ani's weighted blades. "When you left Adsum, why didn't you ever memorize something *useful*, like a medical book?" She wrenched off Ani's ruined leather jacket and pressed as hard as she could on her wound. "Your uniforms. Give me clothing to stop the bleeding!"

Cole's and Maxen's blazers. Rhett's suit jacket and shirt. Crys's and Eli's cardigans. Sage's button-down. All were soaked through by the time Poppy spoke up from the corner of the pod. Her voice was cracked, like the long cry of someone falling. "You shouldn't have disabled her Quest Bot."

Reluctantly, Jade jerked her eyes from Ani to the dean, their supposed guardian. Guilt, doom, rose up her throat. She swallowed each down before she hissed, "Why, what do you know?" *Far* more than she had let on back at Adsum Peak.

"Ani has severe hemophilia," Poppy said. "Her blood doesn't clot normally—"

"So her bot was *protecting* her," Maxen whispered.

Cole peeled off his T-shirt, gently pushed Jade's shaking hands aside, and applied renewed strength to the hole in Ani's torso. His makeshift bandage was drenched in seconds.

Jade's voice was a stripped roar. "So you're telling me we're just going to watch her bleed out right in front of us?"

"I stole bots from Asclepius, Yates's lab," Crys said, raking through the bag strapped across her chest. "Ani's *has* to be in here." She said the last bit like a prayer. Like the Savior they'd all forsaken could still grant this last desperate appeal.

Jade stared at the blood pouring out of Ani like an unstoppable river, spilling from her stomach, brimming over the cloth bandages, Cole's hands, running between his fingers down to the polished wood floor.

Death pooling at their feet.

Ani's face turned white as a burial shroud.

"It isn't here . . ." Crys said in a frustrated cry. "Ani's vial isn't here."

"No student was supposed to die . . ." Poppy moaned. "I cared for each of my charges like they were my own. Maxen, tell them."

Maxen lunged for her, pinning his mother against the blue-lit wall. "You were with my dad this whole time?"

"Of course not," Poppy snapped, her eyes flashing bright. "I was trying to beat Damon at his own game." Her breath caught in her chest. "Hariri . . . the Conservators changed the rules."

"What did you do to Zoe?" Crys seethed, clutching Poppy by her narrow jaw.

Eli loomed over the sputtering Poppy, whose hands were raised as if to yield. But her palms were already stained with blood. "And Khari, did you kill her, too?"

Poppy squeezed her eyes closed, like she could shut out what she'd done. "Khari put herself at risk when she left Adsum . . . she was no longer under my protection."

Crys released her hold on the dean as Rhett staggered from his seat. "Damon had me take care of Khari's resting place. I never learned how she died. But Zoe, I had nothing to do with."

Poppy sobbed, her legs giving way, Maxen's outrage the only thing seeming to keep her upright. "Zoe volunteered with me . . . at the food bank . . . she *knew* not to consume my special quiches . . ." She faltered.

"*Quiche?*" Eli repeated, rubbing at his red-rimmed eyes. "Like the one that fingerless gunslinger tried to shove down my throat at the hospital?"

"Please," Poppy gasped. "Forgive a dying woman."

Crys and Eli recoiled.

Maxen hugged his mother closer. "What do you mean dying?"

"Stay with Hema," Poppy whispered to him. "They're the only one who can help you now."

Maxen jolted back, shaking his head, as the Exiles' onetime dean, mother, guardian, their greatest betrayer, slumped to the floor, her hand moving sluggishly for her thigh. Poppy's dark billowy silks had hidden the blood, but Jade saw it now. The bullet hole. The life gushing from her femoral artery.

"No," Crys screamed. "You don't get the easy way out. Give us answers!"

"The Conservators are everywhere," Poppy gasped. "Beware the cities."

Her final words, a warning. And then she went still.

Jade's swollen eyes sought out Cole. She latched onto that nothing-can-faze-him, happy-go-lucky grin. Tried to lose herself in the galaxy of those hopeful hazel eyes.

It was all the doing of his bot, she knew.

An unnatural, counterfeit calm.

Yet she held on just the same.

"Hang on," she whispered, gripping Ani's hand.

But she could feel her slipping away.

TWENTY-FIVE

The pod slowed. As Crys and the others prepared to enter San Francisco's portal, Poppy's words ran on a hyperloop in her mind.

Beware the cities. Beware the cities.

The Conservators are everywhere.

A cold shiver skipped down Crys's spine. She hardened herself, refusing to tremble or shake, seismically retrofitting her body against the shock. The Exiles had just landed in the second most densely populated city in the Golden State. The city with the most billionaires.

Beware the cities.

Who were these gray-suited Fortunates? What was Damon's role in all of this?

The Conservators are everywhere.

Crys's fingers were numb. For thirty minutes she'd been scouring her bag in a painstaking, indefatigable search for Ani's Quest Bot. She refused to believe it wasn't here. Refused to let Ani go. To let Jade's already black-and-blue heart break anew, as her own had for Zoe.

Ani moaned in Rhett's arms, tried to touch the gash in her stomach. Her eyes rolled back in their sockets as Jade stilled her hand, murmuring through a well of unshed tears to hang on, to stay with her. To fight.

"Two blocks down, on Mission Rock and Third." Sage reiterated the ER's location to Rhett for the fourth time. She'd memorized San

Francisco's map with one look, essentially making her an instant local and consummate guide.

"I'll make it," Rhett promised. He nodded to Jade, who still hadn't let go of Ani's hand. "We'll both make it." He had the least recognizable face of the Exiles, making him the best chance to get Ani into the hospital and, fortune willing, back *out*.

"Are you sure you checked *all* the pockets?" Cole asked Crys after she'd scoured her bag one last time, her hands coming up empty.

That was a question Yates would ask when she'd lose her phone, her favorite ring, her ever elusive wireless earbuds. Crys's blood ran hot at the suggestion now. *Of course* she had. Then her eyes landed on the pile of blood-soaked clothes on the pod floor.

No, she hadn't, Crys realized, pure exultation in her veins.

She sprang forward, kissed Cole hard on the mouth, and dove for her cardigan's inner pocket. "It's here!" she shouted, retrieving the vial with Ani's name written on it. Carefully, she handed it to Jade.

Jade's hard-edged face, taut as a gut-wrenching highwire, went slack. She grabbed Crys's face and held it to hers. "You're a verified savior, you know that?"

Crys didn't wish to be thought of as a mini-Damon, not anymore, but she said nothing, watched with bated breath as Jade carefully poured the clear liquid straight down Ani's throat.

"Arrival in ten," Sage announced, attempting to wipe the blood from her cheeks. Only spreading it further.

Jade tore her attention from Ani and dug in the silk folds of Poppy's skirts. Her hand came away with a gun. Maxen stood transfixed beside his mother's lifeless body. She offered him the weapon. He shook his head, and Jade shoved it into her waistband.

Wily swiped the mayor's pistol from the floor beside the steel doors. Poppy's death would be pinned on them whether they possessed the murder weapon or not. Better to be armed. "How long will it take for Ani's Quest Bot to kick in?"

"For me, it took hours," Eli answered, massaging his neck, his healed spine. He rose to the balls of his feet. Primed to run, block. Swing. Who knew what waited for them outside the confining walls of this pod.

Beware the cities.

Cole's fingers traced his lips as if to impress the taste of Crys onto them. "Mine was instantaneous."

"Mine too," Crys let slip.

Jade's head jerked to her sister. "What do you mean, *mine too?*"

But the doors parted, exposing them to the bright portal platform dotted with nocturnal travelers. A woman shot up from a bench, hand already reaching for her phone. To call the navy suits, or to film the bloodied, half-naked new arrivals, it didn't matter. They were captured either way. Rhett darted out of the pod, carrying Ani, and bounded up the escalator, three steps at a time. Crys watched until her dangling, inert limbs disappeared from sight.

"Uh, is this real or a social-media stunt?" a young man shouted, holding his phone up to record.

They'd all see Poppy's body soon enough. It was no good pretending, no use putting on a show. Not this time.

Jade kept close to Crys as they moved out from the pod, the others pressed shoulder to shoulder behind them. Maxen shot forward, hands scraping through his dark tangled mane, head tilted toward an immense screen on the far wall. A supercut of Yates's face paraded across the screen. *Breaking news,* the caption read. *Billionaire tech mogul and philanthropist reported missing.*

What? How? When? The questions fired off like missiles in Crys's frantic brain before a final thought exploded. Had it been Yates's dried blood on the Soaring Precious?

"Isn't that the missing billionaire's son?" a man gasped, pointing his phone camera at Maxen's bare chest. His blood-soaked hands.

"What, is he *crazy* or something?" a girl cried, backing away as they cut across the platform for the escalators.

"Just keep moving," Jade urged.

But Maxen stopped. Turned and locked eyes first with Jade, then Crys. They were luminous and clear, and for once Crys glimpsed the man beyond the insolent egotist she'd always seen before. He looked focused. Resolute. A stalwart brother.

"Go," he whispered. Demanded. "I can hold them back." His voice sounded stiff, formal, utterly unlike Gen 2. "My family is the cause of all this pain. Please, Jade, let me do this."

Jade shook her head behind her veil of hair. "You don't have to offer yourself up. It doesn't have to be this way."

"Oh, but it does," Maxen answered. His mouth quirked in a sad smile. "You never saw my Quest Bot in your bag, did you, Crys?"

Like a mirror image of Jade, Crys shook her head.

"Hema will figure out how to create more," Jade pressed. "And we can find you mainstream treatments in the meantime."

Maxen sighed. "And how long will all that take?"

No one answered.

"If—*when*—the hallucinations or delusions return, what's to stop me from accidentally hurting you again?" He scanned the crew. "Any of you?" He reached out, gentle and swift, as if to touch Jade's bullet scar, but dropped his hand, thinking better of it. "Let me be the one to do this, for you. And if it's not too much to ask, when you're out there, free, and you think of me, think of me like *this*. Not my past or my future. But *right* now. The me in this moment."

Jade said nothing, but the look that passed between them said it all.

And then he was gone, attracting all the attention, including the cameras. He raised his arms as the city police invaded the platform in their blue-black suits, guns trained on Maxen. "It was all me—" he shouted.

Two officers threw him to the ground before he could make a full confession and bask in his martyrdom. Then the cold reality, the sheer magnitude, of what he'd done set in.

The distraction allowed the remaining Exiles to barrel up the escalators. They'd almost made it out of the portal when a sole baby-faced officer spotted them through the sight of his pistol. Jade clocked it, too, and poised to throw her body in front of Crys, but the officer had already fired.

A rubber bullet carved into Crys's thigh.

Jade screamed, sank to her knees alongside her sister, and before they could think, *act*, they were slammed to the floor by an iron cage of an officer.

"Freeze," the baby-faced officer ordered Cole, Sage, and Wily.

Between the confusion of racing legs, the fallen bodies around her, the faces she didn't recognize screaming in terror, Crys saw the three Conservators stride, unchallenged, off the escalator and across the soaring steel-and-glass main hall, keeping to the outskirts of the mayhem that they themselves had set into motion.

None of the Exiles bothered to cry out for the Conservators' arrest. They knew all too well that to society, to the police, it didn't compute that affluence and violent crime could coincide. Crys watched as the richly dressed trio walked freely out the domed exit, the Soaring Precious sheathed across Hariri's back, while a knee dug into her own.

A fresh wave of fury crashed through her, the *wrongness*, the injustice of it all turning her blood molten. Zoe, Khari, Poppy, and now possibly Ani and even her own adoptive father—all their murders, one way or another, were going to come down on Crys. On the band of homeless orphans. *On the experiments gone wrong.*

"*No*," Crys growled, bucking off the officer. She turned back to the others, who were rushing forward in a suicide charge to recover Jade. "Follow the Conservators, we'll catch up. *Go!*" Another rubber bullet ricocheted off a steel pillar before Wily was able to drag Cole away.

Ignoring the burning ache in her thigh, Crys kicked to her feet and drew the perfume vials from her pockets. "Jade, hold your breath!"

Jade's face knotted in confusion, but Crys saw her chest freeze midinhale.

Wielding two vials, Crys sprayed both her assailant and the baby-faced officer, the latter shrinking back in horror at the sight of Jade's face. Crys pulled Jade to her feet, and they squeezed their way toward the congested exit doors, stopping along the way to gather several jackets scattered across the hall's marble floor, abandoned by hyperloop passengers who'd dropped them in the sudden frenzy.

"We lost them," Eli said when they linked back up in an alley a block from the portal. He took the coat Crys tossed him, his eyes darting around the corner, up to the roof, through the service entrance of a thrift shop. "They could be anywhere."

"Or *everywhere*," Wily said, throwing on a hoodie.

Crys popped her head through the wide neck of a corduroy overshirt. "We need to keep moving."

Sage wrapped an oversize coat around herself, her long lashes rapidly blinking like she was tapping out Morse code. *SOS.*

But Crys knew there was no one to contact for help. They were on their own.

"We've been invisible most of our lives," Cole said with a shrug. "Those moneyed ghouls will get bored and forget about us soon enough." He stood in a pool of streetlight in his borrowed jean jacket, looking like a pale ray of hope. Everyone seemed to gravitate toward him, soaking in his positivity, like it was a power that could be shared.

A screeching patrol car sped past, sending the Exiles flush against the brick wall.

"I know a place to take cover," Jade offered, "but we'll have to get to the Haight."

"Are you talking about *the Panhandle*?" Sage said, horrified.

"That place is supposed to be worse than Dry River," Wily said, a gleam in his eye that Crys recognized from his Quake Tour days. "I'm in."

Jade zipped the leather jacket she'd taken from the portal. Wrong shade, wrong length, but a part of Ani was still with her, sheltering her.

"I'm in, too," Crys said.

Jade nodded, gripping the trompo like a talisman. "We'll stick to the alleys."

Wily stretched his glutes, preparing himself for the city's famously steep streets. "Well, one good thing, my ass is going to look fantastic after this."

Sage stepped forward. "Speaking of rears, everyone get behind me."

Wily grabbed her arm. "You good?"

"Yes, I'm good." Sage shook him off. "Why wouldn't I be good?"

"You haven't listed pop-rock titles since we left the pod," Eli pointed out.

Ignoring the insinuation, Sage charged out of the alley. Crys and the others followed close. She led them through the Mission District, brilliant, colorful murals painted on every building's facade, hipster youth packed outside trendy Mexican restaurants and lining up in front of bars.

"Are *you* feeling okay?" Sage asked Wily when he passed a taqueria without so much as a head turn.

"Are any of us?" Eli panted, grabbing a stitch in his side, eyes still flittering, searching for any sign of their hunters. For signs of the grim symbol. But if the Conservators were near, they were patiently lying in wait before they pounced a second time.

After twenty minutes of power walking, they reached the Lower Haight, and the tents started to appear: on bus-stop benches, street corners, the stoops of churches, outside a construction zone for a condominium complex.

Cole cleared his throat beside Crys. "You know Sage has been secretly using her phone's GPS this entire time, right?"

Yes, Crys had realized. She thought they all had, but no one wanted to say it out loud. To admit her memory power had been her bot.

Jade appeared behind them, tapping Cole on the shoulder. "You mind?" she asked, nodding to take his space.

"Not one bit," Cole answered. "It's good to see you two reunited. It's like when you lose one of your favorite pairs of socks or gloves. You two belong together, you know?"

He pushed ahead as Crys and Jade trudged side by side up a particularly precipitous concrete hill.

"So, are we going to talk about what happened back there?" Jade asked after a while.

"Only Damon and the Gens have print access to the Soaring Precious's display case," Crys panted, punctuating each word with every hard-earned step up. "Maxen was with you, and Gen 1 didn't have the saber at Splendor Park. That means Damon encountered the Conservators, either readily giving them the blade or losing it in a fight . . ."

"You know I'm not asking about the saber," Jade huffed.

Crys knew she was asking about the bots. Her perfume. She just wasn't ready for an interrogation.

They crested the hill, the heavy tread of their shuffling feet locking time with the pulse in Crys's ears as they descended. She shrugged, pretending her thigh didn't burn, her lungs didn't scream for oxygen, her head wasn't pounding. "I'm reclaiming what's mine," she said. "A bit of rebranding, you could say."

Jade sighed. Or was it a laugh? "Ever the business maven."

Crys's hands curled around the warm perfume vials. She counted nine remaining.

"I met the mayor's Gravestone earlier tonight," Jade mused. "I couldn't understand why he smelled like your perfume, or why he cowered from me." Crys realized he'd done the same with her back at Dry River City. He must have used it then pocketed the vial when Wily tossed it out from the tent. "Have you worked out how long the effects of your fear fragrance last?"

"I went through a vial a week," Crys estimated. "Although, who knows how many nanoscopic Quest Bots are swimming around in each."

"So a single spray could last a week, months—"

"Or Damon's design could be that the more of the fragrance, *the bot*, that I directly inhaled, the more powerful my fear became."

Jade chewed her lip, her keen eyes sweeping the still streets, the inky shadows. The steepled roofs and canted bay windows of every Victorian-style building they passed. "Well, your perfume might be the best thing we have to keep Hariri, that rotted soul of a Fortunate, away from us." She rubbed her hands together furiously, trying to scrape away the blood that clung to her skin. "I mean, what kind of vile maniac goes around wielding an ancient emperor's saber?"

One who doesn't like losing to Damon Yates, Crys thought, remembering how Yates had won the precious multimillion-dollar artifact at a competitive Sotheby's auction. Maxen had mentioned that Hariri and his playmates had once been Yates's friends. Before tonight, Crys wouldn't have known them from Adam or Eve. When had their relationship soured? And why?

"Crys?" Jade's voice came out strained, her drawn faced flushed. "I shouldn't have ever left you. I'm sorry."

Crys shrugged. Dug into her left pocket. "I thought you didn't believe in apologies." She placed half of her glass vials into Jade's open hand. "Only in getting even."

Jade grinned like she'd just been handed keys to the latest dragster. Or the passcode to a pioneering weaponry shop. "You'd share, with *me*?"

"What's mine is yours."

"Like old times."

"Like new times."

The crush of domed tents and canopies lined the sidewalk like a disorderly residential neighborhood. In each, a mob of silhouettes huddled closely, lit by bright, naked bulbs connected to wires Crys saw running from open tent flaps to a nearby streetlamp.

Was this place, or one like it, now her home, her life?

Again?

She no longer had her Adsum fortune, her Ivy League future waiting for her. Was no longer an heiress. A daughter. She'd lost everything. Had only what was with her. The stolen clothes on her back. Her bots. The Exiles.

Jade.

Yet, somehow, Crys felt like a billionaire all the same.

She inhaled deeply as she and Jade struggled up another incline. She couldn't say that the air of poverty smelled marvelous, but she was tired of covering up what she'd so desperately sought to forget. Crys breathed in the truth, free and easy, lingering on the crest of the last high hill that overlooked the sprawling Panhandle encampment. She touched the worn, itchy cloth of her shirt above the words tattooed along her ribs. *Always higher.*

And then she made her way down.

TWENTY-SIX

The moment Jade crossed into the Panhandle, the long, narrow park that housed San Francisco's largest city-run tent village, she knew the Conservators had made it there first.

Even just yesterday, Jade would have believed that the unhoused residents shaking all around her, mumbling irritably to themselves, were just living with mental illness, or tweaking. Coming down from a Soot binge. That's what the navy suits, the passing citizen, would see: drug users, not people who had ingested something far more sinister.

But after Dry River City, and tonight's introduction to the Conservators, Jade knew better. "Eli, eyes to the ground," she warned when she spotted a vinyl sticker-tag of three red slash marks stuck to the trunk of a tree, then on a dozen canvas walls.

"Look," Sage said, gesturing toward a mobile food bank parked along Fell Street. Tables were set up around the truck, smiling volunteers in clean collared shirts passing out fresh produce and something that looked a hell of a lot like Poppy's bite-size quiches.

Pockets of screaming broke out across the densely populated camp. Spooked locals began fleeing the park by the tentful.

"Spit it out," Eli cried to a pair of youths, rushing forward to slap the half-eaten quiches out of their hands.

"Think you can steal from me?" The larger young man swung, fighting for what was his.

Eli ducked, and the second youth barreled forward, attempting to land a sloppy punch across the side of his head. Eli pushed him back. "Don't eat the quiches!"

Jade and Wily jumped in, fists up, needing to shut the situation down before they drew too much attention. One look at the dried blood on their hands, the unhealed wounds on both their faces, and the youth turned tail and ran, leaving the bot-laced quiches on the ground.

But the victory was short-lived. Everywhere Jade turned, Panhandlers were devouring the gourmet treats, a bevy of them lining back up for more. Jade watched, helpless, as their gazes fell on the sticker-tag fixed to the truck bed, as the engineered fear took hold, triggering the unstoppable fight-or-flight response. A rising dread washed through Jade, threatened to spill over into panic. Whatever the Conservators were after was bigger than the Exiles. Bigger than Yates testing Quest Bots on his Adsum students.

"We have to shut it down," Crys said, moving for the truck, for the volunteers who were now cowering back in confusion, seemingly unaware of what they were serving. As Zoe must have been.

"There's no point," Jade said, holding Crys back. "This place is already headed for the same fate as Dry River City."

And there was nothing they could do to stop it.

"Incoming," Cole announced. A new set of Conservators, wearing expensive two-piece gray suits and stockings over their faces, strolled through the camp, groups of Panhandlers parting around them like the Red Sea, recoiling from the symbols on their lapels.

"This way," Jade said, blazing the trail through a winding dirt alley between rows of tents.

In the confusing press of bodies, the dark, unfamiliar turf, the mess of collapsed shelters, the growing babel of screams, they lost Eli and Cole.

Crys met Jade's eye, the pair of them of the same mind. They each pulled out a vial of the fear fragrance. "Stay between us," Crys told Sage and Wily.

They retraced their steps, the sisters' trigger fingers primed on the perfume nozzles. They rounded a corner, but still no trace of Eli or Cole. Only more fear symbols, more Panhandlers desperate to desert their homes, like an invading army was at the gates with orders to kill every last person.

Jade cocked her head. "Did anyone else hear that?"

Again, a stifled cry from inside a ramshackle lean-to built against the tall, slender trunk of a eucalyptus tree.

"*Cole*," Crys shouted, voice cracking.

Before they could storm the crude structure, Eli came crashing into it, taking the tarp walls down with him. He was shaking, emitting deep agonized bellows, trapped in the jaws of a fear incursion. Cole was on his knees, palms pressed tight against his eyes. Eli dropped next to him. "That woman got Cole. I tried going after her," he growl-screamed, "but their damn symbol is everywhere."

Jade scanned the perimeter for the Conservator with the handbag and cutting smile.

Crys dove for Cole, checking his body for wounds. "What's happened?" He trembled, his breaths too quick, too shallow, refusing to open his lids. "Tell me you didn't eat the quiche?"

Cole shook his head, a choked scream escaping his lips as he pointed to a soaked rag on the ground. Had the Conservators weaponized a fear bot as a vaporized inhalant?

"Look at me, just keep your eyes on me," Crys repeated. She cupped Cole's cheeks in her hands. "Don't go dark."

The mob of Panhandlers on the far side of the pathway suddenly scattered. Jade looked up to see a barrel-chested Conservator laughing through his stocking mask, high on the power to make those before him cower.

Two can play at that game, Jade thought, grasping the perfume vial in her pocket. "Crys, what do you say we give these suits a dose of their own medicine?"

Crys rose to her feet and drew out two vials, understanding Jade's scheme at once.

"Explain?" Sage said, warily eyeing the Quest-made perfumes.

Another round of terrified shouting broke out. A second Conservator had joined in on the twisted revelry.

"There's no time," Crys said. "Sage, Wily, stay with Eli and Cole."

And then the sisters spilled into the chaos, each taking a Conservator. Light on her toes, stealthy as a shadow, Jade attacked from the man's blind side, spraying him before he could register the breeze at his back.

"Over there," Crys breathed, nodding toward two gray-suited women slapping more fear symbols outside the mobile bathroom doors.

She and Jade crept forward, their approach muffled by the Panhandlers' screams. Jamming their noses and mouths into their elbows, they simultaneously fired a hazy cloud of bot-induced terror at the women. By the time the scent of peonies and cedar hit their nostrils, the sisters were gone. Hidden behind a pile of gutted mattresses.

"Hariri's here," Wily whispered, helping Sage lead a stumbling Eli and Cole, their eyes squeezed shut, to crouch behind the makeshift hideout.

"Another hit-and-run?" Crys asked, unholstering a fresh perfume vial.

The Panhandlers crowding the pathway split, and Hariri and the Unfortunate-repellent symbol on his lapel sliced through them like a cleaver. He ripped away his nylon mask, his hooded eyes aimed dead at the hunkering Exiles.

"No," Jade answered. "We face them." She stepped out from behind the rusty box spring, her palms held up in front of her in a wordless gesture: *empty hands, open minds*.

It was a lie, of course. Jade had two thin razor blades she'd pulled from her bag between her fingers, and such a close-minded condemnation of this man that her anger numbed the red-hot fear telling her to stay back. To hide.

Crys moved in beside her, making Hariri smile. "Crystal and Jade, together again. How charming. I like to think it was all my doing, though it wasn't my intention, I admit."

Crys hurled a glare so cutting, Jade was half surprised the man didn't flinch. "It was *you* who had Zoe's body planted in the Exiles' motor home, then?"

Hariri's smile stretched, his teeth white enough to blind. "Wonderful, I'm glad we're all caught up."

Jade stomped her back heel on the bold sticker-tags that littered the pavement where she stood. "Eye-catching symbol. What's it mean?" She needed to keep him talking. Boasting. She needed to know his endgame before she decided how to play against him.

Hariri slid his jeweled fingers over the leather sheath that held Yates's saber. He seemed amused, in the mood for humoring a wayward Unfortunate who was about to take his secrets to her early grave. "It's an old hobo symbol from the Great Depression. A system of hieroglyphs, if you will, that vagrants once used to communicate. A primitive survival code." He gave a jaunty flick to the enamel pin on his lapel. "We thought we would keep things simple, a sign bums and tramps could read. Understand. *This isn't a safe place.* It's a warning to leave."

Jade laughed. "You make it sound like a suggestion."

Eli grumbled a slew of muffled curses from behind the hand that blocked his eyes.

Hariri's bearded chin drifted toward the woman with the handbag, who'd joined him alongside the maimed redhead. "I don't see any force here. Do you?"

The woman grinned, readjusting her grip on the leather handbag that perfectly matched her platinum-gray suit. How many fear-soaked rags did she still have in there? "No violence, no raids, no arrests. The homeless are leaving their tent city voluntarily."

"All that's left of Dry River City is a storage tent lined with dead bodies," Wily shouted, attempting to get between Jade and Crys to the

Conservators. "You call innocent people getting crushed in a stampede to flee your symbol a *voluntary* choice?"

Sage seized him by the hood of his sweatshirt and yanked him back, plucking the mayor's pistol from his white-knuckle grip. "You have one too many scars already," she whispered fiercely. "For once in your unruly life, stay back and *listen*."

Jade looked at Hariri and motioned to the bedraggled figures evacuating the park all around them. Clutching their hair, tearing at their eyes. Leaving with nothing. Only the fear in their minds.

This isn't a safe place, this isn't a safe place.

Leave.

Even without a bot-laced quiche, Jade's own mind cried for her to bolt. To disappear. Instead, she stood there, a stoic sounding board for a braggart to flaunt his grand plans to. "I expect you think you're going to get away with all of this," she said. A statement, not a question.

Nevertheless, Hariri answered. "Oh, I expect much more than that. Gratitude, favors, *power*." His amber eyes drew Jade in like quicksand. "Our cities were once great. Magnificent jewels, attracting tourists, tycoons. The envy of the world."

The grin that Jade had visions of tearing from his face finally flattened, his lips puckering like the permanent laugh lines that rimmed his sunken eyes. "Look what these soft, indulgent laws have enabled. Crime-infested slums. Eyesores. Humiliations. An invasive community sullying public parks, streets, highways, living off the mandatory mercy of corporate tax hikes, leeching off their industrious betters. For decades, the homeless epidemic has been spreading like a coronavirus, and there isn't a thing anyone can do about it."

"Until now?" Jade guessed.

The smile was back. "Until now. Governors, along with every mayor and sheriff from Los Angeles to New York, will be kissing my feet. I have the cure to the outbreak that has plagued our leaders for nearly a century. I can assuage their naysayers, ensure their reelections . . ." Hariri extended his hand.

Jade felt the fine hairs on Crys's arms stand on end, like raised swords signaling to charge.

But the man's smooth palm was empty. "All with an invisible weapon," he continued. "Under the radar of the press and the masses, the Conservators will purge the overrun cities and reclaim them as our own. We will declare them safe again, and the prestige of the country's formerly prized metropolises will be restored."

"And the millions of unhoused Unfortunates you displace will then be someone else's problem," Jade offered with a sneer.

"Precisely," Hariri cried enthusiastically.

Wily groaned. "I don't know how much longer I can stomach this bullshit."

But Jade continued to press. "Why kill Poppy Szeto?" She wanted answers, a morsel of closure to satisfy Maxen, when she liberated him from wherever the navy suits locked him up.

Hariri shrugged. "Poppy was looking for an out, so I gave her one. She chose her fosters over her equals. She couldn't stomach the sacrifices it took to complete our restoration."

"And Yates?" Crys asked, her fingers itching at the pocket of her torn trousers, a whisper of concern, of sadness, rounding her sharp words.

"That *traitor*," the redheaded man scoffed. The gauze around his maimed hand oozed, and Jade wondered fleetingly whether the Conservator's finger was in a cooler somewhere or lost on the bloody pod floor. Or if he simply had enough money to buy a new one.

"Damon Yates was once one of our foremost members," Hariri revealed. "A preservationist, a visionary, before he abandoned the noble cause to play false Savior. To play father and teacher to a gang of Unfortunate waifs." Was that jealousy in those hooded eyes? An old wound bleeding into his voice, flushing his olive skin a crimson red?

He covered both with his blinding smile. "But we were patient with our revenge, cunning with our ambitions."

"By blowing up Asclepius?" Crys interjected. "Killing Yates's bioengineer, attempting to murder every one of his students?"

"An impactful first reclamation day, wouldn't you say?" Hariri laughed, his cronies echoing his amusement.

Jade needed Hariri to focus. "So Poppy helped you steal Yates's nanobots—"

"Oh, we didn't steal," Hariri corrected. "We upgraded and perfected."

"What's he mean by that?" Eli growled.

Cole clamped a twitching hand on Jade's shoulder, his eyes downcast, locking on Crys's poker face. "It isn't just another fear bot?"

Hariri's beatific smile suggested something far more menacing. A cold sweat slid down Jade's arms. She knew her bag of tricks was empty. She clutched the bullet that failed to kill her with one hand, reaching into her back pocket for the trompo with the other. She unclenched her aching jaw, a demand for the Conservator to elaborate on the tip of her dry tongue, when Crys stormed forward.

"You 'perfected' at the sacrifice of Zoe and Khari!"

Hariri paused, as if he had to pull the names from a void. "The orphan girls?"

Crys's entire body trembled with fiery anger, like an incendiary grenade about to burst.

Then Jade had an idea. Deftly, and out of Hariri's sight, she began to wind the worn string around her wooden spinning top.

"Khari was a test run," Hariri explained. "A little message to the Savior. Zoe was an unfortunate mistake. Their bodies reacted fatally to our nano reform." He shrugged. "A few ripples before smooth sailing ahead . . ."

"Did you murder Yates, too?" Crys strained forward, but Jade had her anchored by a fistful of the stolen corduroy shirt.

"*Wait*," she urged.

To her surprise, Crys listened. Stood still as an opossum in shock, as quiet as when they were kids, buried in the rubble, waiting for their parents to breathe.

"Damon's is a far worse fate, I'm happy to report." Hariri broke the news of Damon's misfortune with the enthusiasm of a journalist tossing out juicy tidbits to a salivating audience. "He's losing his mind."

The Exiles emitted a collective "*What?*" All but Jade. She guessed Hariri's crude meaning. *Could Yates be suffering from schizophrenia like Maxen?* Didn't genetics play a role?

"A benefit of being Damon's former confidant is knowing his vulnerabilities," Hariri divulged, his eyes clouding over. "The open ocean air and a bottle of tequila can do that to a man, induce him to *let slip* what can be used against him."

Jade wanted to point out that she was going to use all of what *Hariri* was so openly exposing against *him*, but she kept her mouth closed. Kept him talking.

Hariri's laugh lines deepened with his glee. "I knew Damon was diagnosed with early onset Alzheimer's. When the years passed and his disease never worsened, I was mistrustful of his miraculous recovery. Tonight my suspicions were verified. His own Quest Bot was keeping his dementia at bay. But that, I'm also pleased to report, has since been rectified."

Yates had a bot.

The words, their meaning, reverberated through Jade like an echoing strike from a meditation gong. *Be calm, relax, unwind,* Damon had tried to teach her at the Quietude, to help her control her restless mind. *Don't. Think.*

She wound the trompo's string, again and again, until the thread was tight. Then positioned her fingers. Waited. Not thinking. Allowing the Conservator's nauseating speech to flow in and out of her mind with every grounding breath she took.

Yates was infected with the nano reform.

Fear symbols were hidden all over his beloved LA.

Soon the entire state. The country.

Yates will be a walking shell of a man. Stripped of home, all power of remembrance . . .

Stripped of his genius, Jade's mind screamed.

"No!" Jade and Crys cried sharply in stereo.

"Clean them out," Hariri ordered his henchmen. The Conservators slinked into view, untucking silk pocket squares from their jackets, dousing them with an unmarked bottle.

Crys raked back her golden hair. Jade jutted out her chin. Exposing their full faces, like unsheathing knives. Cocking guns. But their blades had already landed. Their bullets already buried in their attackers' minds. When the Conservators moved forward to attack, they recoiled back in horror. Jade and Crys had already struck first.

"You're not the only one who can make people fear you," Crys said, holding up her perfume vial.

Hariri's billion-dollar smile returned. Delighted in his unlikely challengers. With a dexterous flourish, he drew the Soaring Precious from its leather sheath. "Perhaps Yates did teach you something at that poor excuse for a school."

"You don't deserve that saber," Crys seethed.

"Is that so?" Hariri goaded, the ornate blade shining against his rings. "I invite you to come and take it."

Be calm, relax, unwind.

They couldn't touch him, and he knew it. He was one of the richest people in the world, an invisible shield of exceptional wealth, of credibility, wrapped around him. Even if they captured him and took him to the navy suits, odds were *they'd* be the ones charged. For kidnapping. For defamation. Attempted murder.

Men like Hariri were to be believed by default.

It's what made the world go round.

Jade gripped her trompo, her uncle's words shouting in her mind. *You gotta be your own quake sometimes. Shake things up.* Her pulse thudded in her ears, and she imagined it to be the steady thump of Ani's heartbeat.

Still alive. Still fighting.

Suddenly, Crys broke ranks, prepared to take matters into her own raised fists. Sage moved behind her with the mayor's pistol, Wily pulling Poppy's gun from Jade's waistband, clearly thinking a bot-less Jade might be too afraid to act.

But Jade was ready.

Calm and relaxed, she unwound.

She launched the trompo onto the paved path between Crys's and Hariri's feet, where it landed, spinning on its point, round and round, hypnotizing.

The woman with the cruel smile moved to crush the trompo with the back of her boot heel. "We don't have time for games—"

"I wouldn't do that if I were you," Jade said, her voice dripping with peril. "I've placed a bomb inside that spinning top. Whenever it stops turning, *boom.*" She emphasized this last point with an explosive motion of her hands. She hoped her reputation preceded her. That the warnings of the scapegrace, the depraved, fearless wretch, had reached even the Conservators' bejeweled ears. "I'd say we've got about half a minute to cut our losses and run, or we're all going to lose a lot more than our fingers."

Hariri threw back his head, a deep howling laughter spilling over the tent city, covering the growing din of the Panhandlers' screams. He locked eyes with Jade.

Five seconds went by. Neither flinched.

Ten seconds.

Then Hariri bought Jade's bluff. "Until next time," he promised, his smile disappearing as he retreated.

Jade turned, rallying Crys and the others to follow. Within seconds they were lost in the crowd fleeing the park. As she ran, Jade imagined the trompo losing its momentum. Falling innocently to its side with nothing but a dull thud. A piece of her shared childhood, left behind, whole. She hoped another Unfortunate kid would stumble across it, use it as a talisman, a guide through the war the Conservators had brought to their doorstep.

"Where are we going?" Crys asked Jade as they cut through the dark, unfamiliar streets. "To the outskirts? We can't stay in the cities."

Jade could hardly believe she would think it, let alone say it out loud, but she knew there was another way to fight. A way to save more than just themselves.

"We're going to find Damon Yates," she answered evenly.

The fortunes of millions depended on it.

EPILOGUE

Damon didn't know where he was.

He'd made it out of the hyperloop tubes. Just barely. Had found a recess, a safe haven, as one of his pods blinked by. He'd walked and walked, his blood spilling from the saber wound on his arm, rolling over his knuckles, dripping from his fingertips. He knew he was leaving a trail. But who would come to look for him?

Hariri and his Conservators wanted Damon's body alive. Only his brain cells dead.

He knew he couldn't return home, even if he wanted to. The Castle in the Air was gone, his lab lost, his Yates Empire overrun with thieves.

Defeat was unexpectedly freeing. The questions he'd spent decades searching, meditating, fighting, to answer—*Am I good enough? Am I worthy?*—were finally clear.

He heard the cruel, bitter voices of his birth parents, his wives, his children, *his Questers,* reply in perfect unison.

No. And he never would be.

All that was left was for him to concede to his exile.

Damon had been wandering for days. His bare feet were blistered; his stomach, empty. Soon, his mind would be empty, too. What was a person without their memories? He was glad he would not be around to find out.

The group he was traveling with now was somewhere outside the metropolis, behind a strip mall, in an alleyway. Three seemed to be a safe number. Too many and you attracted the increasingly horrified residents, and in turn, the increasingly hostile local police. Too few, and you were prey to the other quarry: stripped of clothes, crumbs, and shoes, if you had them to begin with.

Celene groaned as she placed her scrawny weight into her cane, lowering herself onto the grimy pavement. The hardheaded woman was much younger than Damon, but her tight curls were silver, her face pinched like the smashed soda cans he'd started to collect from recycle bins for coins. "You're sure there aren't any of them symbols anywhere here? I'm not waking up in the dead of night to your howling again, having to go range for a new sleeping spot." Celene rubbed at her blind eyes. "Once I'm down, I'm down."

"No, ma'am, it's clear," Lucas answered, curling up in a bath towel he'd found beside a bus bench. The boy was the age of the Adsum first-years. The age Damon had been when his true mother and father had found him. A vanishing part of Damon wondered how long the boy had been alone.

He avoided talking to either of them. He'd told Celene and Lucas that his name was Hicks, the last name from his birth certificate, and they'd left it at that.

Peeling off his sweater, Damon bunched it into a ball and lay back, adjusting the ragged bandages an old combat vet had given him from the last group he'd wandered with. His arm was still sore. Might even have been infected. But he didn't let that bother him now.

Now, he just settled in, waiting to forget.

As Celene and Lucas drifted into dreamland, Damon stared into the night sky. He located *Zoe 1* and *Khari 1*, his nightly routine. Watching the satellites pass, contemplating how many short months, weeks, he had left until his mind left *him*. In the nights to come, with every rotation of the satellites, a piece of him would disappear. Another memory gone. Soon, what made Damon Yates the Savior would die, slowly, and he'd be wide awake for all of it.

Crystal and Maxen had abandoned him. Poppy had betrayed him. Hariri had destroyed him.

What was the use in fighting?

With each passing second the dangerous peptides and plaque formations in his brain were building. Growing. His Quest Bot was no longer there to serve as a powerful cage, trapping them before they could assemble.

Maybe it wouldn't be all that bad. Losing his memory.

He would be no one. Unwanted. Unclaimed. Disconnected from the reality of his situation. No more carrying the pain of the past. No more worrying over the Conservators' future.

Damon had tried so hard to be his own Savior. To hang on to his world-shaking technology. To be its one and only wielder. But there was no point clinging fast to empty air. No use in holding tight to fading memories.

After a time, *Zoe* and *Khari* passed from sight. Damon shut his eyes. And let go.

Authors' Note

When we initially think about what stories we want to tell, we naturally think about twin sisters. For *Exiles*, we were fascinated by the question: What if one sister couldn't stand the sight of her own twin's face? We envisioned a rivalry between sisters that went beyond the average competitiveness or hostility between siblings, one that induced actual terror in one sister at even the thought of being in the same room with the other.

This idea played on a childhood phobia we had of twin experiments, how we're the perfect test subjects to study the importance of environmental and genetic influences. As we grew older, it became less about an irrational fear of being abducted and forced into a twin study and more like "Hey, we could join one to earn a few extra bucks in college." (We could never actually bring ourselves to do it.)

The idea of genetic experiments inspired a different kind of thought experiment: What if it was possible to engineer fear in a person, or even an entire group of people? And who better to test the bounds of that study than twins that share their DNA?

We wrote the bulk of *Exiles* during quarantine in Los Angeles as the devastating effects of the COVID-19 pandemic took hold on the city's homeless population. Tent cities swelled all around us, the affordable housing crisis playing out right before our eyes. Neighbors battled with the unhoused communities over parks, beaches, and sidewalks, and state and local officials had no idea what to do. They still don't. Right now, over

150,000 people in California are unsheltered. And that number is growing. Neighborhood Facebook boards and Nextdoor apps buzz with angry messages about the unhoused. National politicians call these communities a blight on our nation's cities. Who is going to do something about it?

These questions led us to another thought experiment: If a biotechnology existed that really could engineer fear in a person, what if someone weaponized it to "deal" with the urban homeless population?

Thus began our research into nanobots. We'd already read about studies and developments of nanobots as a tool to help fight cancer and mental illnesses, which steered us toward other potential future uses of the biotech, all of which ended up informing and inspiring the various Quest Bots that each Adsum student was given. Although *Exiles* is a work of fiction, it was important for us to have a solid foundation in science. We partnered with an adviser from MIT and had delightfully nerdy Zoom conversations and email threads about nanobots, and whether it was theoretically possible to make someone fear another person's image. Or an innocent symbol. And if so, then how?

When we were brainstorming the initial idea for *Exiles*, our editor Adrienne Procaccini said something that really stuck with us: tech itself is agnostic, and it only becomes "good" or "evil" depending on who employs it, and why, and how. Through talks with our science adviser and other research, we quickly realized that the potential for nanobots to alter humankind is endless, and whoever has access to the new tech will bring a whole new meaning to the concept of "haves and have nots." Without exactly intending it, each of our novels so far seems to be a disaster siren for our future. We can't escape our generation's anxieties about what's ahead: superstorms, increasing viral misinformation, the unintended consequences of revolutionary technology. And there's a belief among some that more science and technology can solve our society's biggest problems. But, really, we believe that humankind's greatest power is our empathy. Technology is only a tool that humans use to effect change, but it will be our humanity that ends up saving us from ourselves.

ACKNOWLEDGMENTS

Writing is a solitary experience, especially in quarantine, but we couldn't have written this novel without the support and encouragement of our friends and family, especially our mom and dad (or dad and mom, if this is you reading, Dad). An endless thank-you to our editor Adrienne Procaccini, for your belief in us and your guidance with this story. Our utmost gratitude to our developmental editor, Jason Kirk, for your sharp, tireless eye and your friendship. To the entire 47North team at Amazon Publishing, we send a wholehearted thank-you for your expertise and collaboration. To Ashwin, thank you for going down the rabbit hole with us about the possibilities of nanotechnology, and to Wyatt and Winston, who have now been our loyal writing mascots for four books and counting.

Publishing a novel requires a team, and we are eternally grateful that we have the dream team on our side.

About the Authors

Photo © 2021 Neal Handloser

Twin sisters Ashley Saunders and Leslie Saunders are the authors of *The Rule of One*, *The Rule of Many*, and *The Rule of All* in the dystopian series The Rule of One. The duo honed their love of storytelling in film school at the University of Texas at Austin. After just under a decade penning screenplays and directing commercials, the sisters deliberately stumbled into the world of novel writing. They vow to never leave it. The sisters can be found with their Boston terriers in sunny Los Angeles, exploring hiking trails and drinking entirely too much yerba maté. Visit them at www.thesaunderssisters.com.